PRAISE FOR REGINALD HILL'S MYSTERY NOVELS

"The real joy of the Dalziel-Pascoe books is in the writing and the characterizations. Mr. Hill has such disparate writers as Trollope, Beerbohm, Sayers, and Shaw in his blood."

—*The New York Times*

"Hill's polished, sophisticated novels are intelligently written and permeated with his sly and delightful sense of humor. . . . More than most other mystery novels, Hill's Dalziel-Pascoe novels are enjoyable as much for their characters as for their complicated, suspenseful mystery plots."

—*Christian Science Monitor*

"Hill never coasts on his well-honed technique, but keeps posing himself new challenges. . . . Score another one for Hill, whose wit thrives on the perversities of human nature."

—*Cleveland Plain Dealer*

"Hill blends civility and m[illegible] most agreeable way."

[illegible] Magazine

"A lot [illegible] stories, but Reg[illegible] who write cla[illegible]

—*Baltimore Sun*

"Hill is . . . the most civilized, clever, and enjoyable crime writer we have."

—*London Sunday Telegraph*

Pascoe's Ghost
and Other Brief Chronicles of Crime

by
Reginald Hill

A SIGNET BOOK
NEW AMERICAN LIBRARY
A DIVISION OF PENGUIN BOOKS USA INC.

PUBLISHER'S NOTE

This is a work of fiction. Names, characters, places, and incidents either are the product of the author's imagination or are used fictitiously, and any resemblance to actual persons, living or dead, events, or locales is entirely coincidental.

NAL BOOKS ARE AVAILABLE AT QUANTITY DISCOUNTS WHEN USED TO PROMOTE PRODUCTS OR SERVICES. FOR INFORMATION PLEASE WRITE TO PREMIUM MARKETING DIVISION, NEW AMERICAN LIBRARY, 1633 BROADWAY, NEW YORK, NEW YORK 10019.

First published in Great Britain
by William Collins Sons & Co Ltd, Glasgow.

SIGNET, SIGNET CLASSIC, MENTOR, ONYX, PLUME, MERIDIAN
and NAL BOOKS are published by New American Library,
a division of Penguin Books USA Inc.,
1633 Broadway, New York, New York 10019

First Signet Printing, May, 1989

1 2 3 4 5 6 7 8 9

PRINTED IN THE UNITED STATES OF AMERICA

Contents

Pascoe's Ghost 11
The Trunk in the Attic 114
The Rio de Janeiro Paper 129
Threatened Species 140
Snowball 168
Exit Line 182
Dalziel's Ghost 195

In *Pascoe's Ghost* all the chapter headings come from the poetical works of Edgar Allan Poe.

Truth is not always in a well . . .
The depth lies in the valleys where we
seek her, and not upon the mountain tops
where she is found.

—The Chevalier C. AUGUSTE DUPIN

Pascoe's Ghost

CHAPTER 1

Oh, the bells, bells, bells!
What a tale their terror tells.

I

The phone rang.

Swithenbank heard his mother answer it.

"John!" she called. "It's for you."

Stuffing the last fragments of toast into his mouth, he rose and went into the hall.

"Hello," he said.

Everything was quiet. It was like being in church. The morning sun could only manage a dim religious light through the circle of stained glass in the front door and the smell of pine-scented polish was as heavy as incense on the dank autumn air. Could he not have noticed how cold it was here in his childhood? He vowed to bring an electric blanket if he came at Christmas. If he came.

"Hello? Hello!" he said and put the receiver down.

"Mother!" he called.

Mrs. Swithenbank appeared at the head of the stairs. Her hair was a deep shade of lavender this month. For a woman in her late fifties, she had a trim elegant figure despite an enormous appetite which she never hesitated to indulge.

"Who was it on the phone?" asked her son.

"Didn't she tell you, dear?"

"She? No, the line was dead."

"Was it? Oh dear. Perhaps she'll ring again."

"Didn't *she* give a name?"

"I think so, dear. I always ask who's calling. In case it's Boris or one of the others so I can say you're out. Though I don't really like to lie."

"It's just the modern equivalent of the butler saying I'm not at home, Mother," said Swithenbank in exasperation. "So, what did this woman say?"

"Well, to tell the truth, I didn't really catch it, she had such a funny voice. Very distant somehow. But it wasn't Boris or any of the others. I mean, I know it wasn't Boris, because it was a girl. But it wasn't Stella or Ursula either, or I'd have said."

"Oh Mother!"

"It sounded a very odd name," she said defensively. "Una something, I think. I'm sorry I missed it, but after all, dear, I'm not your secretary. I'm sure she'll ring again."

The phone rang.

Swithenbank snatched it up.

"Wearton two-seven-nine," he said.

"John, dear fellow! Caught you at last. How are you?"

"Hello, Boris," said Swithenbank, scowling at his mother's retreating back. "I'm fine. I was going to call before I went back."

"I would be devastated if you didn't. In fact that's why I'm ringing really. I'm having a few of the locals round for drinks tomorrow, Saturday, about seven-thirty. I thought I'd ask our old gang to hang on for a bite of supper afterwards. You know, Stella and Geoff, Ursula and Peter."

"I know who the old gang are," said Swithenbank acidly.

"We're all dying to see you again. It's been six months at least since you were last in Wearton. Just before Father died, wasn't it?"

"Yes. I'm sorry I couldn't make it to the funeral, Boris."

"Don't worry. We all understand. It's been difficult for you." The voice dropped a sympathetic semi-tone. "No word yet? On Kate, I mean."

"No," said Swithenbank shortly.

"It must be awful for you. Awful. It's a year now, isn't it?"

"That's right. A year."

"Twelve months, and nothing. Awful. Cheer up, though. I suppose no news is good news."

"I can't imagine why you should suppose that," said Swithenbank.

"I'm sorry. What I meant was . . . look, do try to get along tomorrow night, won't you?"

"I can't promise, Boris. I'll give you a ring later if I may."

"Fine. Good. Excellent.'Bye!"

Swithenbank was smiling as he put down the phone. He went into the kitchen where his mother was washing the dishes.

"That girl on the phone. The name couldn't have been Ulalume, could it?"

"Ulalume? Yes, that sounds very like it, though it doesn't sound very *likely*, does it? By the way, I'm going into town when I've finished these. I'll probably have lunch there."

"Mother," said Swithenbank wearily. "You've been going into town and having lunch there on Fridays for the last twenty years at least. Everyone in Wearton expects it. I expect it. I can only hope that you may be visiting the hairdresser, too. But I cannot be surprised."

"I'm not trying to surprise you, dear," said his mother mildly.

Fifteen minutes later he heard her call goodbye as she passed the open sitting-room door. Almost simultaneously the phone rang.

By the time he got into the entrance hall his mother had picked up the receiver.

"It's that girl again, dear," she said. "I must dash or I'll miss my bus. 'Bye!"

He did not touch the phone till he heard the front door close behind her.

"Hello? Hello?" he said.

For twenty seconds or more there was no reply; then as from a great distance a thin infinitely melancholy voice said, "Ulalume . . . Ulalume," stretching the words out like a street-vendor's cry.

"For God's sake, stop fooling around!" commanded Swithenbank, his voice authoritative and controlled. But the control disappeared when a voice behind him said, "Mr. John Swithenbank?"

He spun around. Standing in the open doorway was a man, tall, slim beneath a short fawn raincoat, early thirties, rather a long nose, mop of brown hair falling over his brow and shadowing the light blue, watchful eyes.

"Who the hell are you?" demanded Swithenbank.

"I met a lady on the drive—she said just to walk in. Something about the bell not working."

He reached out of the door and pressed the bell-push. A deafening chime echoed round the hall. He looked embarrassed.

"I'm sorry," he said. "I'm interrupting your call. I'll wait outside, shall I, till you're finished."

"It is finished," said Swithenbank, replacing the receiver firmly. "What do you want with me, Mr. . . ?"

"Inspector. Detective-Inspector Pascoe," said the man. "Could I speak with you, Mr. Swithenbank? It's about your wife."

"You'd better come in," said Swithenbank. "Hang your coat up if you think it's going to be worth it."

Pascoe wiped his feet, removed his coat, and carefully hung it up on the old-fashioned hall-stand which loomed like a multiple gallows behind the door.

2

Boris Kingsley replaced the phone on the bedside table. He was sitting on the edge of the bed and the mattress sagged beneath his weight. He was naked and he contemplated his bulging belly with the helpless bewilderment of a weak king confronting a peasants' revolt.

"When did you last see your little Willie?" asked Ursula Davenport, snuggling against his back and peering over his shoulder.

He dug his elbow into one of her bountiful breasts.

"About the same time you saw your little Umbilicus," he said.

"Will he come?"

"What?"

"Johnny, I mean."

"Why do you call him Johnny? No one else calls him Johnny. You always try to suggest a special relationship."

"We had once. At least, I thought so."

"But Kate put paid to that," said Kingsley spitefully. "Funny, I often think that both you and Stella got married on the rebound."

"Stella?" She raised her eyebrows.

"Your sister-in-law, dear. There are depths beneath that unyielding surface."

"I'm glad to hear it. I wasn't conscious of a rebound," she said evenly. "Unless it was from Stella moving into the bungalow. I could hardly stay on, could I?"

"I wish you'd stayed and the bungalow had moved," grumbled Kingsley, walking across to the window and peering out.

The lawn had that tousled unkempt look even the best kept grass gets on a dank October morning. He had the sense of peering down at a wild moorland from some craggy height. Away to the right ran an avenue of trees, while straight ahead was a tangle of neglected shrubbery which reinforced the impression of desolation till he raised his eyes a little and the cheerful red-brick of the Rawlinson bungalow some three hundred yards away re-established the scale of things.

"Pa should never have sold your father that land," said Kingsley with irritation. "It ruins the view."

"I dare say Stella will think the same about little Willie if she's out in the garden," said Ursula

"She should be lucky," said Kingsley. "How do you think your brother is since his accident?"

"You are an evil-minded bastard sometimes, Boris," she said.

"And you're the vicar's wife," he mocked. "Is it sermon on the mount time?"

She rolled off the bed as he approached.

"I think it's time to go home and have breakfast."

"Stay here," he suggested. "When's Peter due back from his concert?"

"Not till this afternoon."

"Well then."

"But old mother Warnock is due here in half an hour."

"She'll devil us some kidneys. You can say you dropped in to invite me to address the Mothers' Union."

"Boris, dear, she'd stand up and denounce us before the first hymn next Sunday morning. No, I'll have a quick shower and be off."

She left the room before he could attempt to restrain her by force or persuasion.

He did not appear too frustrated by her evasion but strolled round the room getting dressed. Unhappy at the selection of trousers in the large mahogany wardrobe which occupied half a wall opposite his bed, he took a key from a chest of drawers and unlocked a smaller oak wardrobe in the corner by the window. Here were hanging the heavier twills which the chill of the morning invited.

Here also hung a woman's dress in white muslin with blue ribbons to gather it gently in beneath the bosom. On the shelf above was a wide-brimmed floppy hat in white linen trimmed with blue roses. He touched it lovingly, then caressed the soft material of the dress with his open hand.

When he turned from re-locking the wardrobe Ursula was standing dripping wet in the bedroom doorway.

"I couldn't find a towel," she said.

"I'll come and rub you dry," he answered, smiling.

3

Geoffrey Rawlinson let his binoculars rest on his chest, stood up, collapsed the seat of his shooting-stick and, leaning heavily on it so that he drilled a trail of holes across the lawn, he limped back to the bungalow.

He heard the phone being replaced as he negotiated the high step into the kitchen, and a moment later his wife came into the room, snapping on the light so that he blinked as it came bouncing at him off chrome, tile and Formica. The changes Stella had made in the kitchen never ceased to amaze him. It was, he claimed, more automated than the War Room in the Pentagon. But even in high summer it still needed artificial light till the sun was high in the sky.

"Children off to school?" he asked.

"Yes. Please, Geoff, how many times do I have to ask you? Don't dig up the floor tiles with that thing!"

"Sorry," said Rawlinson. He leaned the shooting-stick against the waist disposal unit and took up his heavy blackthorn walking stick which was hooked over the rack of the dishwasher. It had a thick rubber ferrule which squeaked against the floor as he walked towards his wife.

"Who were you phoning?" he asked.

"The butcher," she said. "Is *she* still over there?"

"I've been looking at the birds," he answered in tones of gentle reproach. "That pair of whitethroats is still there. It's really incredibly late for them. I think one of them may have been injured and the other's waited for it. Touching, don't you think?"

His wife regarded him without speaking. Her face had all the individual features of great beauty, but there was something too symmetrical, too inexpressive about them, as though they had been put on canvas by a painter of great technique but no talent.

Rawlinson sighed.

"I don't know. Just because you saw her walking down the old drive last night doesn't mean she was going to bed down with Boris."

"Don't be a fool," she snapped. "Peter's away singing, isn't he? And why else should she be skulking around out there on a nasty damp evening?"

"You were," he observed quietly.

"I was in my own garden," she said sharply. "If she wanted to visit Wear End, she could easily drive round by the road. After all, she does have her own car, which is more than we can afford."

"It's her own money," said Rawlinson.

"It's the money you had to pay her for half of your own house," retorted Stella.

"We've been over all this before," he said. "I had to

buy her out. And there was something left over from Father's will to pay for all this modernization."

He gestured at the kitchen.

"While she lets her husband freeze in that draughty old rectory and spends all her money on cars and clothes!"

"She has to live there too."

"Not when Peter's away she doesn't."

"Oh, for God's sake," he snapped. "She's my sister, so leave it alone."

"And Peter's your cousin. And you're my husband. But what difference does that make to anything?" she yelled after him as he stumped out of the kitchen.

An hour later she took him a cup of coffee in his study.

The light was on above his draughtsman's drawingboard but he was sitting at his desk with his bird-watching journal. The writing was on the left-hand page. On the other he had sketched with a few deft strokes of a felt-tipped pen a pair of whitethroats in a sycamore tree. In the background loomed the bulk of Wear End House with its windows all shuttered.

She put the coffee down by the drawing.

"Are we going to Boris's tomorrow night?"

"I suppose so."

"Will John be there?"

"He's got the face for it."

"What do you mean?"

"Oh, leave it alone, Stella!"

"I think he deserves all our sympathy and support."

"Last time you said it was the biggest stroke of luck he'd had!"

"I still think that!" she snapped. "But the difference between thinking and saying is called civilized behavior."

"OK. OK. Let's drop it," he answered moodily. "I must try to get some work done or we'll have nothing to put down the waste-disposal unit."

At the door she paused and said, "I don't mean to nag, Geoff, but things. . ."

"Yes, yes. I know."

"How's your leg this morning?"

"The same. And better."

"How can that be?" she asked.

"Nothing changes," he said, reaching for his coffee, "but you learn to live with pain."

4

Arthur Lightfoot leaned on his hoe and watched the young woman in the telephone-box. Her Triumph Spitfire was parked with its nearside wheels on the edge of carefully tended grass which lay in front of the village war memorial. Lightfoot made no secret of his watching. Generations of his family had lived and laboured in Wearton and there was as little chance of a native turning from the close contemplation of a stranger as there was of the soldier on the memorial dropping his rifle.

Lightfoot was a man whose face had been weathered to a leathery mask beneath an unkempt stack of gingery hair. His deep-sunk eyes rarely blinked and his mouth gave little sign of being fitted for human speech. To age him between thirty and fifty would have been difficult.

What nature had done for the man, art had done for the woman. She had blonde hair, a good but not over emphatic figure and a face which happily confessed to twenty-five but left you guessing about thirty-five. It had a slightly preoccupied expression as she came out of the phone-box and took a couple of uncertain steps towards the car. Then, as if feeling Lightfoot's gaze upon her, she turned, looked back at him, and strode with sullen determination across the road.

"Excuse me," she said, then, her eyes caught by a double row of staked dahlias close by the side wall of the old stone cottage, she exclaimed, "Aren't they lovely! Such colours for a murky day."

"Frost'll have 'em soon," said Lightfoot.

"Are they . . . do you sell them?"

Lightfoot made a gesture which took in the full extent of his smallholding.

"I grow what I need," he said. "What I don't need, I sell."

He did not look like a man who needed many dahlias, so the woman said, "May I buy some?"

"Aye. Come in and take thy pick."

He held open the rickety gate for her and she walked along the rows of blooms pointing to her choices which he cut with a fearsome clasp knife taken from his pocket. When she reached the angle of the cottage she stopped and said, "I see you had a fire."

The ground behind the cottage was scorched and blackened and a pile of charred rubbish looking like the remnants of several outbuildings had been shovelled together alongside a wired pen which housed three pigs.

"Aye," he said.

"Not too much damage, I hope," she said, looking at the back of the cottage which also bore the mark of great heat. The window-frames looked as if they'd been recently replaced and reglazed.

"Enough. Nought that money won't mend. Are you done choosing?"

"I think so. Perhaps another pink one. They are gorgeous. Is it good soil?"

"Soil's what you make it," he answered. "Many a barrowload of manure and many a barrowload of compost I've poured into this soil. See there!"

He pointed to where a broad pit which seemed to be full of decaying vegetable matter was sending coils of vapour into the dank autumn air.

"Hot as a curate's dreams in there," he averred, watching her closely.

She glanced at him, amused by the odd expression.

"It doesn't look very appetizing," she said. "What's in it?"

"Everything," he said. "What pigs won't eat yon pit gobbles up. Dustmen get slim pickings from Arthur Lightfoot."

His sudden enthusiasm made her uneasy and she was glad to hear the rickety gate shut behind her.

"That your car?" asked Lightfoot as she regained the footpath.

"Yes."

"Ah."

He didn't offer to say more so she asked, "Could you tell me the way to a house called The Pines? I've got a vague idea, but I might as well hit it first time."

"Swithenbank's house?"

"That's right."

"Them dahlias for Mrs. Swithenbank?"

"As a matter of fact, they are."

"She's not fond of dahlias, Mrs. Swithenbank," said Lightfoot. "She says they're a wormy sort of flower."

"I'm sorry for it," said the woman, irritation in her voice now. "Can you tell me where the house is or not?"

"Second turn left, second house on the left," said Lightfoot.

"Thank you."

When she reached the car, he called after her, "Hey!"

She laid the flowers on the passenger seat before turning.

"Yes?"

"Mrs. Swithenbank doesn't like people parking on her lawn either."

Angrily she got into her car, bumped off the grass strip in front of the war memorial, and accelerated violently away.

Arthur Lightfoot watched her out of sight. Turning to his wheelbarrow, he tossed in a couple of weeds prior to pushing the barrow towards his compost pit and tipping the contents on to its steaming surface.

"Feeding time," he said. "Feeding time."

CHAPTER II

. . . I wake and sigh
And sleep to dream till day
Of the truth that gold can never buy.

Pascoe relaxed in a commodious chintz-covered armchair whose springs emitted distant sighs and clangings like an old ship rolling at its moorings on a still night. He looked, and felt, extremely comfortable, but the watchful eyes were triangulating the man in front of him.

Swithenbank was a slightly built man, almost small, but with an air of control and composure which created a greater sense of *presence* than another six inches might have done. He had black hair obviously carefully tended by a good barber. Sorry, *hair stylist,* corrected Pascoe, whose own hairdresser was very much a barber, still more a butcher according to Ellie, his wife. Ellie would also have used Swithenbank's clothes as the occasion of more unflattering comparisons. Pascoe was smart in an off-the-peg chain store kind of way, while there was something about the other man's thin-knit pale blue roll-collar sweater that proclaimed without the need of a label that it was an exclusive Italian design and cost forty-five pounds.

Show me a poor publisher and I'll show you a fool, as Dr. Johnson may have, ought to have, said, thought Pascoe, forcing his attention from the exquisitely cut slacks back to the man's features. Broad forehead, long straight nose, thick but neatly trimmed black moustache, small, very white teeth, which glinted beneath the dark brush as the man made ready to speak.

"Let's not beat about the bush, Inspector," said Swithenbank.

"What bush would that be?" enquired Pascoe politely.

"You said you were here about Kate, my wife. Have you found her?"

"No," said Pascoe.

"Thank God!"

"I'm sorry?" said Pascoe.

"I thought you were going to tell me you'd found her body."

"No. Not yet, sir."

Swithenbank looked at him sharply.

"Not yet. But you sound as if you expect to."

"I didn't intend to," said Pascoe.

Suddenly Swithenbank smiled and the atmosphere became much more relaxed, as if he had operated a switch. A man of considerable charm, thought Pascoe. He didn't trust men of considerable charm very much.

"So we're really at square one, no further forward than

twelve months ago. You think Kate's dead though you've got no proof. And I, of course, remain Number One suspect."

"It's a position we unimaginative policemen always reserve for husbands," replied Pascoe, content to fall in with the new lightness of manner.

"But my ratiocinative powers tell me there must be more, Inspector. Visits from your colleague, Inspector Dove of the Enfield constabulary, I have come to expect. I think he believes, not without cause, that ultimately the threat of his company could bring a man to confess to anything. But I'm sure it takes more than mere suspicion to get a Yorkshire policeman into motion. Am I beating anywhere nearer the bush, Inspector?"

"The bush is burning, but it is not consumed," said Pascoe with a smile.

"A Biblical policeman!" exclaimed Swithenbank.

"Just carry on with the still small voice," said Pascoe, beginning to enjoy the game.

"Now you disappoint me," said Swithenbank. "Wasn't it Elijah who got the still small voice? While, of course, Moses it was who talked to the trees."

"Both agents of the truth," said Pascoe. "You were saying?"

"It's my guess, then, that something has stimulated your interest in me. A tip of some kind. Phone calls perhaps? Or anonymous letters? Am I right or am I right?"

"You're right," said Pascoe. "That's really very sharp of you, sir. Yes, there's been a letter. And, oddly enough, it came to us here in Yorkshire."

"Why 'oddly'?"

"It's just that it's a year since your wife disappeared and we've had nothing about you before. Except through official channels, I mean. All the usual post-disappearance 'tips' went to your local station at Enfield—or straight to Scotland Yard. We contacted Enfield about this letter, of course."

"And the omniscient Inspector Dove told you I was presently visiting Wearton!"

"Right," said Pascoe. "And as *we* received the letter and you are in *our* area . . . well, here *I* am."

"And a pleasant change it makes from your cockney cousins," said Swithenbank. "If I may say so."

"Thank you kindly," said Pascoe. "And if I may say, you seem somehow less surprised or taken aback by all this than I would have expected."

"I work as an editor for Colbridge the publishers. A condition of service is not being surprised. By anything! But you are very sharp, Inspector. In a manner of speaking, I've been prepared for your visit. Or at least its first cause."

"You've had a letter too?" guessed Pascoe. "Splendid. We must compare notes."

Swithenbank smiled and shook his head.

"Alas, no letter. Just phone calls. They started in London about a fortnight ago, three direct, a couple which just got as far as my secretary and the woman who cleans my flat. So I decided to come up here."

"Why? What did they say?"

"Always the same thing. And again this morning, twice. My mother answered the phone. First time the line was dead by the time I got to it. But she heard the message. And the second time, just as you arrived, I heard the voice myself. Exactly the same as before. Just a woman's name, twice repeated. *Ulalume.*"

"Ula . . . ?"

"Ulalume."

"And the voice was female?" said Pascoe, perplexed.

Swithenbank shrugged and said, "Probably. It's an eerie wailing kind of tone. Possibly a male falsetto."

"And when you spoke sternly in reply?"

"Ah. Of course, you came to the door then, didn't you? The line went dead. End of message."

"Message?" said Pascoe. "I'm clearly missing something. There's a message here, is there? Just what does Ulalume signify, Mr. Swithenbank?"

The other leaned back in his chair, put the tips of his fingers together beneath his chin and recited.

"And we passed to the end of the vista
But were stopped by the door of a tomb—
By the door of a legended tomb;
And I said—'What is written, sweet sister,

On the door of this legended tomb?'
She replied—'Ulalume—Ulalume—
'Tis the vault of thy lost Ulalume!' "

"Remarkable," said Pascoe. "I'm impressed. But not much wiser."

"It's a poem by Edgar Allan Poe. Ulalume was a nymph, the dead love of the poet who inadvertently returns to the place where he had entombed her a year earlier.

And I cried—'It was surely October
On this very night of last year
That I journeyed—I journeyed down here—
That I brought a dread burden down here—
Well I know, now, this dim lake of Auber,
This misty mid-region of Weir.'

I can do you *The Raven* and *Annabel Lee*, too, if you like."

"October," said Pascoe. "Weir. Wearton. So that's what brought you up here! What an apt choice of poem!"

"Had I killed my wife and brought her to Wearton to bury her last October, it might indeed seem so," said Swithenbank coldly.

"Indeed," said Pascoe, catching the man's style. "But that's not quite what I meant. The reference was aptly chosen in that you understood it instantly. To me it meant nothing. Just chance?"

Swithenbank shook his head thoughtfully.

"No, not chance. Among other things I do for my firm, I edit a series called *Masters of Literature*. Slim volumes, a bit of biography, a bit of lit. crit.; nothing anyone's going to get a Ph.D. for, but useful to sixth-formers and the undergrad in a hurry. I've done a couple myself, including one on Poe, accompanied by a selection of his poems and stories."

"I see," said Pascoe. "Would this be generally known?"

"It didn't make any best-seller list," said Swithenbank.

"But people in Wearton could know? Your mother might do a spot of quiet boasting. My son, the author."

"I think when I'm away she tries to pretend I'm still at college," said Swithenbank. "But yes, some of my old friends would know. The only true test of an old friend is whether he buys your books! Boris Kingsley certainly bought a copy—he asked me to sign it."

"Boris . . . ?"

"Kingsley. He lives at the Big House, Wear End House, that is."

"I see," said Pascoe. "Any other particular friends?"

Swithenbank laughed, not very mirthfully.

"I gather that friends come a close second to husbands as popular suspects."

"For anonymous letters, yes," said Pascoe.

"I'm sure you're wrong, but let me see. Of my own close circle there remain, besides Boris, Geoffrey Rawlinson. His wife, Stella, née Foxley—big farmers locally. Geoff's sister, Ursula. And Ursula's husband who also happens to be their cousin, Peter Davenport, who also happens to be our vicar!"

"I see," said Pascoe. "A close circle, this?"

"To the point of inbreeding," said Swithenbank cheerfully. "As good local families, we're probably all related somewhere. Except Boris. They've only been here since the end of the last century."

"So you all grew up together?"

"Oh yes. Except Peter. His branch of the family lived in Leeds, but he used to spend nearly all his holidays here. Surprised us all when he went into Holy Orders."

"Why?"

"No one you've stolen apples with can seem quite good enough to be a priest, can they?" said Swithenbank.

"So apart from you, all your circle have remained in Wearton?" said Pascoe.

"I suppose so. Except Ursula and Peter, of course. They married while he was still a curate somewhere near Wakefield. When was that?—about eight years ago, yes, I'd married the previous year—of course, I'd been working in London for nearly two years by then . . ."

"So you'd be twenty-three, twenty-four?"

"So I would. The others fell in rapid succession. First

Geoff and Stella, then, almost immediately, Ursula and Peter. It wasn't till three years after that that Peter came to Wearton as vicar. Too young for some of the natives but the local connection helped."

"But Mr. Kingsley didn't marry?"

"No. He looked after his parents up at the Big House. They weren't all that old, but were both in poor health. His mother went about eighteen months ago, his father last spring."

"And that's the lot? Of your friends, I mean?"

"Yes, I think so. There's Kate's brother, I suppose. Arthur. Arthur Lightfoot. He was several years older and several ages less couth; certainly not one of the charmed circle that made Wearton the Port Said of the north a dozen years ago. But you'd better prick him down on your interview list."

"Interview list?"

"I presume it's more than idle curiosity that's making you ask these questions, Inspector!" he said acidly.

The doorbell rang. Its chime would not have disgraced a cathedral.

"Your mother?" wondered Pascoe. "I should like to talk to her."

"Never gets home till five on Fridays," said Swithenbank.

The bell rang again. Swithenbank made no move.

"Your mother was mistaken about the bell," observed Pascoe. "It seems to be working very well."

"She hates to be disturbed," said Swithenbank, "so she disconnects it. The first thing I do when I come up here is repair it."

Again the bell.

"You certainly know your business," said Pascoe admiringly. "Yes, I'd certainly say it was repaired. It's just the *tone* you miss, not the function, I gather?"

Swithenbank rose.

"It never does to appear too available," he said, leaving the room.

He pulled the door shut behind him. Pascoe immediately jumped up and moved as quietly to the door as the creaky floorboards would permit, but he needn't have bothered about sound getting out as the woodwork and walls were obviously thick enough to prevent anything less raucous than the bell getting in.

Working on the Dalziel principle that the next best thing to overhearing a conversation is to give the impression you've overheard it, he did not resume his seat but stood close to the doorway, apparently rapt in contemplation of a small oil painting darkened by age almost to indecipherability, until the door opened and he found himself looking at a pretty blonde carrying a large bunch of dahlias.

"Let me take those to the kitchen. Mother will be delighted. They're her favourite. Oh, this is Detective-Inspector Pascoe, my dear. Jean Starkey."

Swithenbank removed the flowers and left Pascoe and the newcomer shaking hands.

With an expertise that Pascoe admired, the woman assessed the seating available and chose the comfortable armchair. Not liking the look of the cane chair Swithenbank had occupied, Pascoe perched gingerly on a chaise-longue which was even harder than it appeared.

"Are you an inhabitant of Wearton, too, Miss Starkey?"

She glanced down at her ringless left hand and smiled approval.

"Oh no. Like yourself, just visiting. At least I presume you're just visiting?"

"For the moment, yes."

"Does that mean you may eventually settle here?" asked the woman, rounding her eyes.

"I think it means the Inspector doesn't consider 'visiting' adequately covers his possible return flanked by bloodhounds and armed with warrants," said Swithenbank.

He came back into the room carrying a huge vase into which the dahlias had been tumbled with no pretence of aesthetic theory.

Placing them on a small table within reach of the big armchair he said, "Do what you can with these, Jean dear. I've no talent for nature."

Then, relaxing into the cane chair which seemed to have been made for a man of his size, he continued, "Mr. Pascoe is here about Kate's disappearance. No, there's been no news, but there's been a new outburst of anonymous activity. Phone calls to me and a letter to the police. By the way, Inspector, you never actually told me what was in the letter, did you? It must have been something pretty striking to get you off traffic duty. Could I see it? I might be able to help with the writing."

"No writing, sir," said Pascoe. "Typewriter. Possibly a Remington International, quite old. You wouldn't know anyone who has such a machine?"

He included the woman in his query. She smiled and shook her head.

"But what did it say?" persisted Swithenbank.

"Not much. Let me see. *John Swithenbank knows where the other is*. Yes, that's it."

Swithenbank and Jean Starkey exchanged puzzled glances.

"I'm sorry, Inspector," he said. "It's like Ulalume to you. I don't get it."

"No, no. I should apologize," said Pascoe. "I haven't been entirely open."

He pulled an envelope out of his inside pocket and from it he took three colour prints which he passed over to Swithenbank. The prints showed from different angles a pendant ear-ring, a single pearl in a gold setting on a thin chain about an inch long.

"Do you recognize that, sir?" asked Pascoe.

Jean Starkey, unable to contain her curiosity, had risen to peer over Swithenbank's shoulder at the photographs. He glanced up at her and she put her hand on his shoulder either for her support or his comfort.

"Kate had a pair like that," he said. "But I couldn't be absolutely sure."

"It matches the specification in your list of clothes and other items which disappeared with your wife."

"Does it? It's a year ago. If you say it does, then clearly it does. This was with that cryptic note?"

"Not so cryptic after all," said Jean Starkey.

"No," said Swithenbank. "No. I see now why you came hot-foot to Wearton, Inspector. This really does point the finger."

"But it means nothing!" protested the woman.

He smiled up at her.

"I don't mean at me, dear. I mean at whoever sent it. If it is Kate's, that is. Could I have a look at the ear-ring itself, Inspector?"

"Eventually," said Pascoe. "Just now it's down at our laboratory for examination."

"Examination? For what?"

Pascoe watched Swithenbank closely as he answered.

"I'm afraid, sir, that there were traces of blood on the fastening bar. As though the ear-ring had been torn from the ear by main force."

CHAPTER III

Much I marvelled this ungainly fowl
to hear discourse so plainly.

"A poem," said Dalziel.

"By Edgar Allan Poe," said Pascoe.

"I didn't know he wrote poems as well."

"As well as short stories, you mean?"

"As well as pictures," said Dalziel. "I've seen a lot of his stuff on the telly. Good for a laugh mainly, but sometimes he can give you a scare."

Pascoe regarded the gross figure of his boss, Detective-Superintendent Andrew Dalziel (pronounced Dee-ell, unless you wanted your head bitten off) and wondered whether the fat man was taking the piss. But he knew better than to ask.

"I've got it here," he said, proffering a "complete works" borrowed from the local library.

Dalziel put on his reading glasses which sat on his great shapeless nose like a space-probe on Mars. Carefully he read through the poem, his fleshy lips moving from time to time as he half voiced a passage.

When he had finished he rested the open book on the desk before him and said, "Now that's something like a poem!"

"You liked it?" said Pascoe, surprised.

"Oh aye. It's got a bit of rhyme, not like this modern stuff that doesn't even have commas."

"Thank you, Dr. Leavis," murmured Pascoe, and went on hurriedly, "but does it do us any good?"

"Depends," said Dalziel, putting his hand inside his shirt to scratch his left rib cage. "Was it meant to be general or specific?"

"Sorry?"

"If it's specific, listen.

It was down by the dank tarn of Auber
In the ghoul-haunted woodland of Weir.

You want to find yourself a bit of woodland round a pond and go over it with a couple of dogs and a frogman. What's the country like round there?"

"Like country," said Pascoe dubiously. "Wearton's a cluster of houses, pub and a church in a bit of a valley, so I suppose there are plenty of woods and ponds thereabouts. But if it's *that* specific, Swithenbank would hardly have mentioned it to me, would he?"

"Mebbe not. Or mebbe he'd get a kick. Playing with a thick copper."

"I didn't get that impression," said Pascoe carefully.

Dalziel laughed, a Force Eight blast.

"More likely with me, eh? But he'd soon spot you're a clever bugger, the way you get your apostrophes in the right place. So if he *has killed his missus and if this Ulalume poem does* point in the right direction, he'd keep his mouth shut. Right? *Unless* he was bright enough to think we might have got a few calls ourselves."

"Which we didn't," said Pascoe. "Just the letter."

"And the ear-ring," said Dalziel. "Remind me again, lad. How'd we first get mixed up in this business?"

Pascoe opened the thin file he was carrying and glanced at the first sheet of paper in it.

"October twenty-fourth last year," he said. "Request for assistance from Enfield—that's where Swithenbank lives. Says he'd reported his wife missing on the fifteenth. They hadn't been able to get any kind of line on her movements after the last time Swithenbank claimed to have seen her. Like him, she comes from Wearton, so would we mind checking in case she'd done the classic thing and bolted for home. We checked. Parents both dead, but her brother Arthur still lives in the village. He's got a bit of a smallholding. He hadn't seen her since her last visit with Swithenbank, two months earlier. Nor had anyone else."

"Or they weren't saying," said Dalziel.

"Perhaps. There was no reason to be suspicious at the time. Routine enquiry. That was it as far as we were concerned. A month later Enfield came back at us. Were we *quite* sure there was no trace? They wrapped it up, of course, but that's what it came to. They hadn't been able to get a single line on Mrs. Swithenbank and when someone disappears as completely as that, you start to get really suspicious. But if you're wise, you double check before you let your suspicions show too clearly."

"Who'd done the checking in Wearton?" asked Dalziel.

"We just left it to the local lad first time round," said Pascoe. "This time I sent Sergeant Wield down. Same result. All quiet after that till this week when the ear-ring turned up."

"How've they been earning their pay in Enfield this past year?" asked Dalziel.

"Saving the sum of things from the sound of it," said Pascoe. "But in between the bullion robberies and the international dope rings, they managed to lean heavily enough on Swithenbank for him to drum up a tame solicitor to lean back."

"Any motive?"

Pascoe shrugged.

"The marriage wasn't idyllic, so the gossip went, but no worse than a thousand others. *She* might have been having a bit on the side, her girl-friends guessed, but couldn't or wouldn't point the finger. *He* wasn't averse to the odd close encounter at a party, but again no one was naming names."

"That's marriage Enfield-style, is it?" said Dalziel, shaking his head. He made *Enfield* sound like *Gomorrah*.

"Give us his tale again," continued Dalziel.

"Friday, fourteenth October, Swithenbank arrives at

his office at the usual time. Nothing out of the ordinary during the morning except that his secretary told Willie Dove, Inspector Dove that is, who was doing the questioning, that he seemed a bit moody that morning."

"How moody? *I shouldn't have cut off her head like that*—that moody?"

"The secretary just put it down to the fact that his favourite assistant was leaving that day."

"Favourite? Woman?" said Dalziel eagerly.

"Fellow. No, it wasn't the fact that he was leaving, more why he was leaving that had got to Swithenbank, it seems. This chap was putting it all behind him, going off to somewhere primitive like the Orkneys to live off the earth and be a free man. There's a lot of it among the monied middle classes."

"He's not bent, is he, this Swithenbank?" asked Dalziel, reluctant to leave this scent.

"No," said Pascoe, exasperated. "It just made him think, that's all. Doesn't it make you think a bit, sir, when you hear someone's had the guts to opt out? It's a normal sociological reaction."

"Is it, lad? You ever find yourself fancying somewhere primitive, I'll send you to Barnsley. What's all this got to do with anything?"

"I'm trying to tell you. Sir. They had a party for the dear departing at lunch-time. It started in the office and finished on platform five at King's Cross when they put their colleague on his train. Swithenbank was in quite a state by this time."

"Pissed, you mean?"

"That and telling all who would listen that he was wasting his life, that materialism was going to be the death of Western society, that any man who was brave enough could sever his chains with a single blow . . ."

"What kind of chains did he have in mind?" wondered Dalziel.

"I don't know," said Pascoe. "Though I should say from the way he dresses that he's decided to hang on to the chains and go down with the rest of Western society. Anyway, those sober enough to remember anything remembered this outburst because it was so uncharacteristic of him. An intellectual smoothie was how his secretary rated him."

"A loyal girl, that," said Dalziel.

"Willie Dove has his ways," said Pascoe. "Where was I? Oh yes. From King's Cross they, that is the survivors, walked back to the office, hoping to benefit from the fresh air. It's near Woburn Place, so not too far, and they got back about two-thirty. But Swithenbank didn't go in. Despite all attempts to dissuade him, he headed for his car."

"His mates didn't think he was fit to drive?" said Dalziel. "He must have been bad, considering most of these southern sods drive home half pissed every night!"

"Possibly," said Pascoe, as if accepting a serious academic argument. "The thing was, it wasn't home that Swithenbank was making for, but Nottingham."

"Nottingham? He really must've been drunk!"

"I'm sorry," said Pascoe. "Didn't I say? He was due up in Nottingham that evening for a conference with one of his authors. He'd taken an overnight bag to the office with him and planned a gentle drive north at his leisure that afternoon. But as we've seen, events had overtaken him. So far, his story's been confirmable. After this, there's only Swithenbank's word for what happened, and most of that he claims to have forgotten! He says he'd only driven about half a mile when he came to the conclusion he must be out of his mind! He says he didn't really make a conscious decision, but somehow instead of heading for the MI, he found himself on the way home to Enfield. He can't recollect much about the drive, or getting into the flat, but he's pretty certain his wife wasn't there."

"If she was, he'd be the last person she'd be expecting to see," said Dalziel. "Think about that!"

"I believe Inspector Dove has thought about it," said Pascoe patiently. "All Swithenbank does remember positively is waking up some time after five, lying on his bed and feeling rough. He had a shower and a coffee, felt better, tried to ring Nottingham to apologize for his lateness but couldn't get through, wrote his wife a note saying he'd been home, and set off up the MI like the clappers. Like I say, there's no support for any of this. But one of the neighbors definitely saw him arrive back the following afternoon about five p.m. His wife isn't in and Swithenbank gets worried."

"Why? She never missed *Dr. Who*, or what?"

"His note was still there," said Pascoe reprovingly. "Untouched. He does nothing for an hour or two, then rings around some likely friends. Nothing. Finally late on Saturday night when she still hasn't returned, he contacts the police. And the wheels go into motion. Routine at first. There's a suitcase and some of his wife's clothes missing. So they check the possibilities. Friends, relatives, etc.—that's where we first came in. Her passport's still at home. A month later she's made no drawing upon her bank account. So now Willie Dove moves in hard."

"Started digging up the garden and chipping at the garage floor, did he?" said Dalziel.

"He probably would have done except that they lived in a flat and he parked his car in the street," said Pascoe. "But he found nothing."

"So what's he think?"

"He thinks Swithenbank's a clever bugger and has got the body safely stashed. He's kept on at him ever since, but nothing."

"So why's he think Swithenbank's the man?"

"Intuition, I suppose."

Dalziel snorted in disgust.

"*Intuition!* Evidence plus an admission, that's what makes detective work. I hope I never hear you using that word, Peter!"

Pascoe smiled weakly and said, "He's not making a big thing out of it. He just feels in his bones that some time between leaving the party and getting to Nottingham, Swithenbank did the deed and disposed of the body."

"What's wrong with the night before?" asked Dalziel. "Put her in the boot. That'd explain his bit of depression that morning."

"So it would," said Pascoe. "Except . . ."

"All right, clever bugger," growled Dalziel. "What's up?"

"Except, she went to the hairdresser's on Friday morning. Last reported sighting," said Pascoe.

Dalziel was silent for a while.

"I ought to thump hell out of you twice a day," he said finally. "I take it because you've said nowt much about it that this Nottingham visit was confirmed."

"Yes," said Pascoe. "Jake Starr, some science fiction writer. He was doing a bit on Jules Verne for Swithenbank's *Masters of Literature* series. He confirmed Swithenbank arrived a lot later than arranged, about eight p.m. They worked—and ate—till the early hours. Got up late the next morning. Swithenbank left after lunch. We know he was back in Enfield by five."

Dalziel pondered.

"All we've got really is a cockney cop's feeling that he did it. Right?"

"And the phone calls. And the letter and ear-ring."

Dalziel dismissed these with a two-fingered wave of his left hand.

"This lass who turned up today. His fancy piece, you reckon?"

"Could be," said Pascoe cautiously.

"Perhaps she's the other lass in the poem, that Psyche."

"I think Psyche represents the poetic soul," said Pascoe.

"Poetic arsehole," said Dalziel scornfully. "What's it say?—*so I pacified Psyche and kissed her.* That sounds like flesh and blood to me. Mind you, if she is his fancy woman, it's a funny thing to do, bringing her up to Wearton like that. It's like flaunting it a bit, wouldn't you say?"

Pascoe indicated that he would say. Jean Starkey had been much occupying his mind since he left Wearton that morning. He had made a note of her car number and asked for it to be traced as soon as he got back to the station, but since vehicle licensing had been computerized, this process could now take several hours.

"Well, it all seems bloody thin to me" said Dalziel, rising from his chair and scratching his left buttock preparatory to departure. "Some old mate trying to stir things for Swithenbank. Did you check on his old acquaintance in the village?"

"Didn't have a chance this morning," said Pascoe. "I had to be back here for a meeting at lunch-time. But I'll go back, I suppose, and have a word. Or send Sergeant Wield."

"That's it," approved Dalziel. "Delegate. You've got plenty to keep you occupied, I hope. *Our* problems. This is nowt but an 'assist,' after all."

"If Kate Swithenbank's lying in a hole near Wearton, it's more than an assist!" protested Pascoe.

"If Jack the bloody Ripper's opening the batting for Yorkshire (and I sometimes think the buggers who are look old enough), it's still someone else's case," said Dalziel. "They'll be open in an hour. You can pay for my help with a pint."

"Dear at half the price," muttered Pascoe as the fat man lumbered from the room.

He spent the next twenty minutes going over his notes on the background to the case. On the left-hand page of his notebook he had made a digest of the facts as he knew them. The right-hand page was reserved for observations and comments and was woefully blank. He managed by an effort of will to break the blankness with a couple of question-marked words, but it was reaching beyond the limits even of that intuition which Dalziel so scorned and he hastily turned the page as though the fat man might be peering over his shoulder.

He was now among the notes on Swithenbank's "friends" in Wearton. The tedious business of chatting with each of them would have to be done some time. He wondered whether his conscience would permit him to send Sergeant Wield again. Perhaps, if only the woman Jean Starkey hadn't turned up. There was a false note there somehow. It could be, of course, that Swithenbank wasn't expecting her. He was cool enough to carry it off. Perhaps she was a bit on the side who felt it was time to claim a more central position. But there had been nothing in her manner to suggest that her arrival was an act of defiance. Another hyper-cool customer? Like calling to like? John Swithenbank. Jean Starkey. Same initials. Not something you could really comment on in a report, though Dalziel had once told him he could squeeze significance out of a marble tit. Jean Starkey. John Swithenbank. And . . . and . . . there was something there . . . the marble tit was yielding . . .

"Excuse me, sir."

"Oh, damn!" said Pascoe, roused from his reverie just on the brink of revelation.

"Sorry, sir," said Sergeant Wield. "That car registration you wanted checked. They've broken all records. Here you are."

He placed a sheet of paper on the desk and withdrew. Pascoe looked down at it, unseeing at first, then the words hardened into focus.

Miss Jean Starkey,
38A Chubb Court,
Nottingham.

"Well," said Pascoe. "Well."

The marble was like a wet bath sponge now.

He picked up his telephone and rang the public library. That done, he asked his exchange to connect him with Inspector Dove at Enfield.

"Hello, Peter. What's up? Don't say you've corralled our boy!"

"Not yet," said Pascoe. "Look, Willie, that statement from the writer Swithenbank went to visit, Jake Starr. Who took it?"

"Hold on. Let's have a look. Here we are. We did what we did with you lot, relied on Nottingham. Why? What's up?"

"Do you know if anyone at Nottingham actually met Jake Starr?"

"Hang about, there's a note here, can't read my own writing. No, in fact I don't think they did. I remember now. They spoke to his secretary, who said Starr was on his way to New York. But she remembered Swithenbank arriving and she was there on Saturday morning when he left. She got in touch with her boss who sent a statement confirming this and having Swithenbank in his sights till bedtime. The secretary was around most of the time too. So we didn't ask them to follow it up when this Starr fellow got back. Why?"

"You don't happen to have a note of the secretary's name, do you?"

"Yes. I've got a statement from her here. I'm sorry,

Pete, we could have sent you photo-copies of all this stuff but knowing how much your boss hates paper, I thought the brief digest would do. Jean Starkey. Miss Jean Starkey. There we are. Now tell me what this is all about."

"With pleasure," said Pascoe. "I've just been on to our library where they have useful things like a Writers' Who's Who. Jake Starr is a pseudonym. And no prizes for guessing that the real name is Jean Starkey. But there's more. Miss Starkey's a very personable blonde who at this very moment is in Wearton visiting Swithenbank. And it didn't look like business to me!"

Dove whistled.

"That leaves us with a bit of egg on our face, doesn't it?" he said cheerfully. "Does it get us much farther forward, though?"

"Try this," said Pascoe. "If somehow Swithenbank did contrive to have his missus in the boot when he drove north that afternoon, with Starkey alibi-ing him, he had all the time in the world to dispose of the body somewhere a long, long way from Enfield. Naturally he'd want somewhere as safe as possible. What if his childhood memories put him in mind of the perfect hiding-place up here?"

"Hidden cave, secret passage, that sort of thing?" said Dove, making it sound like something out of Enid Blyton, much to Pascoe's irritation.

"OK then. Where do *you* think she is?" he asked."Stuffed up the chimney in his flat?"

"First place we looked," laughed Dove. "Thanks for ringing, Pete. It could be helpful and at least it gives you something better to do than chasing cows out of cornfields. Keep up the good work and let's know when he's planning to come back, then I'll see what a bit of real pressure can do. Anything else I can do for you?"

He can do for *me!* thought Pascoe indignantly. As he flicked through the pages of his notebook, his eye fell on his question-marked words. Never mind what Dalziel said, everyone had one good intuitive guess coming and even Dalziel would reckon this was in a good cause.

He made a mental choice, crossed out one of the words and said in a studiously casual voice, "Just one thing.

Kate Swithenbank's last reported sighting was at the hairdresser's. Did anyone ask what she had done there?''

There was a pause and a rustling of papers.

''It's not here if they did,'' said Dove. ''Any particular reason?''

'Just part of the steady plod us yokels go at,'' said Pascoe. ''I don't really imagine that you lot have overlooked anything. Else.''

''Get stuffed,'' said Dove. ''I'll see if I can find out. Cheers now.''

''Cheers.''

Pascoe sat back in his chair and felt pleased with himself. His social science degree enabled him to regard such phenomena as inter-regional rivalries with academic objectivity. On the other hand you couldn't get away from it, there was something very pleasant about getting one up on those smart-alec sods in London. Dalziel would, in his own phrase, be chuffed to buggery.

There was still the problem of tactics. There was no question now of sending Sergeant Wield to Wearton. This was his affair, right to the bitter end. The question was when? And how?

The answer came from the most unexpected source.

His telephone rang and the constable on the exchange said a Mr. Swithenbank would like to speak to him.

''Put him on,'' commanded Pascoe.

''Inspector, glad to have caught you.''

His voice sounded higher, lighter on the telephone.

''I was just thinking about you, Mr. Swithenbank.''

''I'm flattered. And I about you. A thought struck me—you hinted a desire, or rather an intention, of talking about this business with my old acquaintance in the village. Are you still keen?''

''It's on my schedule,'' said Pascoe cautiously.

''The thing is, Boris Kingsley is having a little get-together at the Big House tomorrow evening. I was just going to ring him to make it OK to take Miss Starkey along with me. All my old chums will be there. So it occurred to me, if you'd like to take them all in one fell swoop, I'm sure Boris wouldn't mind. He's always had a taste for cheap fiction and a real life detective questioning his guests in the library would be right up his street.''

Pascoe thought about it, felt the silence growing long enough to be significant and decided he didn't mind. After all, Swithenbank mustn't be allowed to think the law was so easily organizable.

"Deep thoughts, Inspector," said Swithenbank. "Penny for them."

"Something about Greeks bearing gifts," replied Pascoe. "Yes, I think that might prove very useful, Mr. Swithenbank. Thank you."

"Oh good. Why don't you call here about seven and then you can have a drink and a chat with Mother before we set out."

"Fine," said Pascoe. " 'Bye."

"Cheeky bugger," he said to the replaced telephone. You had to admire the man's nerve, he thought with a smile. Setting him up like Hercule Poirot.

Then his eyes fell on the still open volume of Poe and he pulled it towards him and read:

And I cried—"It was surely October
On this very night of last year
That I journeyed—I journeyed down here—
That I brought a dread burden down here—"

He glanced at his desk calendar. Tomorrow was Saturday, 14 October.

"Cheeky bugger," he said again. But there was no humour in his voice this time.

CHAPTER IV

From childhood's hour I have not been
As others were.

I

"And she caught him by his garment saying, Lie with me."

Peter Davenport was so engrossed in what he was writing that he had not heard his wife come into the study and he started violently as she grabbed his cardigan.

Ursula laughed.

"Wrong text, dear?" she said. "It might produce a livelier sermon than some of your recent efforts."

"It might," he agreed, smiling with an effort. "I'm sorry, my dear, I'm just a bit busy and there might not be time later . . ."

"For what? I should have listened when they told me a counter-tenor was a kind of eunuch."

She shivered violently and drew her thin silken robe more closely around her.

"You'll catch your death. Here, take my cardigan."

"*And he left his garment in her hand, and fled, and got him out.* No, you keep it. You must be frozen to the marrow sitting here. God, when are they going to do something about the heating in this place? Or flog it and put us in a nice cosy semi?"

In the summer the big Victorian rectory was a source of delight to Ursula most of the time. Then she could enjoy the role of vicar's wife, enjoy supervising the annual garden party on the huge bumpy lawn, enjoy entertaining various ladies' committees in the cool, airy drawing-room, enjoy discussing with them the recipe for her famous seed cake (purchased at Fortnum and Mason's whenever she went to London), enjoy their resentment of her, their memory of her wild young days, their suspicion that their husbands still lusted after her. And on long warm summer evenings as hostess to more secular groups of friends, she enjoyed throwing open the french windows and leading them into the garden after dinner, walking barefoot across the lawn, laughing and talking and sometimes turning from vicar's wife to essential Eve and back again within the compass of a cloud's passage across the moon or the circumvention of a rhododendron bush.

But when summer's date was done, the draughty old

rectory quickly grew chill beyond the reach of its antiquated radiators or the economic flame at the back of its huge open fireplace. She was not altogether joking when she told Boris Kingsley she slept with him for warmth whenever Peter was away at one of his choir concerts, though in truth she had no more real idea of the reason than she had of her reason for marrying her cousin eight years earlier. Perhaps she had needed to show Kate Lightfoot and John Swithenbank that their alliance meant nothing to her. But she lacked the temperament for self-analysis, managing to find even in the worst day something that made the next day seem worth waiting for. She knew there was something wrong between her and her husband, even had a notion of what that something was, but had no solution to offer for the problem other than to wait and see and enjoy herself as best she could along the way.

Peter Davenport on the other hand believed he understood all too well his reasons for marrying Ursula and had long since recognized them as inadequate and selfish. But other more pressing matters had been occupying his mind and his conscience in recent months. Like Ursula, he had lived from day to day, but unlike her, he felt an impulsion to definitive, even desperate action, which he could not resist much longer.

"I've got nothing to wear tonight," she averred.

He thought bitterly of the stuffed wardrobes upstairs, then dismissed the uncharitable thought. Ursula had been eager to put her inherited money into the common pool; he had resisted. He was glad he had. At least that couldn't be held against him.

"It'll be very informal, surely," he said.

"Informal doesn't mean scruffy," she retorted.

"No, it doesn't," he said. "Lexicographers the world over would agree with you. Who's going to be there anyway?"

"The usual lot," she said. "The usual conversations, the usual tedium."

"Isn't John going to be there?" he asked.

She looked at him sharply.

"What difference will that make?"

"A breath of fresh air from the great outside world."

She laughed and said, "You may be right. I was talking to Boris earlier. He hinted at a surprise but wouldn't say what. You know how he loves being mysterious. Perhaps Kate has come back from the . . . wherever she's been."

Davenport put down his pen sharply and stood up.

"Not even Boris would keep back such news just for effect," he said sternly. "Poor John. A whole year now. It must have been hell for him."

"That depends on what the previous year was like, doesn't it?" said his wife. "Let's have a drink, shall we? It might warm us up."

"All right. What time do we have to go?"

"Half seven, something like that," she said vaguely. "I thought we'd walk it. Along the old drive."

"What on earth for?" he protested strongly. "It looks like rain. And it'll ruin your shoes."

"I just feel like the exercise. Besides, it's traditional. Vicars and their ladies must have taken that route when summoned to the Big House for a couple of centuries at least."

"Perhaps. It's not a pleasant walk. At this time of year, I mean."

He shivered and she regarded him curiously.

"Shouldn't a vicar know how to put ghosts in their places?" she mocked.

"What do you mean?"

"Joke," she said. "Though come to think of it, sometimes there does seem a rather excessive amount of noise and movement in the churchyard. Not just foxes and owls, I mean, though some of it's so overgrown it could hide a tiger. You really ought to insist that something's done about it, Peter."

"Yes, yes. I'll have a word," he said. "Let's have that drink."

He poured the gin with a generous hand and was pouring himself another before his wife had done more than dampen her full red lips on her first.

2

"My name's Pascoe. I'm a police inspector. Could I have a word with you, Mr. Lightfoot?"

Arthur Lightfoot viewed him silently, then went back into the cottage as though indifferent whether Pascoe followed or not.

Reckoning that if he waited for invitations round here, he was likely to become a fixture, Pascoe went in, closed the door behind him, pursued Lightfoot into a square, sparsely furnished living-room and sat down.

The room occupied the breadth of the building and Pascoe could see that the uncurtained windows at the back were new and the plaster on the wall had been recently refurbished.

"You had a fire?" he said conversationally.

"What do you want, mister?"

Pascoe sighed. One of the more distressing things about his job was the frequency with which he met Yorkshiremen who made Dalziel sound like something from Castiglione's *Book of the Courtier.*

"It's about your sister, Kate. I've got no news of her, you understand," he added hastily for fear of creating a false optimism.

He needn't have worried.

"I need no news of our Kate," said Lightfoot.

"I don't understand. You mean you don't want to hear anything about your sister?"

It was a genuine semantic problem. Lightfoot's face showed a recognizable expression for a moment. It was one of contempt.

"I mean I need no news. She's dead. I need no bobby to come telling me that."

"Well, if you know that, you know more than I do," rejoined Pascoe. "What makes you so sure?"

"A man knows such things."

Oh God, that awful intuition again. No, not intuition, superstition. This was a medieval peasant who stood before him, but without any feudal inhibitions.

"We can't be sure," insisted Pascoe gently. "Not till . . . well, not till we've seen her."

"I've seen her."

"*What?*"

"What do you know, mister? Nowt!"

Lightfoot spoke angrily. It was clearly only the gentler responses that were missing from his make-up.

"I've heard her voice in the black of night and I've risen from my bed and I've seen her blown this way and that in the night wind," proclaimed Lightfoot with terrifying intensity.

Pascoe began to regret that he had sat down as the man loomed over him describing his lunatic visions. Looking for an excuse to get to his feet, he spotted a framed photograph on the mantelpiece.

"Is this your sister, Mr. Lightfoot?" he asked, rising and edging past the man. The picture showed a slim girl in a white dress and a wide-brimmed floppy hat from beneath which a pair of disproportionately large eyes looked uncertainly at the photographer. Like a startled rabbit, thought Pascoe unkindly. The background to the picture was a house which could have been The Pines, but identification was not helped by the fact that the print had been torn in half, presumably to remove someone standing alongside the girl.

Lightfoot snatched the frame from his hands, a rudeness perhaps more native than aggressive.

"What do you want?" he demanded once more.

"I'm on my way to see your brother-in-law," answered Pascoe, deciding that the more direct he was, the quicker he could make his exit. "There have been some phone calls, and a letter, suggesting that he knows more about your sister's disappearance then he's letting on. We're eager to find the person who's been making these suggestions."

"So you single me out!" said Lightfoot accusingly.

"No," said Pascoe. "I was in Wearton yesterday, and I spoke to Mr. Swithenbank then, but I didn't have time to contact anyone else. Later on tonight I'm going to see a variety of people at Wear End, Mr. Kingsley's house. I thought I'd drop in on you en route, that's all."

"You guessed I wouldn't be at t'party then?" said Lightfoot.

Pascoe looked uncomfortable and Lightfoot laughed like a tree cracking in a strong wind.

"Yon bugger wouldn't invite me to suck in the air on his land," he said.

"Mr. Kingsley doesn't care for your company?" said Pascoe redundantly.

"He cares for nowt but his own flesh," said Lightfoot. "Like father, like son."

He replaced the photograph on the mantelpiece with a thump that defied Pascoe to touch it again.

"Is it your brother-in-law that's been torn off the picture?" enquired Pascoe.

"I wanted none of his face around my house," said Lightfoot.

"Why's that?"

"No reason."

"Do you not like him either?"

"They're all the same, them lot," said Lightfoot. "Kate'd be still living to this day likely if she hadn't got mixed up with them."

"Surely they were her friends," protested Pascoe.

"Friends! What need of friends when there's family? Are you done, Mr. Detective? There's others have to work late hours besides t'police."

On the doorstep Pascoe turned and said, "Have you made any calls to Mr. Swithenbank or sent the police a letter, Mr. Lightfoot?"

"That's direct," said Lightfoot. "I wondered if you'd get round to asking. The answer's no, I haven't. If I knew definite who'd harmed her, I . . ."

"You'd what?"

"I'd know, wouldn't I? Do you question Swithenbank so direct?"

"If the occasion demands," said Pascoe.

"Then ask him this. What was he doing skulking around the churchyard at midnight night before last? You ask him."

"All right," said Pascoe. "As a matter of interest, what were *you* doing skulking round the churchyard, Mr. Lightfoot?"

The door was shut hard in his face. Pascoe whistled with relief as he strolled through the gate and got into his car. There was something frightening about Lightfoot in a primal kind of way. A man who had commerce with ghosts must be frightening! Though a man so certain of his sister's death might have other reasons for his certainty, and that was more frightening still.

Behind him in the comfortless cottage Lightfoot returned to the job which Pascoe's arrival had interrupted. Seated at the kitchen table, he oiled and polished the separated parts of his shotgun till he was satisfied. Then he reassembled it and sat motionless for a long time while outside the light faded, rooks beat their way homeward to the nest-dark trees, a light mist drifted out of the dank fields till a wind began to rise and bore it away and drove the darkness over the land.

Then Lightfoot stood up, put on a black donkey jacket, set his gun in the crook of his arm and went out into the night.

3

Arthur Lightfoot was in many people's minds that night.

Geoffrey Rawlinson as he shaved in preparation for the party at Wear End found himself thinking of Lightfoot. Even in his democratic teens when as a matter of faith such things were not allowed to matter, he had always been conscious of a vague distaste for calling on Kate at her brother's cottage. There was something so brutishly spartan about the place, and in that atmosphere Kate herself, so unnoticing of or uncaring for the near squalor, seemed a different person. By his early twenties, Rawlinson was openly wrestling with the choice he had to make. If he married Kate, he was marrying a Lightfoot. The two major elements of his make-up—the draughtsman's love of order and shape and the naturalist's love of energy and colour—clashed and jarred against each other like boulders in a turbulent sea. His sister looked pityingly at him but refused to speak. It had to be his own choice and he was ashamed of himself for having such a superficially Victorian reason for hesitating.

Then Ursula told him one morning the news she had learnt the previous night and he realized to his amazement that his sense of critical choice had been fallacious.

Now he lived in a framework of meticulous order which he felt both as a scaffolding and a cage.

But even now, even when he regretted the past most passionately, the memory of Arthur, spooning stew into his mouth at the kitchen table with the encrusted sauce bottle and the curded milk bottle on guard before him, made Rawlinson twitch with distaste.

But that memory was just a mental feint to keep his mind from contemplating—as now he did, looking into his own reluctant eyes in the shaving mirror—the events of a year ago, and the pain, mental and physical, he had suffered since that dreadful night.

Stella Rawlinson thought of Arthur, too, and wondered for the thousandth time, with a cold self-analysis which had nothing to do with control, why the humiliation of a fourteen-year-old girl should lay marks on her which persisted throughout womanhood. It was not unusual for a pubescent girl to have a crush on her best friend's elder brother. Nor could it be too unusual that recognition of this should cause dismissive and hurtful amusement. But rarely could this amusement be couched in such terms or such circumstances as to create a hatred stretching beyond maturity.

Only one other person had ever been aware of what she suffered. What were best friends for? But a sharing is as likely to mean a doubling as a halving, she had long ago decided. It was a mistake to be rectified if possible, certainly not one to be repeated. So even with her husband she kept her peace and when he showed signs of wanting to commit the same error of confidence, she turned away.

And Boris Kingsley, too, thought of Arthur as he arranged the chairs and filled the decanters in his library. But he thought of many other things besides as he opened the wardrobes in his bedroom and dressed for his party.

And for a while as his guests arrived he thought of nothing but making them welcome. He didn't like most of them but there are less expensive ways of manifesting dislike than over your own drink in your own house, so he smiled and chatted and poured till a clock chimed and he glanced anxiously at his watch.

Then he smiled again but this time secretively, excused himself, closed the door firmly behind him, and picked up the telephone.

CHAPTER V

The angels, whispering to one another,
Can find, among their burning terms of love,
None so devotional as that of "Mother."

"You've met my mother?" said Swithenbank.

"Briefly," said Pascoe. "How do you do?"

He shook hands with the woman and wondered if he was being conned. Surely this wasn't the woman he had spoken to outside the house the previous day. There had been something distinctive . . . yes, her hair had been a sort of purpley-blue, not the rich auburn of the woman before him.

"You approve of my coiffure, Mr. Pascoe?" she said and he realized he was staring.

"Very nice," he said. "It's very . . . becoming."

"I changed it at my son's behest," she said. "He didn't care for my last colour, did you, John?"

"It seemed inappropriate," said Swithenbank.

"And this?" said his mother, striking a little pose with her left hand behind her head. "Is this appropriate?"

"If not to your age, at least to your genus," he said drily. "I'll leave it to you, Inspector, and put the finishing touches to my own coiffure. Mother, Mr. Pascoe might like a drink."

"What would we do without our children to teach us manners?" wondered Mrs. Swithenbank. "Scotch, Inspector?"

"Please. Some water. Your daughter-in-law went to the hairdresser's on the day she disappeared."

It was not quite the way he had intended to open the

interview but Mrs. Swithenbank was not quite the woman he had expected. She took the transition with the ease of a steeplechaser spotting that the ground fell away on the other side of the hedge.

"Did she now? That would be a year ago today, you mean, Inspector?"

"That's right. Thought it was a Friday last year."

"Yes, I've always found that rather confusing. Though it's nice to have one's birthday shifting around; it's easier to miss. Not that birthdays bother me yet. I had John young, of course. And he looks older than he is. Here's your drink, Mr. Pascoe. Do you find me absurd?"

"I don't think so," said Pascoe gravely.

"Not just a trifle?"

He considered.

"No," he said. "Amusing, yes. But not absurd."

"Good. Neither do I. What did Kate have done at the hairdresser's?"

"Shampoo. Cut. And she bought a wig."

Dove had phoned through with the information at lunch-time, admitting as cheerfully as ever that perhaps a year earlier they should have been asking questions about a frizzy blonde as well as a straight brunette.

Pascoe was not one to kick a man when he was down but he had no qualms about applying the boot to someone as reluctant to fall as Dove.

"This could knock your Swithenbank fixation into little pieces, Willie," he had said. "She could have got to the other end of the country without being noticed."

"And stopped unnoticed? Bollocks," Dove had replied. "All it means is she could have left the flat without being spotted and been picked up somewhere else by Swithenbank, who knocked her off on his way north. Keep at it, Pete. You're doing good. For a provincial!"

"Did your daughter-in-law habitually wear wigs?" he now asked Mrs. Swithenbank.

"Never to my knowledge. She had longish straight hair. Reddish brown, a rather unusual colour. She hadn't changed the style much since she was a girl. She wasn't a one for following fashions, not in her clothes either. Always the same kind of dress, whites and creams, soft materials, loose-fitting—she hated constraint of any kind.

But she always managed to look right. What colour was the wig, by the way?"

"Platinum blonde."

"Never," said Mrs. Swithenbank emphatically. "I can't imagine that . . . unless you mean she could be walking around somewhere *disguised* as a blonde."

"Any idea why she might do that?" enquired Pascoe.

"She was a strange girl in many ways," answered the woman slowly. "There was something about her—a kind of feyness. There were three girls in John's gang, Kate, Ursula Rawlinson and Stella Foxley. Kate was the ugly duckling. The other two . . . I gather you'll be meeting them tonight so perhaps I shouldn't anticipate your reactions . . ."

"A kind thought," said Pascoe, "but I'll just be chatting. It's not an identity parade! Please go on."

"You'd have thought the other two would have walked away with all the boys. Ursula was a big well-made girl, full of life—still is! Stella—well, she was pretty too, but in a rather stiff kind of way. It was strange; before the village drama group folded up, she used to appear in nearly every production and on the stage she really came to life, but off it she's always been . . . no, perhaps the competition she offered was a lot less stiff, but she was still much prettier! And Ursula! As I say, she was the belle. Little Kate Lightfoot with her skinny body and big frightened eyes, she faded away alongside her. Yet . . ."

"Yes?" prompted Pascoe.

"You know how it is when you're young, Mr. Pascoe. There's always a lot of chopping and changing of boy-friends and girl-friends in any group. I used to think Ursula called the tune, passing on her discarded beaux to Kate or stealing hers if the fancy took her. But eventually I began to wonder if the reverse weren't true!"

"And what did you decide?"

"Nothing," said Mrs. Swithenbank, sipping her scotch. "Kate always did things too quietly to give the game away. She moved around like a ghost! And Ursula, though she might behave as if her brains were in her brassiere, had far too much sense to make a fuss."

"Were you surprised when your son married Kate?" asked Pascoe.

She looked at him reprovingly as though the question were too impudent to be answered, but when Pascoe put on his rueful look, she said, "John had already been working for Colbridge's in London for two years. He seemed to breaking links with his Wearton friends, though if he had got engaged to Ursula, I should not have been surprised. In face I might even have been pleased. She has many good solid qualities. I sometimes think she may have regretted her marriage, too."

"As your son regretted his?" said Pascoe.

"As I regretted it, Inspector," she said acidly. "John has never by word or sign indicated that he had any regrets. And I can't give you any good reason for my own regrets, except perhaps the unhappiness of this past year. I never knew my daughter-in-law well enough to understand her. I tried, but I couldn't get close to her. I even started buying flowers and vegetables from her brother after the marriage, to sort of integrate the families, and *that* required an effort of will, I tell you. Have you met him? He's real Yorkshire peasant stock with something a little sinister besides. His family were all farm labourers, good for nothing, but, God knows how, he bettered himself and runs a smallholding in the village. I stopped going there a couple of months after Kate disappeared. I couldn't bear the way he looked at me."

She shuddered. Pascoe looked around the room and noticed that the dahlias had been removed.

"But you didn't find Kate frightening, too?" he said.

"Only in the sense that what we don't know frightens us," she said. "Perhaps there *is* nothing to know. Perhaps that's the truth of it, that underneath she's just an ordinary dull little girl. Marriage is abrasive, Mr. Pascoe. John would find out the truth of her sooner or later."

"And . . . ?"

"And if what he found bothered him so much that he wanted rid of her, he would ring his solicitor! One of the things I envy your generation is that divorce is there for the asking. Any other reaction is unthinkable!"

"I'm afraid that not everyone would agree with you," said Pascoe.

This woman was certainly not absurd, he had long decided. And she was only as amusing as she wanted to be. Most important of all, despite the apparent freedom with which she poured out her impressions of her daughter-in-law and others, Pascoe suspected that they were measured with a most exact and knowing eye.

"Meaning what?"

"You took a phone call for your son yesterday morning."

"Did I?"

"A woman's voice. Don't you remember?"

"The funny name. Is that the one you mean?"

"Yes, that's right," said Pascoe. "Ulalume. You didn't recognize the voice?"

"No," she replied. "I don't think so, though I am a little deaf, especially on the phone. It's easier when you can observe the lips. I certainly didn't recognize the name."

"Was there anything distinctive you can recall about the voice?" persisted Pascoe.

"Not really. As I say, I'm a little deaf and the line wasn't very good. It sounded terribly distant."

"What exactly did this woman say?" asked Pascoe.

"Hardly anything, that I can recall," said the woman. "I gave our number, she said *John Swithenbank,* I said *who's calling?* She said *Ulalume,* is that right? I said *who?* She didn't say anything else so I went and got John. What does all this signify, Inspector?"

Quickly Pascoe explained, reasoning that if Swithenbank didn't want his mother to know, he shouldn't have left her to be interrogated alone.

"I don't like the sound of this," she said sharply when he'd finished.

"No?" he said.

"Someone's trying to make trouble. There were one or two nasty calls a year ago when the news first got out. People in the village and round about—old maids with nothing better to do, I usually guessed their names and that made them ring off pretty quickly! But this sounds more organized, as if someone's been thinking about it. Not just an impulse like some old biddy filling the gap between *Crown Court* and *Coronation Street.*"

"That's very astute of you," complimented Pascoe. "Any ideas?"

"I can't fathom the precise aim," said Mrs. Swithenbank, "but I should be surprised if she, or he, were a thousand miles away from you tonight."

She glanced at her watch and pursed her lips impatiently.

"I hope John isn't going to keep you waiting much longer, Inspector. There's a film I particularly want to see on the television and he promised to have you on the way before it started."

Taken aback by the sudden change in the objects of her concern, Pascoe downed his untouched drink in one to demonstrate his readiness to be off and said, "Perhaps it's Miss Starkey who's holding him up."

"*That* wouldn't surprise me," she said significantly.

Not quite certain whether she was really underlining the *double entendre*, Pascoe asked if she had known Miss Starkey long.

"I never saw her before in my life. I came home last evening and there she was. I was then consulted about whether she could stay or not, but not in a manner which admitted the possibility of refusal."

"Despite which, you didn't refuse?" said Pascoe, tongue in cheek.

She glanced at him sharply, then smiled.

"No, I didn't."

"A business colleague of your son's, perhaps?" said Pascoe casually.

"I'm glad you don't even pretend to believe that!" said the woman. "No, I imagine she's precisely what she appears to be. His mistress."

"Here by invitation?" said Pascoe, with doubt bordering on incredulity in his voice.

"No, Inspector. Not by invitation, but certainly by design," said a new voice.

Jean Starkey was standing by the half-open door, amusedly self-conscious at the dramatic effect of both her timing and her appearance. She wore a scarlet dress of some soft elastic fabric which clung so close that the finest of underwear must have thrown up its contours. None could be seen to break the curving lines of her body and when she moved forward into the room muscle and sinew rippled the scarlet surface like a visual aid in an anatomy class.

Pascoe sighed and she smiled her appreciation.

"Even at court they never go in for more than a year's public mourning," she said. "I decided that it was time Wearton became aware of my existence. So here I am."

"And John?" said Mrs. Swithenbank.

"Took me in his stride," said Jean Starkey. "He usually leads—don't misunderstand me—but he's not hung up about it. He recognizes a useful initiative when it sticks out before his eyes."

"You certainly do that," said Mrs. Swithenbank.

"Mourning," said Pascoe. "That's for the dead, Miss Starkey."

"Marriages die, too, Inspector," she replied. "I don't know where Kate is now, but the point is, if she were to come through that door now, it would make not one jot of difference."

They all looked at the door, which she had left ajar. Footsteps were heard coming down the stairs. They got nearer, moving without undue haste, and suddenly Pascoe felt tension in the room.

Then the telephone rang.

The door was closed reducing the telephone to a distant vibration of the air. A moment later this, too, was shut off and as Pascoe had discovered that morning, the walls shut out human speech.

"You need good hearing in this house," said Pascoe conversationally.

"The Swithenbanks don't miss very much," said the old woman. "I do hope you enjoy the party tonight, Miss Starkey. You mustn't mind if John's friends stare a little at first. Remember that while he's been away getting acquainted with the big wide world, they've been stuck here in tiny old Wearton."

"I'll make allowances," smiled Jean Starkey.

The door opened and Swithenbank came in. He was wearing cream slacks, a cream jacket and a golden shirt with a huge collar and no tie. Pascoe felt very conscious that his own suit had come from C and A, but sought revenge in telling himself that the other man looked like an advert for the Milk Marketing Board.

"All ready?" enquired Swithenbank. "We're rather late, I'm afraid. But we can always compensate by coming away early. Good night, Mother. Don't bolt the door if you got to bed, will you?"

"No," she said. "Who was on the phone, dear?"

Swithenbank smiled.

"Just a friend," he said, holding the door open for Jean Starkey and Pascoe.

"Who was it, John?" insisted his mother.

"I told you," said Swithenbank. "A friend. The same one as rang yesterday morning, remember? She told me she was lonely and impatient. She said her name was Ulalume."

CHAPTER VI

And travellers, now, within that valley,
Through red-litten windows see
Vast forms that move fantastically
To a discordant melody.

It was only a short drive to Wear End or the Big House as Pascoe now found himself thinking of it. It didn't look that big, he thought as he got out of the car, but certainly over-large for one man's occupation. Several windows were lit up and in their light and that of a rusty ornamental lantern hung in the portico, his assessing eye picked out signs of decay and neglect—blistered paint, flaking stone, a broken shutter and a narrow crack which zig-zagged up the façade till it disappeared in the dark shadow under the pediment. All the best Gothic decor! sneered Pascoe to reassure himself of his own indifference to the atmosphere, then felt his hair prickle on his neck as distantly, eerily, somewhere in the darkness a woman's voice cried, "John! Oh Johnny!"

Swithenbank stopped in his tracks and all three of them

peered in the direction of the noise. The night sky was clouded and the darkness made thicker by the electric glow above their heads. At first all Pascoe could do was separate the trees from their fractionally lighter background. There seemed to be a double row of them running away in symmetry with the sweep of the drive that had brought them from the roadway. They swayed and soughed in the slight but chilling wind and as his night vision improved Pascoe became aware of another movement. Between the trees something white fluttered and billowed and came towards them with a kind of ponderous bounding gait. Two sounds accompanied it, that breathless female cry of "John!" and a most unfeminine tread of galloping feet.

Then the oncomer was off grass and on to gravel and with more relief than he would have cared to admit, Pascoe saw it was a woman running with the skirts of her full white satin evening dress kilted up to reveal a pair of muddy Wellington boots.

A final spurt took her into Swithenbank's arms with a force that anyone not a gentleman might have staggered under. Dalziel, for instance, thought Pascoe, would probably have stepped aside and let her hit the front door. But the slight figure of Swithenbank bore the brunt without flinching and as Pascoe got a better concept of the new arrival under the lantern light, he observed that it was a brunt worth bearing.

This was most probably that Ursula whose considerable charms Mrs. Swithenbank wished had conquered her son, a theory confirmed as the said son now asked with incongruous politeness, "How are you, Ursula?"

"Johnny! Why have you been hiding from us? I'm so pleased you've come tonight. I can't tell you how disappointed I would have been!"

Over his shoulder her eyes were drinking in Pascoe and Jean Starkey with unconcealed curiosity while behind her another figure came out from between the trees, a tall thin man with a flop of dark hair over pale defeated eyes. He wore a dark overcoat and, like a disingenuous Prince Charming, carried in either hand a silver shoe.

"Hello, John," he said.

"Hello, Peter. Cured many souls lately?"

"Not many. And you—edited any good poems lately?"

"Not much since Poe," said Swithenbank.

"Oh, let's get inside where I can see you properly. Has anyone rung? Boris! Boris! Don't let your guests hang about in the cold!"

Ursula opened the front door as she spoke and entered with the familiarity of old acquaintance. The others followed. Davenport, Pascoe noticed, seemed as uninterested in the identity of the newcomers as his wife was curious. She had now seated herself at the foot of a flight of stairs which ran up from the center of the small but pleasantly proportioned hall. Pulling back her skirt above her knees, she thrust forward what, even accoutred as it was, appeared to be a very elegant leg and said, "Johnny, dear, help me off with my wellies."

A fastidious expression skimmed his face, but he obediently seized the proffered boot by heel and toe and began to lever it free.

"Oh, you've started the fun without me, you naughty children, and it's my party, too!"

A balding, portly man, nautical in a brass-buttoned blazer, advanced upon them, his face shining with sweat and *bonhomie*.

"John! How are you? So elusive! I must have spent a fortune trying to ring you. Even tonight, I began to get so worried!"

"We're not the latest, Boris," replied Swithenbank, glancing at the woman on the stairs.

"Oh, the poor parson and his starving wife, you can always rely on *them* to turn up for supper," said Kingsley dismissively. "Ursula, Peter, welcome aboard. Good concert the other night, I hope? And last but not least, these must be . . ."

He shot an interrogative glance at Swithenbank, who said sardonically, "Surely you can tell which is which."

Kingsley laughed. He really was doing the jovial host bit, thought Pascoe. A trifle hysterically perhaps?

"Miss Starkey! Jean. Any *dear* friend of *dear* John's is welcome here. And Detective-Inspector Pascoe! Or should I call you mister?"

"As you will," said Pascoe, who was wondering whether the look of shock on Ursula Davenport's face was caused by the revelation of his job or Starkey's status. Her husband seemed indifferent to both bits of information and Pascoe, seeing him now under the more revealing lights of the hall, began to suspect that he was held very lightly together by drink.

"Ursula, you know your way around, show Jean where to put her things while we go forward and prepare some drinks for you."

As they went along the hall towards an open door out of which came a hubbub of voices raised to combat James Last on the stereo, Kingsley seized Pascoe by the elbow and slowing him down a little murmured, "I don't know how you'd like to work, Inspector, but most of these people will be going within the hour. Only those you want to see, or so I believe, that is the Rawlinsons, the Davenports and, of course, myself, will be staying on for a bite of supper. Perhaps you'd like to start by having a couple of drinks and getting a general impression of our local community, leaving the close grilling to later? Less embarrassing, too. I'll just say you're an old chum!"

Pascoe nodded agreement, wondering what it was that made a man he could imagine getting wrathfully indignant if the police tried to breathalyze him so eagerly cooperative.

There were about twenty people in the room, mostly dressed with the relative informality of the age, though none was quite so fashionably casual as Swithenbank. Pascoe observed him as he said his hellos to people before settling quietly against the mantelpiece with a drink, his eyes on the door. A couple approached him, a man with a curious limping gait and a woman wearing the kind of drab black dress in which nineteenth-century governesses hoped to avoid arousing either the envy of their mistress or the lust of their master. Swithenbank greeted her with a non-contact kiss, him with a pre-fifteen-rounds handshake and spoke animatedly, saying in a voice suddenly audible right through the room, "No, *glad to be back* would hardly be accurate."

The reason for this sudden clarity was that the end of a James Last track had coincided with an almost total cessation of social chit-chat. Even as Pascoe turned, the hubbub resumed, but cause of the hiatus was there for all to see. Jean and Ursula had made their entrance together. It was neck and neck which was the more eye-catching—Ursula voluptuous in virginal white or Jean outrageous in clinging scarlet. Either alone was worth a man's regard. Together the effect was a golden-days-of-Hollywood dream.

Swithenbank abandoned the limping man and the governess and advanced smiling on Jean.

"Darling," he said, "come and meet a few people."

Ursula came and stood by Pascoe.

"If you don't want people to know you're a policeman," she said, "you shouldn't hang around so close to the drink. But pour me a gin as you're here."

Pascoe obeyed. When he turned from the sideboard, the lame man was talking to Ursula.

"Who is that woman?" he demanded, sounding very angry. "What the hell is John playing at?"

"Everyone's entitled to friends, dear brother," she answered.

"You know what I mean, Ursula. It's not decent, not here in Wearton."

"Because of Kate, you mean? A man's got to make up his own mind what's decent, Geoff. Wouldn't you agree, Mr. Pascoe?"

"He might consult the feelings of those close to him," said Pascoe provocatively, though what exactly he was provoking he did not know. "It's Mr. Rawlinson, isn't it?"

The man turned away without reply and limped back to the woman in black, who hadn't moved from the fireplace.

"His wife?" asked Pascoe.

"That's right. Stella. Not that she twinkles much."

"What happened to his leg?"

"An accident. He fell out of our belfry."

"What?"

"You heard right. Geoff's a great one for watching birds. He draws them, too, he's got a beautiful touch. Wouldn't you say Geoff's got a beautiful touch, dear?"

Her husband, who was refilling his glass from the gin bottle, shot her a glance of bewilderment, not at her remark, Pascoe judged, but at something much more general. It bothered Pascoe; vicars were paid to be certain, not bewildered.

"Well," continued Ursula as her husband wandered away, "Peter, my husband, he's the vicar, gave Geoff permission to go up to the tower and make observations, take pictures, whatever these bird-men do. And one dark autumn night about a year ago, he fell!"

"Good God! What happened?"

She shrugged, a movement worth watching.

"He couldn't remember a thing. It was a frosty night and I reckon knowing my brother that he'd be balancing on a gargoyle or something to get a better view. And then he slipped, I suppose. Fortunately Peter went out at midnight just to check whether Geoff wanted coffee or a drink before we went to bed. He found Geoff unconscious. Luckily he'd missed the tombstones and landed on grass but he was pretty badly smashed up."

"As a matter of interest, when precisely was this, Mrs. Davenport?"

"I told you. A year ago. In fact I'd say, precisely a year ago. It was a Friday night and it was the weekend Kate Swithenbank went missing. Not that we knew about that till later. Is that why you're here, Inspector?"

"Sh! Sh!"

It was Kingsley who had stolen up behind them.

"We can't have everyone knowing the police are in our midst. Most of these people are respectable law-abiding tax-evaders and as such deserve to have their sensibilities protected."

"Then what *shall* I call you?" said Ursula.

"Try his name," urged Kingsley. "I'm Boris. This, as you've probably gathered, or if you've been bold, grasped, is Ursula."

"Peter," said Pascoe.

"Peter. It's my fate to meet Peters. The rocks on which I foundered," said Ursula lightly. "Where is my revered husband, by the way?"

"Being all parochial in the corner. Circulate, circulate; you'll have plenty of time, too much perhaps, for close confabulation later."

From the far side of the room there came a little scream.

"Oh lor," said Kingsley. "It'll be the colonel up to his Wimbledon tricks."

But when he got across there with Pascoe not far behind, it turned out to be the colonel's lady, who claimed to have seen a face at the window.

"It peered at me though the hydrangea bush," she claimed.

"No need to worry, dear lady," Kingsley assured her. "It was probably one of the local peasants, drawn by rumors of wild festivity and your great beauty."

"There was a man. I think he was carrying a gun," insisted the woman.

"I shall organize a posse," promised Kingsley and moved away.

"Silly ass," said her grey-haired companion, presumably the colonel. "Soft at the centre. He'll end up like his father. Time we were off, old girl."

He glowered suddenly at Pascoe to show he resented his eavesdropping. Pascoe smiled embarrassedly and turned away to find himself confronting Peter Davenport, who had obtained a larger glass for his gin.

"What are you after?" he demanded, his light tenor voice scraping falsetto. "How can the law help? Your law, I mean?"

"What other law is there?" responded Pascoe, thinking to steer the exchange into areas which might sound conventionally theological to those around.

But instead of the hoped-for sermon, Davenport's reply was to laugh shrilly, drawing the attention of everyone in the room and, shaking his head, to say, "What indeed? What indeed?" before turning abruptly away and making for the bottle-laden sideboard. Geoffrey Rawlinson, his face full of concern, tried to interrupt his progress but was shouldered aside.

Thank God it's not my problem, thought Pascoe as he observed Kingsley join the vicar at the sideboard and talk animatedly to him with his hand resting familiarly on his shoulder.

A few moments later, Kingsley was taking the same liberty with his own person.

"Mr. Pascoe, Peter, I wonder if I could ask for your help?"

Pascoe shook his head firmly.

"Not if it involves arresting drunken vicars or chasing gunmen through the shrubbery."

"No, please. I'm seriously concerned about Peter, the other one I mean. I've never seen him hit the booze like this before, and there are those here quite capable of sending anonymous letters to the bishop."

"I dare say. But what do you want me to do about it?" asked Pascoe, who was beginning to feel as if he'd strayed on the set of a 1940s British film comedy.

"Just have a word. Something's bothering him and he seems to want to talk to you."

"He could have fooled me."

"No, really," insisted Kingsley. "If I put you in the library and tell him you'd like a chat, I'm sure he'd go. And it'd be a real favour to the dear chap getting him out of here before he starts falling in the fireplace."

The library! thought Pascoe. They really are bent on making a little Poirot out of me!

"If you think it would help . . ." he said.

"I'm sure of it."

Pascoe cast a last look about the room before he left. Swithenbank, his hand resting familiarly on Jean Starkey's back, just above the swell of her buttocks, was talking animatedly in the centre of a much amused group; Ursula was being serious with Stella Rawlinson, whose husband was standing apart by himself with all the animation of a pillar of salt. The colonel and his lady, hovering to pay their dues to their host, were watching the Reverend Davenport mixing himself a gin and tonic without much tonic. Rather to Pascoe's surprise, their expressions were more regretful than disapproving. *Seen it all too often in the mess,* Pascoe guessed. *Damn shame. Good man. Damn shame.*

Was it? and was he? And did whatever was burning up inside Davenport have anything to do with the Swithenbank case?

The library was a disappointment—an ugly square room with a single wall lined with glass-encased books that looked as if they'd been bought by the yard. In the opposite wall an electric fire had been placed in the fireplace but its dry heat did nothing to dissipate the stale smell of long disuse. Encircling the fireplace were a chesterfield and a pair of upright armchairs in hard red leather. Before the room's solitary window was a large desk with a chair on either side of it. Kingsley gestured ambiguously, saying, "Please, sit down," and Pascoe suspected he was being watched with amusement to see whether he would opt for the formal or informal set-up.

"Thank you," he said, peering through the glass front of one of the bookcases at a series of leather-bound collections of *The Gentleman's Magazine* for the years preceding the First World War.

"Help yourself, do," said Kingsley, referring, Pascoe hoped, to the decanters and glasses which stood on a pair of small wine tables rather than to the contents of his bookshelves.

"Right," said Pascoe.

Kingsley left and Pascoe immediately poured himself a large scotch and tried to recall what the hell he was doing here. It all seemed very unreal. Kate Swithenbank, possibly—*probably*—dead somewhere; *that* was the thing to hang on to. Alcoholic vicars with voluptuous wives were probably totally irrelevant. He wasn't sure whether even this Ulalume business meant anything.

He studied a framed map of the West Riding, dated 1786, which hung on one side of the fireplace. It was no more helpful than the O.S. 2½ inch sheet he had examined on Dalziel's suggestion. There were a few patches of woodland around Wearton but the nearest thing to a "dank tarn" was a small reservoir in open country some three miles to the north.

No, the thing was a mess or at best a confusion. His mind was trying to draw connections which could easily be coincidences, as for example Geoff Rawlinson's accident occurring on the very night Kate *may* have disappeared. Well, at least that gave Rawlinson an alibi, if he needed one. Unless, of course, he had *jumped* from that tower because of something on his conscience. Or perhaps was *pushed* because of something he had seen. *Seen?* Where? In the churchyard, of course. That's what he'd be looking down at—from a vantage point no one would expect to be occupied at midnight. Or perhaps someone had remembered too late that there was a chance it would be occupied, and gone up to check, and . . .

No, he was straining; too much speculation and too little evidence was a bad diet for a policeman. But there was something else about the churchyard. Arthur Lightfoot claimed to have seen Swithenbank skulking about there—which meant Lightfoot himself had been skulking about there.

And where else were you likely to find "the door of a legended tomb?"

"Rapt in thought, Inspector?"

Unheard, Peter Davenport had entered the room. He had a full glass in his hand but seemed to have taken at least temporary control of himself.

"I was just wondering how far the church was from Wear End. You walked here tonight, didn't you?"

"Yes. We came down the old drive that used to be the Aubrey-Beesons' private route to church."

"The who?"

"The old squires of Wearton. They died out in the nineteenth century and by the time Boris's family bought the place, the road had been metalled and motor cars were the new status symbol. It's no use looking at that map, you'll see it much better on here."

He indicated a picture on the other side of the fireplace in an ornate gilt frame matching that of the map.

"You know a lot about this," observed Pascoe as he approached.

"Local history's easy for parish priests," said Davenport. "We've got most of the records."

He was making a real effort to sound normal as though eager to postpone an unpleasant moment. But Pascoe lost interest in the vicar's state of mind as he looked more closely at the picture before him.

It was entitled *A Prospect of Wear End House 1799* and as from a fair elevation showed the house and its estate: The tree-lined drive was clearly marked running up to the churchyard but close by the churchyard wall a much denser area of woodland was indicated with a small lake in the middle of it.

"These woods, are they still there?" asked Pascoe.

"No. They've all gone. It's a wonder the avenue survived."

"Why's that?"

"Economics," said Davenport shortly, as though beginning to feel rather piqued that his reluctance to bare his soul to Pascoe was matched by Pascoe's present indifference to the baring.

"You mean they were sold?"

"Not just them. The Kingsleys had wool money when they came here, but the last two generations, Boris's father and grandfather, were better at spending than making. The estate's nearly all gone. There's a housing development *here*, a new road *there*, the village sports and social club playing field are *here*, Geoff Rawlinson's bungalow's *there* . . . all Boris is left with is this thin triangle with the old drive running up to the corner *here.*"

His long forefinger, its whiteness stained with nicotine, stubbed viciously at the *Prospect*.

"And the lake?"

"What? That pond? Drained and filled in when the Kingsleys were still spending money on improvements. About the same time as the 'library' was refurbished, I expect. There *are* limits to what money can buy, aren't there, Inspector? I mean, you can't buy culture. Or peace of mind."

The hysterical note was beginning to return to his voice, but Pascoe wasn't done with the *Prospect* yet.

"The old drive—what kind of trees are they?"

"Beech mainly."

"No cypress?"

"There's a pair of cypress trees by the old lych-gate at the end of the drive, but they're in the churchyard itself. What's your concern with trees, Inspector? Stop trifling, man! Come out with whatever it is you want to say. It's no secret to me why you're here!"

Now Pascoe gave him his full attention. The problem of why the anonymous phone-caller's geographic references should be a century out of date would have to wait. Perhaps (could it be as easy as this?) it wouldn't be a problem in a few minutes. Whatever it was that was devouring this man would soon be revealed. All he had to do was wait. But he wasn't sure if he would have time.

He glanced at his watch. Already he'd heard a couple of cars pulling away from the house. Pretty soon he was likely to be interrupted. So, although his judgment told him to sit quietly opposite this man and wait till he spoke of his own accord, instead he took an aggressive feet-apart stance before the fireplace and said sharply, "All right. If you don't want to talk about trees, suppose you tell me exactly what did happen in the churchyard last October?"

The man looked at him, a curious mixture of relief and wariness in his eyes.

"Happen? What does happen mean to the dead?"

"The dead? Which dead?" asked Pascoe urgently.

"The churchyard's full of the dead, Inspector. In a way since last October I have been one of them."

"You can drop that rubbish!" said Pascoe scornfully. "You're here and now and as alive as me. But who's dead, Davenport? Who *is* dead?"

The vicar held out his glass. Obediently Pascoe slopped it full of gin. The man opened his mouth, was seized by a fit of coughing, drank as though to relieve it, coughed the more, recovered, drank again and made ready to speak.

The door burst open.

"Thank God that's over!" said Boris Kingsley. "Once one goes, the others soon follow. It's the sheep principle. Mr.—Inspector—Pascoe, how would you like us—one by one or all at once?"

CHAPTER VII

There the traveller meets aghast
Sheeted memories of the Past.

Some women cross their legs provocatively. Stella Rawlinson crossed hers like a no-entry sign and regarded Pascoe with all the distaste of an assault victim scanning an identity parade.

"It's kind of you to talk to me," he said with as much conviction as he could manage. His mind was still on the kind of admission or confession Davenport had been about to make before Kingsley's ill-timed entrance. After that the vicar had risen and withdrawn without another word and Pascoe, deciding it would be poor policy at this time to invite the man along to the station to "help with enquiries," had exercised his only other choice and pretended nothing had happened. He'd get back to Davenport after he had chatted to the others, by which time another half-bottle of booze might have put him in the talkative mood once more.

He had picked Stella Rawlinson first on Kingsley's advice. Evidently when the last of the drinks-only guests had gone, Swithenbank had told the others precisely why it was that Pascoe was here. Pascoe would have liked to have done this himself to observe reactions, but he made no complaint and accepted Kingsley's diagnosis that the only likely non-co-operator was Mrs. Rawlinson and it might be well to get her in before her indignation had time to come to a head.

"Can we start by going right back to this time last year?" he said. "Most people would have a hard time remembering anything after twelve months, but in your case it shouldn't be difficult."

"What do you mean?" she demanded as if he had accused her of immorality.

"Just that it was the time of your husband's unfortunate accident and I know how an unpleasant experience like that sticks in the mind," said Pascoe soothingly. "It must have been a terrible shock to you."

"I thought you wanted to talk about Kate Swithenbank," she said.

"You knew her well?" said Pascoe, abandoning charm.

"We grew up together."

"Close friends?"

"I suppose so."

"What was she like?"

She looked genuinely puzzled.

"I don't know what you mean."

"What words describe her?" said Pascoe. "Plain, simple, open. Devious, reserved. Emotional, hysterical, erratic. Logical, rational, cool. Et cetera."

"She kept herself to herself. I don't mean she wouldn't go out or was shy, anything like that. But she didn't give much away."

The woman spoke slowly, feeling for the words. She was either very concerned to be fair or very fearful of being honest.

"I believe she was sexually very attractive as a young girl," he probed.

"Who said that?" she asked. "John, was it?"

"You sound as if that would surprise you."

"No. Why should it? It would be natural, wouldn't it? He married her."

"In fact it was his mother," said Pascoe. "It's interesting when a woman says it. That's why I wondered what your opinion was."

"Yes," she said, not bothering to conceal her reluctance. "She was very attractive. In that way. When she wanted to be. And sometimes when she didn't want to be."

Pascoe scratched his head in a parody of puzzlement.

"Now you're bewildering me," he said.

"A bitch in heat's got no control over who comes sniffing around," she said viciously, then relenting (or at least regretting) almost immediately, she added, "I'm sorry, I don't mean to be unkind. She was a nice quiet ordinary girl in many ways. We were truly friends. I should be very distressed to think anything had happened to her."

"Of course. How terrible it must be for all her

friends,'' said Pascoe fulsomely. ''But if what you say is true, there might be no cause for worry.''

''If what I say . . . ?''

''About her sexuality. Another man, perhaps; a passionate affair. She takes off with him on a sudden impulse. It's possible. If what you say . . .''

''Oh, it's true all right,'' she said. ''Right from the start. Ten or eleven. I've seen her. In this room.''

She tailed off. Funny, thought Pascoe. Everybody *wants* to talk, but they all want to feel it's my subtle interrogative techniques that made them talk!

''This room?'' He glanced at the *Prospect of Wear End.* ''You used to play in here as children?''

''Oh no. When we visited Boris, this was one room we were never allowed in,'' she answered. ''But I was looking for Kate. We'd lost her. I just opened the door and peered in. She was . . .''

''Yes?''

''She was sitting on his knee. Her pants were round her knees.''

Pascoe gave his man-of-the-world chuckle.

''So? Childhood inquisitiveness. A little game of doctors with Boris. It's not unusual.''

''It wasn't Boris. It was his father.''

Pascoe tried to look unimpressed.

''Who is dead, I believe?'' he said. ''Just as well. It's a serious offence you're alleging, Mrs. Rawlinson. Very serious.''

''I felt sorry for him,'' she said vehemently.

''For him?''

''And for Kate, too.'' It was relenting time again. ''She couldn't help what she was. Her parents died while she was young. Her brother brought her up. That can't have helped. He's an animal. Worse!''

Dear God! thought Pascoe. Incest is it now?

''I've met Mr. Lightfoot. He seems an interesting sort of man. He's very sure his sister's dead.''

She shrugged uninterestedly.

''He says he's seen her ghost,'' continued Pascoe.

''He's a stupid ignorant animal,'' she said indifferently.

"Perhaps so. But he may be right about his sister. She could very well be dead."

She laughed scornfully.

"Because some yokel sees ghosts? You must be hard up for clues these days!"

"No," he said seriously. "Because what you've been insinuating about the missing woman's morals makes it seem very probable she could provide her husband with a good motive for killing her."

Her mouth twisted in dismay and for a moment this break in the symmetry of that too well balanced face gave it real beauty.

"No! I've said nothing! I never meant . . . that's quite outrageous!"

She stood up, flushed with what appeared to be genuine anger.

"But what did you imagine we were talking about?" asked Pascoe.

"You're trying to find out who's been suggesting these dreadful things about John."

"Oh no," said Pascoe, shaking his head. "That would be useful, of course. But what we're really trying to discover is whether or not these dreadful things are true!"

Rawlinson looked angry when he came into the room and Pascoe prepared to deal with a bout of uxorious chivalry.

"What have you been saying to Peter?" demanded the limping man. "He's in a hell of a state."

"Nothing," said Pascoe, taken by surprise. "Why should anything I say disturb him?"

The question seemed to give the man more cause for rumination than seemed proportionate as he subsided into an armchair and Pascoe moved swiftly to the attack.

"Tell me about falling off the church tower," he invited.

Rawlinson gripped his right knee with both hands as though the words had triggered off more than the memory of pain.

"Have you ever fallen off anything, Inspector?" he asked in reply.

"Yes, I suppose so. But not so dramatically. A kitchen chair, I recall, when replacing a light bulb."

"Chair or church, it's all the same," said Rawlinson. "One second you're on it, the next you're off. I must have over-reached."

"What precisely were you doing?" asked Pascoe.

"Watching a pair of owls," said Rawlinson. "I'm a draughtsman by training, a bird illustrator by inclination. I watch, note, photograph sometimes, and then do a picture. It had never struck me as a dangerous hobby."

"It's enthusiasm that makes things dangerous," observed Pascoe sententiously. "The Reverend Davenport found you, I believe."

Rawlinson frowned at the name.

"Yes. It was a good job he came when he did. There was a sharp frost and if I'd lain there till morning, I'd probably have died of exposure."

"And immediately before falling, you remember nothing?"

"I remember arriving at the church, unlocking the door to the tower. Nothing more."

"How did you get to the church that night?"

"I walked along the old drive, I suppose. I usually did. My bungalow's right alongside."

"Mr. Kingsley didn't mind?"

"Boris?" said Rawlinson in surprise. "Why should he? I don't think I ever asked him."

"Technically a trespass then," smiled Pascoe. "Do you recall seeing or hearing anything unusual along the drive or in the churchyard that night?"

"Well now," said Rawlinson slowly. "I'm not quite certain it was the same night—it's a long time ago—but once I rather thought I heard a crossbill in one of the cypress trees over the lych-gate. Probably I was mistaken."

He spoke perfectly seriously, but Pascoe did not doubt he was being mocked.

"Your father built the bungalow, you say," he said abruptly. "So there's money in the family."

"A little. He was a jobbing gardener by trade. I earn my own living, if that's what you mean."

"I'm pleased to hear it," said Pascoe, faintly sneering. "Mr. Kingsley now, does he also have to find ways to eke out the family fortune?"

If they start being funny, hit 'em hard, was a favourite maxim of Dalziel's.

"I don't see what this has got to do with anonymous letters, Inspector," said Rawlinson.

"Don't you? Well, I'll explain. I want to get a clear picture of the missing woman. One thing that's starting to emerge is that she came from a very different background from most of the people she called her friends in Wearton. Just *how* different isn't quite clear to me yet."

Rawlinson looked unconvinced but replied, "All right, there's no secrets. Me you know about. Boris has some inherited money, but not much. I believe it came as something of a shock to find out just how little when his father died earlier this year. But in addition he's a "company director," whatever that means. You'd better ask him. John you'll know about, too . . ."

"Not his family. What did his father do?"

"He was a solicitor, rather older than Mrs. Swithenbank, I believe. He died ten years ago. The Davenports—well, Ursula's my sister, of course . . ."

"And therefore shared in the family fortune?"

"We split what little there was," said Rawlinson acidly. "When I married, I bought out her share of the bungalow. Shortly afterwards she married Peter, who is also one of the family. A cousin. His family live in Leeds. He had delicate health as a child and used to come down here for the good country air nearly every holiday. No real money in the family, and a damn sight less in his job! Now let me see. Anyone I've missed out?"

"Yes," said Pascoe. "Your wife."

"I thought you'd have quizzed her yourself," said Rawlinson. "Stella's from farming stock, one of the biggest farms in the area."

"Well off?"

"Oh yes. Though show me a farmer who'll admit it!"

Pascoe laughed, though the attempt at lightness came awkward from Rawlinson's lips.

"So I'm right to say that Kate Lightfoot was the odd one out? Everyone else had some kind of well-established financial and social background."

"Village life is surprisingly democratic," protested

Rawlinson. "We all went to the same schools, no one bought their way out."

"Democracy works best where there's a deep-implanted pecking order," observed Pascoe cynically. "Everybody can be equal as long as we all know our places. What was the Lightfoots' place, do you think? Her father was an agricultural labourer, I believe."

"That's right. He used to work for Stella's father, in fact. Not that he was much of a worker at the end. He boozed himself to death. The mother took off soon after and there was some talk of putting Kate in care, but she made it clear she wasn't going to leave her brother easily. He was about twenty at the time, working on the farm like his father. Then suddenly he gave up his job and the tied cottage that went with it and bought up a small-holding just on the edge of the village, opposite the war memorial, you might have noticed it as you drove in?"

"No," said Pascoe. "The way you say 'suddenly' sounded as if you meant 'surprisingly.' "

"Did it? This was a long time ago. I was only a lad, but in a village you learn early that all business is conducted in public. There was some talk of insurance money from his father's death. But knowing the old man, it didn't seem likely."

"And what were the other speculations?" asked Pascoe.

Rawlinson looked at Pascoe as if for permission, then poured himself a glass of sherry.

"If you were a farm labourer in those days, you didn't save. The only handy source of a bit of extra income was fiddling your employer. Bags of spuds, petrol for the tractor, that sort of thing. Not that it could come to much, and with a Yorkshire farmer like my father-in-law watching over you, I hardly believe it could come to anything! But Stella, my wife, believes wholeheartedly that Lightfoot's fortunes such as they are were based on robbing her father rotten!"

"So he brought his sister up," said Pascoe. "Were they close?"

"You might way so," said Rawlinson cautiously.

"What would *you* say?"

He shrugged and rubbed his knee again.

"Kate was—is—very much her own person, Mr. Pascoe. I was—am—very fond of her. We went out together for a while—nothing serious, all our gang tried various combinations till we settled as we are. I think I got to know her as well as anyone, but there were points beyond which you were not permitted to go."

"Physically, you mean?" said Pascoe, acting stupid.

"Physically you went precisely as far as Kate was in the mood for," replied Rawlinson drily. "But I mean mentally, emotionally even. She shut you out. It was difficult to guess what she felt about Arthur, even when they were together."

"And about the rest of you?"

"Friendly tolerance."

"Even John Swithenbank?"

"No. No," said Rawlinson, a spasm crossing his face as he rose suddenly to stretch his leg. "John was different. I'd have said she disliked and despised him with all her heart."

"I thought as host you'd have saved me for last, Inspector," said Boris Kingsley in a hurt voice.

"Why? Aren't you ready for me?" asked Pascoe.

Kingsley laughed.

"On the contrary, I'm perfectly rehearsed. *What do I know about the letter and phone calls?* Nothing at all. *What do I know about Kate's disappearance?* Ditto. *Do I think John might have murdered her?* No. *Do I think anyone else here tonight might have murdered her?* Improbable but not impossible. *Who am I not one hundred per cent sure about?* Mind your own business."

He sat back looking vastly pleased with himself.

"Why were you left on the shelf, Mr. Kingsley?" asked Pascoe as if the man hadn't spoken.

"What do you mean?"

"The Wearton Six. Rawlinson gets his Stella, Swithenbank gets his Kate. Symmetry requires that you end up with Ursula, Mrs. Davenport. But she opts for an outsider."

"Hardly an outsider," protested Kingsley. "Peter spent most of his hols here. And he's Ursula's cousin. We knew him almost as well as each other."

"Almost," said Pascoe. "Still, you did end up unattached."

"What the devil's this got to do with anything?" demanded Boris.

"I don't know," said Pascoe. "Probably nothing. But if, say, you didn't get married because all your life you'd nursed a passionate but unrequited love for Kate Lightfoot, it might mean much."

"Who's been talking to you? Has someone been saying something? Who was it? Geoff?" He sounded genuinely angry.

"No," said Pascoe. "That wasn't one of the things Mr. Rawlinson told me. Where were you a year ago tonight, Mr. Kingsley?"

The anger subsided and Kingsley shook his head like a boxer who has walked into a sucker punch and now means to take more care.

"I can't be sure. I'd need more notice of that question."

"I'd have thought by now everyone here had notice of it," remarked Pascoe drily. "It was the weekend Mr. Rawlinson fell off the church tower. Remember?"

"Of course. Yes. Dreadful business. I remember wondering . . ."

"What?"

"Mustn't even hint these things, of course, but Geoff had been behaving rather oddly for some time before. You know, very moody. Self-absorbed."

He paused invitingly. Pascoe made a note. He distrusted invitations.

"You mean he may have been upset because his affair with Kate was coming to some kind of climax, so when they met on the Friday evening he killed her, hid the body and then tried to commit suicide in a fit of remorse?" he asked with mild interest.

It was a long time since he'd seen a man splutter, but Kingsley spluttered now.

"*Please.* No! Don't say such things!"

"All right," said Pascoe indifferently. "What about you? What were you doing that night?"

"I've no idea. I didn't hear about it till next day, so I

wasn't directly involved. Probably sitting in front of the television at home."

"Alone?"

"If that was what I was doing, yes. Surely people who have the alternative of human conversation never watch television, do they, Inspector? It's a kind of mental masturbation, essentially a solitary pursuit."

He had stopped spluttering. Pascoe yawned widely.

"Where do you think Kate Swithenbank is now?" he asked through the yawn.

Boris rolled his eyes upward and slapped the arm of his chair.

"I do wish you'd stop trying to confuse me with these changes of direction," he said. "They're irritating without being effective. Unless, of course, your aim *is* merely to irritate."

"Do you think she's dead?"

"I've no idea. How should I know?"

"I didn't say *know*. I said *think*. Only one person could really *know*. Except her brother, of course."

"Why him?" said Kingsley sharply.

"Hadn't you heard? He's seen her ghost."

Kingsley laughed merrily.

"What a cretin!"

"Why do you dislike him, Mr. Kingsley?"

"Who says I dislike him?"

"He says. It hardly seems worth denying. I mean, is there anyone who can really be said to like him? I'm just interested in reasons. Irrational Dr. Fell prejudice? Aesthetic repugnance? Or perhaps, like Mrs. Rawlinson, you think he cheated your father?"

The reaction was astonishing.

"What the hell do you mean?" demanded Kingsley, his face suddenly twisting in porcine ferocity. "What've they been saying to you? Come on, Inspector, spit it out. You'd do well to remember this is my house and you'd be wise to watch what you say!"

There seemed to be something contradictory in this simultaneous demand for frankness and caution but Pascoe, who had been completely innocent of subtle intent, was not long in finding a hypothesis to resolve the contradiction.

"Come on, Mr. Kingsley," he said with the weary certainty of one who knows exactly what he is doing. "I'm a policeman, remember? That means I've a job to do. It also means that I know all about discretion. In any case, there can't be any question of charges, not now. Not either way."

He held his breath and hoped he was making sense. Kingsley's features gradually resumed a more normal colour and expression.

"You're right," he said. "I'm sorry. It's just that it makes me angry, even thinking about it."

"How long have you known?" enquired Pascoe, still feeling his way.

"I never liked the man," said Kingsley, "but it wasn't till after Father died. I was going through his papers. The figures told the story. Then there was a diary . . . well, God, he was wrong, of course. But to suffer like that all those years!"

"This was how Lightfoot bought his smallholding?" pursued Pascoe.

"That's it. And how he's compensated for its inefficient running ever since! You wouldn't think he needs money to look at the man! But he's got expensive habits—drinking, women, too. God, he'd need to pay well to get any half-decent woman near him!"

Ignoring the curious scale of values this suggested, Pascoe went the whole hog and said, "So Arthur Lightfoot steadily blackmailed your father ever since he discovered he'd been interfering with an under-age girl, to wit, his sister Kate."

Kingsley nodded. It seemed to be some relief to the man to hear someone else say it openly.

"I went to see him, of course, when I realized. I didn't know what I was going to do, but it was going to be bloody extreme!"

"And."

"And he said nothing. Admitted nothing. Denied nothing. He just sat there cleaning that blasted shotgun of his. I ran out of words! There was nothing to do. I couldn't get him through the law—there was some evidence, but nothing certain enough, and besides even though he was dead, my father had paid for peace and quiet and a good name."

"So what did you do?"

"Do, Inspector? Do? I did nothing."

Kingsley was now back in full control.

"I hope one night I may catch him poaching on the bit of land that remains to me. Or that he might catch food poisoning from his own disgusting cooking. Yes, I can only sit and pray for some happy accident."

"Like his cottage burning down, for instance?"

"Yes, that was a real tonic when I heard about it. A pity our fire service is so efficient."

"He didn't come to see you afterwards?"

Kingsley regarded him shrewdly.

"Now why on earth should he do that? You're not suggesting I had anything to do with the fire, Inspector?"

"Of course not," smiled Pascoe. "But he'd need money for repairs. He doesn't sound as if he'd carry much insurance."

"You may be right," said Kingsley indifferently. "He certainly wouldn't get it here. I only wish he'd had the cheek to try!"

"And now we come to the sixty-four-thousand-dollar question," said Pascoe.

"And what's that?"

"Did Kate Swithenbank have any idea what her brother was up to all those years?"

There was a long silence.

"And if she did, what then, Inspector?"

"What indeed, Mr. Kingsley? Something perhaps that some people might call a motive."

There was a knock on the door.

Jesus! thought Pascoe. They time their interruptions here better than a French farce!

"Come in," called Kingsley.

A wizened old head with eyes like a blackbird's thrust itself round the door.

"Can ah see thee about t'supper?" it demanded.

"Just coming, Mrs. Warnock," said Kingsley.

The blackbird's eyes regarded Pascoe unblinkingly for twenty seconds, then the head withdrew.

"Hostly duty calls," said Kingsley, rising. "Motive,

you say? Hardly for me, though. I mean, I didn't find out about Lightfoot's bit of nastiness till six months after Kate disappeared, did I?"

"So you say, Mr. Kingsley," agreed Pascoe.

"But as for the others, well, I'll leave you to find your own motives there, you're clearly so good at it. Must fly now. Work up an appetite, dear boy. I'll send Ursula in, shall I? *That* should start the juices running!"

"Boris seemed very pleased to get away from you," said Ursula, rippling into the red leather armchair. "What were you talking about?"

"I'm not sure," said Pascoe. "He was on occasion a trifle obscure. Though he seemed to find no difficulty in accepting that someone in your little group might have been capable of murdering Kate Swithenbank. But he wouldn't say who he had in mind."

"Me," said Ursula promptly.

"Really? Why should he think that?"

"He likes playing Noel Coward, does Boris, but in fact he's terribly straightforward and conventional. His wisdom is proverbial in the strict sense. I mean his mind works in maxims. *Hell hath no fury like a woman scorned* has all the ring of eternal truth to Boris."

"Meaning you have been scorned by . . . ?"

"John Swithenbank, of course. And it's true. I was furious. But only for a time."

"How long a time?"

"Till the wedding. John so clearly regarded the whole business as farcical and whatever Kate regarded it as just as clearly had nothing to do with all those loving vows they made at the altar. Resentment has to have an object. I seemed to have lost mine on that day."

"So you don't think the marriage was happy?" said Pascoe.

"What's happy?"

"I don't know *what*, but I know *where*. It's somewhere this side of either running off or committing murder," said Pascoe.

She didn't seem to feel this required any answer. She was probably right, he thought. He was beginning to see possibilities but the problem was like one of those trick drawings beloved of psychologists—sometimes he saw a rabbit and sometimes he saw a goose. A frightened rabbit that had nothing to do with the missing woman, or a Christmas goose being led to an early slaughter.

"Why do you think he married her?"

"She wanted him to."

She spoke as if this should have been obvious. Was it an answer? There were women, and men, too, in whom volition and achievement appeared contiguous. This Kate Lightfoot was emerging as a formidable woman.

"And Kate, why should she wish to marry a man she didn't love, perhaps even like?"

Ursula leaned forward and opened her arms and knees to the electric fire. Pascoe shuddered but not from the cold.

"John offered her an escape route from Wearton."

"Why should she need that?" he asked. "No one was keeping her prisoner."

"Strictly speaking, no. But she had no training, no employment. She left school and looked after Arthur's cottage, that was all. She'd been doing it for years, and taking care of the business paperwork, too. She was surprisingly ignorant of the world in many ways. She asked my advice once . . ."

"About what?" interrupted Pascoe.

"Getting away, of course. She wanted to go to London. I told her there were two ways for a country girl to go to London, as a typist or as a tart. Unless, that is, she could find some nice well-heeled fellow and marry him! Next thing she and John were engaged."

Ursula laughed ruefully and rubbed her hands together, then crossed her arms and rubbed her bare shoulders, making a sound which Pascoe found very disturbing.

"That was, what? Nine, ten years ago?"

"Something of the sort."

"And since their marriage, what have your relations with her been?"

"Excellent," she said promptly. "Why? You don't really think I killed her, do you? I used to see her a couple of times a year in Wearton, and on the odd occasion I saw her in London. She was always the same, me too, I hope. I enjoyed her company and she never had occasion to push me around. No, that's the wrong phrase. There was never anything Kate wanted me to do except be myself, so I never got taken over."

"And your feelings for Mr. Swithenbank?"

"I'm very fond of John," she said. "I might have had an affair with him if he'd suggested it, but he never did. And Kate never showed the slightest interest in Peter."

"What about your brother?" enquired Pascoe. "Did she ever show any interest there?"

Now her expression turned cold as though the electric fire had been switched off.

"I'm sure you've discovered they were once very close, Inspector," she said. "But I'm equally sure you know that Geoff has the perfect alibi for that weekend. He was lying in hospital half dead."

"Yes. Did you notice anything odd in his behaviour before the accident?"

"Odd? No. Why do you ask?"

"Just that Mr. Kingsley said he was rather moody at that time. That's all."

She laughed.

"Boris! The great psychologist now! It must do dreadful things to your ears, having to admit so much rubbish."

Pascoe decided the time was ripe for a hard push.

"I think you're being rather unkind to Mr. Kingsley," he said. "After all, it was he who took care of your husband tonight."

"What's that mean?" she asked fiercely.

"Nothing, except that he got him out of the way when he started drawing attention to himself. He brought him to talk to me. Mr. Kingsley seemed to feel your husband wanted to get something off his chest."

That was stretching things a bit but Boris was big enough to look after himself.

"He said *what?* Then obviously Boris was talking even more stupidly than he usually does." She stood up abruptly. "I'll go and have a word with him and with Peter. That is, if you're finished with me, Inspector?"

There was clearly no way that he was going to get her

to stay—the words were a challenge, not a request for permission to leave—so Pascoe shrugged philosophically.

At the door she paused.

"One thing I will tell you about Kate. She was the same in London as she was in Wearton. If she wanted out and I think she did, she wasn't just going to walk off alone into the great unknown. There'd have to be someone to go *with* or go *to.*"

"From what I've heard of her, I agree," said Pascoe. "Which means, if she came to Wearton . . ."

"What?"

"Well, the Wearton men seemed to be all alive and well and still living in Wearton. So, unless she's locked in an attic somewhere . . ."

The anger left her face.

"Yes, I see that," she said softly. "I don't think . . . no, not that."

The door closed quietly behind her.

Pascoe studied his notes for ten minutes. They were sketchy. He tended to use his book as some men use a pipe—to occupy the hands, permit significant pause and accentuate dramatic gesture. Much of his scrawl meant nothing. But as he jumped from one page to the next, his mind traced a line between the points where his scrawls quavered into sense and a shape began to form. But he still couldn't see if it were a goose or a rabbit.

He was interrupted by a discreet tap on the door.

"Come in, Miss Starkey," he called.

When she entered, smiling and saying, "Wow, that was clever. Wasn't that clever, John?"

Swithenbank, close behind, agreed.

"I knew he was clever the first time I laid eyes on him," he said.

"You two seem very pleased with yourselves," said Pascoe.

"We've been watching their faces after you'd finished with them," said Swithenbank, "and they've all looked so wrought up, I've been certain you've got something out of them."

"And that's what you've come to tell me?"

"No," said the woman. "Boris says supper will soon

be ready. A trifling foolish banquet which some ancient crone is slowly hauling up from the kitchen. I think he's hoping that between the *hors-d'oeuvres* and the cheese you will reveal all and sent the guilty party screaming out of the window into the police net you've doubtless cast around the house.''

''It's no joking matter, Jean,'' said Swithenbank, frowning.

She made a mock penitential face but slipped her hand into his and gave it an affectionate squeeze as though to express real apology.

Pascoe sighed and wondered what to do. It was like being a blacksmith surrounded by hot irons. Which should he strike first?

''I think I'd like another word with Mr. Davenport before supper,'' he said finally.

With a bit of luck the alcoholic reverend would once more be ripe for the confessional. Pascoe was ready to make a fair guess at what he would say, but like all good detectives he basically distrusted deduction. Evidence without admission was of as doubtful efficacy as works without faith. To hypothesize from clues was fine so long as you remembered the basic paradox that the realities of human behaviour went far beyond the limits of human imagination. Intuition was something else, but you kept it well in check if you worked for Dalziel!

Swithenbank said, ''I'll fetch him, shall I? You will be fairly quick, though, else Boris's goodies will get cold.''

Pascoe said, ''As quick as I can, but do start without me.''

Swithenbank left but Jean Starkey hesitated at the door.

''Yes?'' said Pascoe, shuffling his notes.

Suddenly he knew what was coming and would have preferred not to receive it at this juncture. But there's no evading a woman determined to make a clean breast of things.

''You know that I'm Jake Starr, don't you?'' she said.

He looked up now. ''Clean breast'' had been the right image. She was leaning back against the jamb, one knee slightly raised and the foot planted against the woodwork behind her in the traditional street walker's pose. The red dress seemed to cling more tightly than ever and her nipples, tumescent from the room's coldness or (could it be?) some more personal sensation, were blatant beneath the taut material.

He wondered if she was about to make him an offer he would have to refuse and he wondered why the certainty of his refusal didn't prevent his mouth from going dry and his leg muscles from trembling.

"Yes, I know it," he managed to reply.

She laughed and came and sat down on the chesterfield, but her approach diminished rather than intensified the sexuality of the moment.

"I told John you'd found out," she said triumphantly. "He wouldn't believe me, but I could tell. You were puzzled by me yesterday, but not tonight."

He realized now, not without disappointment, that he'd been mistaken and no offer for his silence was going to be made. She was grinning at him slyly as if she could read his thoughts and he said coldly, "You didn't imagine you could get away with it for ever, did you?"

"I didn't imagine I could get away with it at all!" she replied. "It's no secret. I mean, you get lists of pseudonyms in half a dozen reference books. I even got mentioned in a colour supplement article last May—don't policemen read the Sunday papers?"

"Not in Enfield it seems. OK, so you fooled us. Why?"

She looked at him closely and shook her head in reproach.

"Nothing sinister," she said. "It's just that ever since I started using a male pseudonym, I've found it very useful to pretend to be my own secretary. When people ring who don't know me, it's useful to be able to say Mr. Starr's not available, can I take a message? That way I get time to think about offers, check up on things generally; as myself I'm a lousy negotiator, always say yes too quickly, never dream of trying to up the price of a story or an article. As Mr. Starr's secretary, I pass on the most devastating messages without turning a hair. So when the police contacted me I automatically responded in the same way. Even when I realized it wasn't about not paying a parking fine, I didn't let on. I was due in New York the following day and I'd no intention of letting a bumbling bobby delay me. So I made a statement as Jake Starr's secretary, rang John to find out what the hell was going on, told him what I'd done, and sent another statement as Jake Starr from America. It all seemed a bit of a laugh, really."

"A woman goes missing and you're amused?" said Pascoe.

"Hold on! I thought she'd merely taken off with some boy-friend. And I was glad. John had seemed to be hedging his bets a bit, I thought. Always on about his marriage being on the rocks but never getting close to *doing* anything about it. So if she'd made the break, what do you expect from me but a big *whoopee!*"

"And later? When she didn't show up?"

She shrugged expressively.

"We got worried, naturally. I couldn't understand why the police weren't on to the Jake Starr thing, you really have been pretty inefficient, Inspector. But I could see no profit in doing your work for you. John was being given a rough enough time. So I lay low and hoped that Kate would turn up again. Funny that, isn't it? I was delighted to learn she'd gone. Now here I was desperate to have her come back."

Pascoe nodded approvingly. It was a good story. He had no idea whether he believed it or not, but in the circumstances it was a very good story. He must try some of her books.

"One more thing," he said. "Why have you come to Wearton?"

She warmed herself at the fire, reminding him of Ursula. Two women; similar problems? Then she smiled widely and the problems whatever they were seemed defeated.

"I changed my mind about doing the police's job for them," she said. "Come with me."

She rose and took him by the hand like a small child, or a lover, and led him out of the library, across the hall, up the stairs and into a bedroom.

"Am I to go to bed without any supper?" he asked.

She laughed and taking up a nail file from a huge mahogany dressing-table, she approached a small oak wardrobe which didn't match anything else in the room. Sliding the file into the crack between the door and the jamb, she forced it upwards till it met the lug of the lock and made half a dozen sideways twisting movements.

"*Voilà!*" she said triumphantly and opened the door.

"Why did you bother to lock it after you last time?" enquired Pascoe, regarding the scarred woodwork which advertised forced entry like a neon sign.

She looked hurt.

"I didn't want Boris to know I'd been in here," she said. "But look inside."

With a sigh, Pascoe obeyed.

And the sigh turned into a whistle of appreciation as he spotted the white muslin dress with blue ribbons and the floppy white hat trimmed with cotton roses. In his mind's eye he saw again the half-photograph he had examined in Arthur Lightfoot's cottage just a few hours ago.

"You've broken the law, you realize," he said casually to Jean Starkey, who was standing beside him with the repressed smugness of one who anticipates congratulation.

"*I've* broken the law?" she began indignantly, but stopped as she heard rapid footsteps on the stairs and a man's voice calling, "Pascoe! Pascoe!"

A moment later Swithenbank appeared at the door, his customary calm surface considerably ruffled.

"Pascoe, you'd better come," he said urgently. "It's Peter Davenport. I don't know what the hell's going on but he's been having the most tremendous scene with Ursula and now he's taken off back towards the church. He seems quite hysterical.

"Ursula thinks he's going to kill himself!"

CHAPTER VIII

While from a proud tower in the town
Death looks gigantically down.

The night had grown wilder during the hours since their arrival. There were flurries of rain in the gusty wind which tore at the clouds and sent bunches of stars scurrying across the sky. The ancient beeches rustled and groaned and swayed like an old Disney forest, and underfoot the long grass laid ankle-twisting traps over the forgotten coach ruts.

Here once through an alley Titanic
Of cypress I roamed with my Soul—

Pascoe found himself jogging to the contrived but controlled rhythm of Poe's poem. Behind him, impeded by the woman's dress and shoes, ran Swithenbank and Jean Starkey. Far ahead in the tunnelled darkness he caught an occasional glimpse of a swaying light as though someone were holding a torch.

At the end of our path a liquescent
And nebulous lustre was born.

And there it was, not the pin-prick of a torch but a distinct glow hazed through the fine mist of rain. Pascoe paused and the pursuing couple came up with him.

"Someone's switched the Christmas floodlights on," said Swithenbank. "God, they'll have half the village at the church!"

As though this were a congregation devoutly to be missed, he abandoned the hard-panting woman to Pascoe's care and sprinted ahead. Hard panting became Jean Starkey, Pascoe suspected, and normally he would have accepted the charge gladly, but he wanted to be at the church on time before the voices of reason and discretion had a chance to prevail.

"You OK?" he asked.

A change of note in the heavy breathing and a vague movement of the shadowy head seemed affirmative, so abandoning chivalry and the woman together, he pressed on.

In the darkness of the great outdoors a very few yards can make the difference between good vision and total obscurity. Suddenly what lay ahead swam into close focus—a gateway, a pair of looming evergreens immediately beyond, and fifty yards further on the bulk of the church, its grey stone silvery in the light which flooded its tower.

The wrought metal gate hung open between its two stone posts. Pascoe leapt lightly through on to a neglected weed-snagged gravel path which curved among a forest of mossy and sometimes drunkenly angled tombstones. Leaning against one of these was a figure which might have been taken for an exuberant mason's impression of Grief had it not moved and said, "Pascoe!"

His recognition of Rawlinson was almost instantaneous but that "almost" had his skin crawling chilly.

"Give us a hand," said Rawlinson, groaning as he pushed himself up from the headstone. "I came out in such a hurry, I forgot my stick and the leg's gone."

"Look," said Pascoe. "Shouldn't you hang on here till I can rustle up a stretcher?"

"For Christ's sake, man! Peter's up that fucking tower! I've got to get there!"

Dalziel would not have let such an opportunity pass, but Pascoe knew he was of more tender and humane stuff than his gross superior.

It was this knowledge that made him regard himself with some surprise and distress as he took half a step backwards from Rawlinson's grasping hand and said coldly, "Why? Why have you got to get there?"

"Why? Because it's my fault," the man cried in anguish. "I was as much to blame. And I said I forgave him, but he knew I didn't. Knowing that, where could he turn for help?"

Pascoe nodded. He felt rather disappointed. The picture was going to show a frightened rabbit after all.

"He didn't find you by accident," he said. "He was up on the tower with you. He pushed you."

"No, no, *that* was an accident," insisted the distraught man. "Please help me while there's still time."

"Come on," said Pascoe, suddenly full of self-disgust, an emotion which won the wholehearted support of Jean Starkey, who had arrived soon enough to catch the drift of the exchange and who now said to him as she lent her strength to getting Rawlinson upright, "That was a shitty thing to do."

"Don't you preach at me, lady," he snapped back. "Not you."

In silence, supporting Rawlinson between them, they made their way to the church.

Here Kingsley came to meet them.

"Thank God you're here," he said to Pascoe with what sounded like genuine relief. "He's on top of the tower. He's locked the stair door behind him and he won't speak to anyone."

"Who put that floodlight on?" demanded Pascoe.

"I did," said Kingsley rather proudly. "It's just used at Christmas really but I thought . . ."

"Switch the bloody thing off!" commanded Pascoe, easing Rawlinson against an old rugged cross. "Leave the outer porch light on. Then see if you can break the tower door open."

"It's five hundred years old," said Kingsley, shocked.

"Then with a bit of luck it'll have woodworm," said Pascoe. "Hurry!"

A moment later the bright light faded, leaving the tower as a black monolith while those below stood in the gentler glow which spilled out of the church porch.

"Why've you switched it off?" demanded Ursula. She looked wild and distraught, her gown sodden, her make-up smeared like an action painting by the driven rain. All her sexuality had gone, whereas even in the stress of the moment Pascoe had noted under the floodlight the amazing things dampness was doing to Jean Starkey's scarlet dress.

"If he looked down, all he'd be able to see was the glare," said Pascoe. "Like being on a stage. We don't want him to feel he's on a stage. I want him to be able to see us—and what he's likely to hit. And I don't want a crowd here either. Now tell me, has he said anything?''

''No, not a word.''

''But he's definitely up there?''

''Yes. We nearly caught up with him. He had to unlock the outer door of the church.''

''Where was the key to the tower?''

''Hanging up in the porch with all the other keys.''

''Is the outer door always locked?''

''It has been since last year, since Geoff's accident. But what's all this got to do with getting Peter down from there?'' Ursula demanded angrily.

She was right, thought Pascoe guiltily. He must keep his eyes on the rabbit for the moment and forget the goose.

He took the woman by the arm and led her unresisting to where Rawlinson was standing by the cross peering helplessly upwards.

''Listen,'' he said. ''I think I know why he's up there, but I'm not sure what'll bring him down. You'd better tell me. Is it just the drink talking? I mean, when the rain and the cold sobers him up, will he come down of his own accord?''

Brother and sister exchanged glances.

''No,'' said Ursula. ''Drinking's an escape. The soberer he gets the worse it'll be.''

''I guessed so,'' said Pascoe. ''Then you two had better talk to each other fast. Whatever you know, you've both got to know it, because he's got to know you both know it.''

Ursula managed to raise a wan smile.

''That's a lot of knowing.''

Pascoe regarded her seriously.

''Too much for you?''

She shook her head, then to her brother said gently, ''Geoff, I'm a good guesser. And I'm Peter's wife.''

Rawlinson rubbed the rain off his face or it may have been tears. Then he began to talk rapidly, in a confessional manner.

''When he used to come and stay with us, we always shared a bed. Some time, it must have been in our early teens, I don't remember, but one summer when he came, well, we'd always played and wrestled before like boys do, only now puberty was well under way and we started exciting ourselves and each other with talk and pictures. For me, I believe for most adolescents if it happens, it was just a sort of marking time. I'd have been terrified to go near a girl but that was always the image I had in my mind. Later, as I got older and started making dates with girls, I wanted to stop. It would have been earlier but for Peter; but in the end we did stop. We did our college training, settled down to our careers. I got married, John and Kate got married and finally Ursula and Peter married. I was delighted. I liked him, we were close friends, our childhood was far behind us, then last year . . ."

"It was after the harvest supper, wasn't it?" interrupted Ursula with the certainty of revelation.

Rawlinson nodded glumly, unsurprised that she knew.

"Yes. We were clearing up together, alone. I was . . . unhappy. Well, that's my affair. I talked to Peter. He touched me. And what we did seemed natural, innocent almost. Till next day. I was so full of guilt it almost choked me. I couldn't believe it of myself. The only thing to do seemed to be to pretend it hadn't happened. I made sure I was never alone with Peter during the next couple of weeks. He made no sign that anything was between us, and when he told me about the owls in the tower, I didn't think twice about asking if I could go up there at night. The first three nights I was by myself, getting them accustomed to my presence. The fourth, that was the Friday, he came up with a flask of coffee for me. What happened then—well, all you need to know is the falling was pure accident. My own fault. I was stupid. But stupid or not, it did this . . ."

He slapped his damaged leg in anger and frustration.

"We've got to get him down," he said desperately. "Yes, I've blamed him for this and he knows it. But I never wished the same on him. Never!"

Pascoe was looking at the woman. She put her arm round her brother's shoulder.

"It's OK, Geoff. It's OK. I know, I know. Or at least I guessed. It's OK."

"And your husband, have you talked about it with him?" asked Pascoe.

"No, not directly. It's a myth, isn't it, that everything's solved by bringing it out in the open? We have a kind of jokey relationship about sex. It's a delicate balance but we keep it, we keep it."

She sounded desperate for reassurance.

"Something's upset the balance," urged Pascoe gently.

"Yes, I know. Three or four months ago something, I don't know what. And tonight. Perhaps it's something to do with you being at Boris's!"

She flashed this at him furiously as though delighted to have found a target.

"My God!" cried Rawlinson, who'd never taken his eyes off the tower. "He's there!"

Pascoe screwed up his eyes against the now driving rain. The figure leaning over the parapet could have been part of the stonework, some graven saint, so still and indistinct it was.

"Peter! Peter!" screamed Ursula, cupping her hands in an effort to hurl her words skywards. So strong was the wind now that Pascoe doubted if anything but the thin edge of that cry sounded aloft the tower. His training told him he should already have summoned the fire brigade, at least got them on stand-by. But this story could destroy those concerned just as much as the fall could destroy Davenport.

A figure darted from the church porch. It was Swithenbank, excited but controlled.

"We've got the door open," he said. "What next?"

Pascoe thought rapidly.

"What's at the top of the stairs?" he demanded of Rawlinson.

"Another door out on to the tower."

"Does it have a lock?"

"Just a hasp and a padlock."

"So he can't lock it from above. OK. Mr. Rawlinson, can you manage to move forward a bit, get on to the path right beneath Davenport? Ursula, give him a hand."

Rawlinson clung heavily to his shoulder and limped into position.

"Now stand there the pair of you and bellow at him.

He may not be able to hear, but keep on bellowing. I want him to see you two side by side. And I don't want him to be able to jump without risking landing on one of you. If he shifts position, follow him!"

Accompanied by Swithenbank, he dashed into the church porch. Jean Starkey was there, so wet she might as well have been naked. By contrast Stella Rawlinson was relatively dry. She had found time to put on a raincoat and headscarf before coming out, though her patience had not stretched to moving at her lame husband's pace. Pascoe wondered how much she knew and what the knowledge was doing to her. She it was who carried the torch he had spotted in the distance. He took it from her hand without speaking and pushed his way past Kingsley, who was peering through the tower door with all the nervous excitement of a subaltern about to go over the top.

"You come second," said Pascoe to Swithenbank. "Keep three steps behind me. If I stop, you stop. No talking. I'll try to go through the door at the top quietly. If I can't, I'll go at a rush. Come quick then, I may need help."

"What about me?" said Boris eagerly.

"Stay at the bottom," ordered Pascoe. "If he gets past us, stop him."

It was an unlikely contingency, an unnecessary job. But he didn't want Boris's bulk creaking up those wooden stairs and past experience had taught him that the fewer men you had making an arrest in the dark, the less chance there was of ending up with each other.

The original staircase of the tower must have long since rotted away, but this one was quite antiquated enough. It consisted of five steep wooden steps to each narrow landing and when he gripped the banister, the newel post above rocked so alarmingly in its joint that he ignored the rail thereafter and proceeded bent double to test the stairs by eye before weight. The air smelt musty and what little light came through the narrow windows was hardly reinforced by the dim glow of the torch. Soon Pascoe could see neither the floor he had left nor the roof he approached. He remembered a ghost story in which a girl counted three hundred steps going up a tower, but coming down soon found herself far beyond that figure without any sign of the bottom. Perhaps this was the way it ended for him, too. He flashed his torch downward to seek reassurance in the presence of Swithenbank, but the sight of that narrow intense face with its high forehead, blank eyes and black moustache brought little comfort. For all he knew this man was a murderer. It was still very much a possibility. Though his theory that Rawlinson had been hurled from the tower because of what he had seen had proved a non-starter, that meant nothing. The rabbit could co-exist with the goose.

On the other hand, if Swithenbank were a murderer, he had been too successful so far to need to risk attempting to dispose of a suspicious policeman. Indeed, if one of Pascoe's other hypotheses proved true . . .

But speculation was terminated by the sudden awareness that the next landing was the last. Ahead was the door leading to the top of the tower.

There was no latch on it, only an empty hasp with the discarded padlock lying on the floor.

Gently Pascoe pushed at the door. He felt a resistance and for a moment thought that Davenport must have wedged it shut from without. Then he realized that it was only the force of the wind which pressed against him, and as he pushed again that same wind, as if delighted to get a grip on what had so long resisted it, caught the partly opened door and flung it wide with a tremendous crash that almost tore its hinges out of their post.

The dark figure against the furthermost parapet started and turned.

Pascoe hurled himself forward. The figure placed one foot on the parapet and thrust itself upwards. What might have been a shriek from below or merely a new crescendo of wind cut through the air. Pascoe sprang to the parapet, gripped one of the castellations with his left hand and caught Davenport by the jacket pocket. He felt the material begin to tear but dared not release either handhold to try for a better grip.

Where the hell was Swithenbank?

He heard the steps behind him, glanced back, saw that intense, controlled stare, and for a long ghastly moment wondered how he could have been so wrong about his own safety.

Then with a strength unpromised by his slight frame, Swithenbank caught Davenport by the shoulders and bore him easily backwards.

There was no resistance.

"I wouldn't have jumped," he said mildly as they thrust him before them through the doorway. Pascoe half believed him but not enough to relax his grip as they clattered down the wooden stairs.

Once in the church porch he released him to Ursula's equally tight clasp and thought ruefully that of them all Davenport probably looked the least distraught, though what emotion it was that twisted Stella's face as she watched her husband talking earnestly to Davenport was hard to say.

"Is he all right?" asked Kingsley anxiously.

"I doubt it," said Pascoe. "We'll get him home, call a doctor and get him sedated. After that . . ."

He shrugged.

"Terrible, terrible," said Kingsley. "Look, Ursula won't want us all tramping around the rectory. Shall I take the main party back to Wear End to dry out? Oh, and there's the supper! It'll be ruined! And you can come on as soon as decently possible."

Pascoe sought for some way of saying that, as the matter was not official, a close friend would be more suitable company for the Davenports than an intrusive policeman, but nothing came to mind.

"All right," he sighed.

And in any case, he was still curious to discover what it was that had sparked off Davenport's extraordinary behaviour.

He found out in the next ten seconds.

"All right everybody," called Kingsley. "Here's what we're going to do."

But nobody was listening. Behind him the big church door, closed against the violent weather, was swinging slowly open.

Into the lighted porch stepped a dark-clad figure in a dripping shapeless cap. In the crook of his arm was a shotgun.

Pascoe saw the glance of hatred that came from Davenport's eyes even before the newcomer spoke.

"Evening, Vicar," said Arthur Lightfoot. "Here we are again, then."

CHAPTER IX

But see, amid the mimic rout
A crawling shape intrude!

"How do, Inspector?" continued Arthur Lightfoot. "Have you got him yet?"

"Got who?" asked Pascoe.

"T'chap who killed our Kate," said Lightfoot.

"Mr. Lightfoot, as I've explained, there's no real evidence that your sister's dead."

"There's the ear-ring," interrupted Kingsley. Pascoe regarded him curiously and wondered what his game was.

"Come on, Peter. Let's be getting you home. Whatever the rest of this lot think, you're in no fit state for a metaphysical discussion."

It was Ursula who spoke but when she moved forward with her arm round her husband's waist, Lightfoot made no effort to step aside.

"Do you mind, Arthur!" she said clearly and savagely.

"Just hold on there, missus," said Lightfoot. "I asked Mr. Detective here a question. No one sets foot out of here without I get an answer."

"You've had your answer!" said Ursula. "And in any case, you can't imagine my husband could have anything to do with Kate's disappearance."

"I know what t'vicar can and can't do as well as any," said Lightfoot with a note of vicious mockery in his voice. "And you too, missus, I know what you're capable of. All on you, I know as much about all on you as'd fill a Sunday paper through till Friday."

He raised his voice as he spoke and there was no mistaking the note of threat.

"There's been notes, has there? And telephone calls, has there? And it's you that's been getting them, brother-in-law?"

"That's right," said Swithenbank calmly. "But . . ."

"Who's she? What's she to you?"

The barrel of the gun rose slowly and pointed at Jean Starkey.

"This is Miss Starkey. She's a writer and . . ."

"I can see *what* she is," said Lightfoot scornfully, his eyes running up and down the soaking clinging red dress. "I said, what's she to you?"

"A friend."

"A friend, is it? And our Kate not yet properly buried!"

"And what makes you so sure she's dead?" burst out Swithenbank.

Lightfoot looked at him with a baring of the teeth which might have been a smile.

"I've seen her through glass and I've heard her in the night. Oh, she's dead, she's dead, never have doubt of that."

A spasm of awful grief crossed his face.

"She shouldn't have left, she shouldn't have left," he keened softly, almost to himself.

"I didn't make her leave," protested Swithenbank.

"Not *you*, you girt fool! Wearton. Her home. *Me*. It were you as caused all this. Like as not whoever wrote that letter knew the truth. It were you, weren't it? Tell us where she's hid, you owe her that. Tell us where she's hid!"

Now the barrel was pointing straight at Swithenbank's chest.

"I wish I knew, Arthur, believe me," protested Swithenbank in tones of sweet reasonableness whose only effect was to bring the gun stabbing at his rib-case.

"Liar! I've watched you in this churchyard at dead of night. Is she laid here? Is she? I feel her close!"

Pascoe shivered with more than cold. The animal intensity of this man was terrifying beyond the reach of middle-class neurotics, or even suicidal vicars!

"I don't know!" Swithenbank's voice had the ghost of a tremor now, as though he was just beginning to admit the possibility that the trigger might be pulled.

"Tell him what you were doing here, Mr. Swithenbank," Pascoe suggested. He could see no way to disarm the man without risking a reflexive tightening of that gnarled brown finger.

"I just thought, if Kate did come to Wearton, she might be here, somewhere, in the churchyard. I thought perhaps the tomb of the Aubrey-Beesons . . . we used to play round there as kids . . . once we went in . . . there was a key at Wear End, Boris got it . . . but there was another in the bunch of keys hanging in the porch here, only Peter had started locking the door, so I couldn't get in."

He was definitely gabbling now.

"You mean you thought that stupid poem might be true?" asked Ursula.

"Why not?" Swithenbank demanded.

"Why not indeed?" echoed Pascoe. "I mean, the man responsible for the telephone calls ought to know what precisely they signify, oughtn't he?"

There was a moment of puzzled silence which involved Lightfoot, too, and Pascoe was glad to see that though the direction of the shotgun remained unchanged, the man took half a pace backwards and switched his unblinking gaze to the detective's own face.

"What on earth can you mean, Inspector?" enquired Kingsley.

Swithenbank and Jean Starkey exchanged looks. She smiled fondly at him and nodded encouragingly, like a mother to a shy child.

"All right," he said defiantly. "It's true. There were no anonymous phone calls."

"A couple," corrected the woman. "I made them to John's mother and his secretary. Just to provide a couple of independent ears."

"And I sent the letter and the ear-ring," said Swithenbank as though eager to claim his share of the credit.

"But the blood?" said Ursula.

"Cow's. Probably off the weekend joint," said Pascoe cheerfully. "We have very good laboratories."

"Sod your laboratories," said Lightfoot in angry bewilderment. "What's going on?"

"Arthur, listen to me," said Swithenbank. He spoke urgently, but he was back in full control. "I'm like you. I believe Kate's dead. A year, no sign, it's too much. The police think so, too. And they think I'm responsible, but I swear I'm not! But they're fixated; result is, my life's permeated with suspicion while the real murderer gets off scot free. They're not even looking for him, just watching me!"

Willie Dove really got to him, thought Pascoe.

"But why this charade?" demanded Rawlinson.

"It was my idea," said Jean Starkey defiantly. "I'm a writer. I used my imagination. We wanted something to stir the police out of their stupor and to get the killer worried at the same time."

"But why up here?" retorted Rawlinson. "You know how much we loved Kate, John; some of us, that is. Why bring this trouble up here?"

His wife looked at him with disgust, then turned away.

"Because I believe this is where the trouble belongs, Geoff," said Swithenbank. "Up here. In Wearton. Where else would Kate come? Where else might there be someone to meet her?"

"She lived with you in London for years!" protested Kingsley.

Swithenbank shook his head.

"I've checked and double-checked the possibilities there. Not many. She liked a quiet kind of life, Kate. Well, you all know that. No, I'm almost certain she came back here. And was not welcome. And got killed for her pains."

"But who would kill her? And why?"

It was Ursula who spoke, her husband's needs momentarily forgotten.

Swithenbank smiled humourlessly.

"Killing's not so difficult, Ursula dear. We've been pretty close a couple of times tonight, haven't we? You know what Kate was like. Simple, direct, impulsive. Insensitive. If she was sick of me, of our life in London, and wanted to come back to Wearton, she'd just set off. Suppose she has a choice here. Arthur in his cottage or a lover, someone she's been sleeping with on and off for years, perhaps. A man who thinks she takes it as casually as he does, a bit of sensual titillation when the chance offers. A man who doesn't want a scandal, certainly doesn't want a permanent relationship. She goes to him, rather than Arthur. Obvious choice it seems, till this man laughs at her, tells her to go back to London. She wouldn't make a fuss, not Kate. She'd get up quietly and say she was going. But not back to London, no; back to her brother."

Arthur Lightfoot groaned from the depths of his being. The others regarded him uneasily, except for Swithenbank, who went relentlessly on.

"Angry husbands are one thing, but the prospect of an angry Arthur was quite another. Look at him, for God's sake! And so, one thing leads to another . . ."

"But not to murder!" protested Ursula. "It makes no sense!"

But her words were subsumed by Lightfoot's groan which had swollen to a cry of rage.

"It's sense to me!" he cried. "And there's only one here that fits the bill. The stud, him as has covered every mare hereabouts. Like father, like fucking son!"

Oh God. Here we go again, thought Pascoe as the black barrel rose once more and this time came to a halt against Boris Kingsley's ample belly.

To his surprise, Kingsley showed not the slightest sign of fear.

"Come off it, Lightfoot," he sneered. "You're not going to fire that thing. That's not your way. A bit of sneaky poaching of another man's game. Or even dirtier ways of getting your hands on another man's money. That's all you're good for. So put that thing away."

"Did you kill my sister?" demanded Lightfoot.

"Oh go to hell!"

"And whoever did kill her, she probably asked for it!" hissed Stella Rawlinson with a venom that shocked even Lightfoot into silence for a moment.

"Listen who's talking!" he rejoined eventually. But before he could elaborate Swithenbank said in his most casual voice, "Yet it's a question which needs answering, Boris."

Now everyone was quiet. Lightfoot had stepped further into the porch, leaving the door unguarded, but Ursula made no effort to shepherd her husband through it, nor from the expression of rapt attention on his face would he have allowed himself to be removed if she'd tried.

Strange therapy! thought Pascoe.

"What do you mean, John?" asked Kingsley courteously.

Swithenbank was standing under the arch of the doorway up to the tower and the light from the single small bulb that lit the porch scarcely reached him so that his voice came drifting out of the shadows.

"It's an odd place, Wearton, Mr. Pascoe," he said. "You try to escape it but it comes after you. And I was foolish enough to take one of the oddest pieces of it away with me! On, don't be shocked, friends. Even among your outstanding oddities, Kate stood supreme! And when she left me, I knew that sooner or later she'd come back here, as long as she was alive, that is."

"Or dead."

Arthur Lightfoot spoke so solemnly that no one dared even by expression to show disbelief.

Swithenbank ignored him.

"You know what I did when Jean and I first started brooding on schemes to start our rabbit?"

"Goose," muttered Pascoe to himself.

"I wrote down the names of everyone here, you excepted, of course, Inspector. And I started to cross out those who I couldn't bring myself to believe capable of killing Kate. Do you know, I sat for an hour and hadn't crossed out a name!"

"Oh, come on, John," said Ursula.

"Not even yours, dear," he said regretfully. "So I made a league table instead. And do you know, Boris, however I constructed it, you kept on coming out on top!"

"Well, you know me, John," said Kingsley. "Always a winner."

"Shut up!" snapped Lightfoot, prodding him with the gun.

This had gone far enough, thought Pascoe. This lunatic could accidentally fire that thing at any moment.

He coughed gently and was flattered to note that he immediately had everyone's attention. He also had for the first time a full frontal of Lightfoot's shotgun. He reached out, took the barrel fastidiously between thumb and forefinger and moved it aside.

"Mr. Lightfoot," he said quietly. "If that weapon is pointed once more at anyone here, and most especially at me, I shall arrest you instantly for threatening behaviour. Lower it and break it!"

The man gave him a look full of hatred, but obeyed, and Davenport, as though the action held some personal symbolism for him, suddenly stepped away from Ursula and in best vicarial tones said, "Please, everybody, hasn't this gone far enough? You're all soaking and it's mainly my fault. I don't want pneumonia on my conscience as well. You're all welcome to dry out at the rectory. Mr. Pascoe, I'd like a private word with you later, if it's convenient."

He was looking at Lightfoot as he spoke these last words and it was the smallholder whose hitherto unblinking gaze shifted first.

Pascoe made an educated guess at what Davenport was going to tell him. He'd lay odds that a year ago Lightfoot, out on a poaching trip perhaps, had witnessed Rawlinson's fall from the tower. He had kept out of sight when the vicar descended—he would hardly want to draw the local bobby's attention to himself—and his curiosity had later been whetted by the discrepancy between what he had seen and the official version. But he'd done nothing about it till the summer when he needed money after the fire. With Kingsley senior's death, his old source had dried up, but a visit to the vicarage, a few dark hints of deep knowledge (he had the perfect manner for it), and he had found a new supply of funds to tap. What precisely he did know hardly mattered. He emanated evil intent like few men Pascoe had met.

He made a mental vow that whatever else came out of this extraordinary evening, Arthur Lightfoot was going to get what was coming to him.

But there were still many other questions to be answered. Obviously Swithenbank had deliberately angled his campaign toward Kingsley, with how much justification was not yet clear. Perhaps he just had a "feeling." Like Willie Dove had a feeling! Or perhaps he knew more than he had yet said. There was still the dress to be explained. He suddenly felt very tired.

There had been a general movement to the doorway. Outside the wind still gusted fitfully but for the moment the rain seemed to have stopped. Not that that mattered, Pascoe thought ruefully. He was so damp that nothing short of total immersion could aggravate his condition.

"Hold on a moment. I don't think we're finished here yet!"

It was Jean Starkey and her words were greeted with a groan of exasperation in which Pascoe joined. He guessed what she was going to say, but he judged that the moment for dramatic revelation was past. What had been an atmosphere of high emotion in a Gothic setting had now become one of damp and discomfort in a draughty church porch. The time had come for warmth and whisky, followed by some hard questioning in a police interview room. He wanted to save his knowledge of the woman's dress in Kingsley's bedroom till then.

But the woman insisted.

"Tell us about the dress, Boris. You haven't told us about the dress."

"What dress?"

"The white muslin dress and the big straw hat. Kate's favourite gear, wasn't it? How does it come about that you've got a woman's dress hidden in a locked wardrobe in your house?"

Now the audience's attention was engaged once more. Kingsley made no effort to deny it but asked indignantly, "How does it come about you know what I've got locked up in my house?"

"It's true, then?" said Lightfoot, who had been smoulderingly subdued for the past few minutes.

"Why shouldn't it be true?"

Whether because of Pascoe's threat or out of personal preference, Lightfoot didn't try to use his gun this time but jumped forward and seized Kingsley one-handed by the throat, bearing him back against the opened door which lay against the wall. No one seemed inclined to interfere, not even when the enraged assailant started using the fat man's head as a knocker to punctuate his demands, "Where-is-she? Where-is-she?"

It was constabulary duty time once more. Pascoe stepped forward and said, "That's enough."

When Lightfoot showed no sign of agreeing, Pascoe punched him in the kidneys and stepped swiftly back. The blow was a light one and Lightfoot swung round as much in surprise as pain. Kingsley, released, staggered out of the church holding his throat, but he could have suffered no real damage for he was able to scream, "I'll tell you why I've got the clothes! It's Kate's ghost, you superstitious cretin! Do you really think anything would come back from the grave to an animal like you in that sty of a cottage?"

He even managed a derisive laugh but it stuttered off into a fit of coughing.

"You'd better explain yourself, I think, Mr. Kingsley," said Pascoe, putting himself between the fat man and Lightfoot.

Though the man was genuinely angry, Pascoe could see the quick calculation in his face. He wasn't about to admit anything illegal, but what was illegal about a practical joke?

"He had it coming to him, that bastard," snarled Kingsley, adding weakly, "It was just a kind of joke."

"To convince him that the sister he loved was dead and he was partly responsible? Very amusing," said Pascoe. "But hardly a one-man show? You must have had a leading lady."

He let his eyes run down Kingsley's corpulent figure.

"You mean, it were play-acting?" said Lightfoot, who seemed far more affected by this news than by Pascoe's punch.

"That's right," said Kinglsey with malicious satisfaction. "If ever a man deserved to be haunted, it was you."

"Play-acting!"

"But where does the acting end, the truth begin?" said Swithenbank. A trifle melodramatic, thought Pascoe, but a good question nevertheless.

"There's still one theory untested, Inspector. Remember the tomb I mentioned? The resting place of the Aubrey-Beesons, the old squires of the Wear?

And I said—'What is written, sweet sister,
On the door of this legended tomb?'
She replied—'Ulalume—Ulalume—
'Tis the vault of thy lost Ulalume!' "

He held aloft a large metal ring with several keys which chimed together as he shook it.

"I can't get it out of my mind that perhaps by accident when I chose that poem, I was closer than I knew to the truth. What say you, Boris? I'm going to take a look before I leave this churchyard tonight. Are you coming, Inspector? Anyone for menace?"

There was a note of hysterical bravado in his voice which caused the others to stir and draw closer together. He took a few paces down the path towards the old lych-gate, which itself was not visible, though the wind-swayed arch of cypress trees loomed dark against the grey wash of the sky. Suddenly the wind dropped altogether; the sough and scrape of branches, the rustle of dried leaves among the headstones, the buffets of violent air against the old stones of the tower, all these sounds ceased and were succeeded by a silence so complete that the screech of the lych-gate opening might have been heard had it been twice the distance.

No one moved.

No one spoke.

Out of the dark at the end of the path a figure was emerging with the strange marking-time approach of someone on a film screen. It was a woman, slight of form and light of step, for she came forward with scarcely a sound, her loose white dress floating softly about her.

Swithenbank, a few yards ahead of the rest, was first to speak.

"Who's there?" he called uncertainly. "Who is that?"

"Hello, John," returned a soft, distant voice. "Arthur, is that you?"

Pascoe felt himself shouldered violently aside.

"More play-acting!" bellowed Lightfoot.

The gun came up, the barrel locked and the cartridge exploded all in an instant.

The woman's form swayed and fell without a sound, making such a small heap on the ground that Pascoe would scarcely have been surprised to find nothing there but a white muslin dress.

But the world of physical reality was not to be denied by churchyards and tombs and arches of cypress.

It was a woman who lay there. Swithenbank knelt at her head, horror and amazement on his face. Lightfoot took one fleeting look but needed no more. Pascoe paused for a second to check the pulse, then plunged into the darkness after him, but stopped when he heard the second shot. Some things there was no need to rush towards.

Ah! what demon has tempted me here?
Well I know, now, this dim lake of Auber—
This misty mid-region of Weir—
Well I know, now, this dank tarn of Auber,
This ghoul-haunted woodland of Wier.

CHAPTER X

Thank Heaven! the crisis—
The danger is past.

"It was like the last act of *Hamlet Meets Dracula,*" said Pascoe.

Some things were far too serious for anything but flippancy.

"And they're both dead?" repeated Inspector Dove at the other end of the line.

"He died instantly. Well, he would, his head was mostly missing."

Pascoe remembered his promise that he would see that Lightfoot got what was coming to him.

"He doesn't sound much of a miss," said Dove cynically.

"He was a blackmailer twice over," agreed Pascoe.

"Though now he's dead, Davenport won't need to talk and Kingsley's backtracking like mad. There'll be more tight mouths around Wearton than at a lemon-suckers' convention. Not that it matters. My guess is that Stella Rawlinson played the ghost. She hated the Lightfoots and Kingsley may or may not have been screwing her into the bargain."

"Into the what?"

"Oh, for God's sake!"

Pascoe found that he was sick of the jokes and the lightness. It was eight-thirty in the morning. He had got home at three but been unable to sleep. Dalziel had observed his arrival at the station with nothing more expressive than an upward roll of his eyes, then suggested that even southern pansies should be awake by this time and he might as well put Dove in the picture.

"I'm sorry," said Dove.

"So am I," said Pascoe. "I'm a bit knackered. It's all turned out so badly. This Lightfoot, he seems to have been a nasty bit of work all round. But he loved his sister. God, even that sounds like the cue for a crack!—and it shouldn't have come to this. Not for anyone. He was the only one she asked for in the ambulance. Arthur, Arthur, all the time."

"And she said nothing else before she died?"

"Not a thing. The only people she'd spoken to were Swithenbank's mother and Kingsley's housekeeper. She must have gone straight to Arthur's cottage when she arrived. We found her stuff there. Arthur was out, of course. She rang Swithenbank. His mother answered. She was flabbergasted naturally, told her about the party, asked where she'd been but got no answer. Kate went up to Wear End, learned from the housekeeper that everyone had taken off towards the church, so she set off after them along the old drive."

"Where the hell had she been?" asked Dove in exasperation. "You say you found some things of hers at Lightfoot's. Any clue there?"

"Nothing obvious," said Pascoe wearily. "At first glance it looks about the same as that list of things she took when she left Swithenbank last year. But it doesn't matter much now, does it?"

"I suppose not. Well, we were dead wrong about Swithenbank. Thank God I stopped this side of pulling his floorboards up! Still, you can't win 'em all."

"No," said Pascoe.

"Cheer up, Pete, for God's sake! You sound like it's all down to you. It was just an 'assist,' remember? You can't legislate for maniacs!"

"I know. I just feel that if I'd handled things differently . . ."

Dalziel had come into the room with a sheet of paper in his hand and when he heard Pascoe's remark, the eyes rolled again. It was like a lesson with the globes in an eighteenth-century schoolroom.

"Pete, it wasn't your job to find out where she'd gone. That was our job, it's down to us. Like I say, OK, we missed out. I feel bad about it, but not too bad. I mean, Christ, she came back and we still don't know where the hell she's been! It's our fault. How could you be expected to work it out if we couldn't? Can't!"

"Too bloody true!" bellowed Dalziel, who had come close enough to eavesdrop on Dove's resonant voice.

"What's that, Pete? Someone there with you?"

"Mr. Dalziel's just come in," said Pascoe hastily. "I'll keep in touch."

"You do that, old son. I'm avid for the next instalment. I used to think it was just a joke about you lot north of Watford having bat-ears and little bushy tails, but now I'm not so sure. Love to Andy-Pandy! Cheerio now!"

Pascoe put down the phone.

"I don't know what he's got to be cheerful about," said Dalziel malevolently. "Or what you've got to be miserable about either."

"Two people dead," said Pascoe. "That's what."

"And that's your fault?"

"Not court-of-law my fault. Not even court-of-enquiry my fault," said Pascoe. "It's just that, I don't know, I suppose . . . I was enjoying it! Secretly, deep inside, I was enjoying it. Big house, interviews in the library, chasing up to the churchyard, stopping the vicar from jumping, uncovering all kinds of guilty secrets—you know I was thinking, gleefully almost, wait till I get back and tell them about this! They'll never believe it!"

"I believe it," said Dalziel. "And I'd have done much the same in your shoes. You did it right. The only thing you couldn't know was that she was alive. That's what you call a paradox, you philosophers with degrees and O levels, isn't it? If you'd known she was alive, she'd be alive! But you didn't. You couldn't!"

"Someone should have done," said Pascoe. "They should have looked harder."

"Too true," said Dalziel with grim satisfaction. "Cases like these, you follow up every line. One line they didn't follow."

"What?"

Dalziel scratched his backside on the corner of the desk, a frequent preliminary to one of his deductive *tours de force,* which one of his more scurrilous colleagues had categorized as the anal-lytical approach.

"What was Swithenbank doing on the day his missus disappeared?"

"The Friday, you mean?"

"Aye."

Pascoe opened his notebook at the page on which he'd first started jotting down notes on the Swithenbank case.

"He was at a farewell party at lunch-time."

"Who for?"

"One of his assistants."

"Name?"

"I've no idea," said Pascoe.

"Cunliffe. David Cunliffe," said Dalziel triumphantly. "Thought you'd have known that."

"It wasn't in any of the papers Enfield sent me," said Pascoe defensively.

"Bloody right it wasn't," said Dalziel with relish. "They've a lot to answer for. This fellow was heading for the good life, back to Mother Earth, do-it-yourself, all that crap, right?"

"Yes. Up in the Orkneys, I think."

"That's right," said Dalziel. "One of the little islands. Him, a few natives, a lot of sheep; and his wife."

"His wife?"

"Oh yes. Only, suppose she wasn't his wife! They don't take kindly to living in sin up there, so it'd be better for community relations to *call* her his wife. But suppose that on that Friday your Kate packed her few things, put on her new blonde wig and set off for the Orkneys!''

Pascoe shook his head to fight back the waves of fatigue, and something else, too.

''Why the wig?'' he asked.

''She was meeting her boy-friend at King's Cross, on the train. She had the wit to guess there might be a mutual acquaintance there to see him off and she didn't want to be spotted. As it happened, the whole bloody party came along, including hubby, so she was very wise. Imagine, there's Swithenbank shooting all that shit about how he wished he had the guts to up and leave everything, meaning his missus, for a better life, and there she is sitting only a few carriages away, doing just that!''

''Oh Christ,'' said Pascoe. ''Is this just hypothesis, or have you checked it out?''

''What do you think I am, bloody Sherlock Holmes?'' exploded Dalziel. ''No, there's no way any of us could have worked out any of that. It was up to Dove and his mates, as I'll make bloody clear! What we've got is this. Arrived this morning.''

He handed Pascoe the sheet of paper he had been carrying.

It was a request for assistance from Orkney Police HQ in Kirkwall. They were holding one David Cunliffe on suspicion of murdering his ''wife,'' whom he now claimed was not his wife but Katherine Swithenbank, formerly of Wearton in the county of Yorkshire, where, he suggested, it was most likely she would return after leaving him.

It was clear the Orkney constabulary had no great faith in his claim. No one had seen her leave the small island on which their croft was situated. No one had spotted her on the ferry from Stromness or on a plane from Kirkwall Airport. Pascoe got a distinct impression that the croft which Cunliffe had so lovingly repaired was now being taken down again, stone by stone, and the land which he had tilled was now being dug over again, spadeful after hard-turned spadeful.

''She was a right little expert at the disappearing trick,'' said Dalziel admiringly. ''When she gets fed up she just packs her bag and goes. And no one ever notices!"

"Someone noticed this time," said Pascoe.

"Belt up! Think on—there's going to be some red faces this morning! Which do you want to do—Enfield or Orkney? Best you do Orkney; Dove'll try to shrug it off, well, the bugger won't shrug *me* off in a hurry!"

He sounded really delighted, as though the whole of the Wearton business had been arranged just so that he could crow over the inefficiency of the effete south.

But before he left the room, he made one more effort to cheer up his dull and defeated-looking inspector, who was sitting with his head bowed over his open notebook.

"I'll say it one last time, Peter," he said. "It wasn't your fault. You reckoned she was dead, everyone reckoned she was dead, her brother, her husband, that Enfield lot. You *had* to go ahead as you did. You'd have needed second sight to know where she was hiding herself. I mean, inspired guesses are one thing, but to work out she was in the Orkneys on the basis of what you knew, you'd have needed a miracle. Right?"

"Right," said Pascoe.

"Good," said Dalziel. "Come twelve, you can buy me a pint for being right. Again."

He went out.

Pascoe closed his eyes and saw again the white-clad woman floating up the path from the lych-gate.

Why had she come back? What had she hoped for?

He shook his head and opened his eyes.

He would never know and he had no intention of trying an inspired guess. Dalziel was right. A detective should have no truck with feelings and intuitions.

He looked at his notebook, which still lay open at the first page of his scribblings on the Swithenbank case, made as he talked to Dove on the telephone two days before.

On the left-handed page there were two words only. One was *HAIRDRESSER?*

The other lightly scored through was *ORKNEY?*

He took his pen now and scratched at the word till it was totally obliterated.

Then he closed the book.

The Trunk in the Attic

The first letter came before I found the trunk. I didn't notice it was addressed to Mrs. M. Evans and my first thought as I drew out the single sheet of paper was, who do I know in Her Majesty's Prison at Wakefield?

Then I read "Dear Marion" and realized my mistake. I suppose I should have stopped there, but the eye is quicker than the conscience and it *was* a very short letter.

> Dear Marion,
>
> Sorry you couldn't make it up here last month and hope nothing's wrong. I just wanted to say if you had plans to come on Tuesday next week, come on Wednesday instead, as on Tuesday I'm seeing the parole board, so keep fingers crossed.
>
> All the best,
>
> Ken

The hand was childish but very firm and bold. I replaced the letter, wrote *opened in error, address unknown* on the envelope, and dropped it in a pillar-box. A week or so later, another letter in the same hand arrived and I treated it in the same way, except that I didn't open it.

Some people are very inconsiderate when they sell a house. I'd never met the Evanses, the previous owners, who had already moved out when the estate agent showed me round. But they should have made some arrangement with the Post Office for forwarding their mail. I had better things to do than worry about other people's letters. And I had other cause to dislike my predecessor in the house.

It was clear that Frank Evans had been an enthusiastic

do-it-yourselfer. And a good one, too. For instance, he'd removed all the fireplaces in the house, bricked them up, papered them over and installed central heating himself. Naturally I had the Gas Board check it over, but they assured me it was perfectly sound. And doors, cupboards, window-frames, etc., were all in excellent condition. Unfortunately, craftsman though he might have been, he was no artist. Indeed, he must have been colour blind. His taste in wallpaper and paint ranged from the merely bright to the positively explosive! Something had to be done about it and while my wife, Ann, remained in London with the children tying up the loose ends of our house sale there, I was camping out here in the north. Decorating isn't bad therapy after a day in an accounts office and I have the kind of systematic mind which was able to devise a work schedule which would see the work finished by the time Ann joined me.

With three days to go, I had completed the ground floor and the children's bedrooms and was just putting the finishing touches to my masterpiece, the main bedroom. I had subtly altered its dimensions with ceiling tiles and plaster cornicing. The paintwork was a soft white with just a hint of pink and now I was putting on the paper, a discreet but sensuous Scandinavian pattern.

The telephone rang just as I was starting the last wall. I had a length of pasted paper in my hands which I laid carefully on the table. It was certainly Ann, I thought. I had rung her from the office earlier to tell her that at last the telephone had been reconnected. Another of Frank Evans's little tricks had been not to pay his bill and the Post Office had disconnected the phone before I arrived.

"I want to talk to Marion," said a man's voice, very brusque.

"Do you?" I said. "You must have got the wrong number."

"Is that Frank?"

"No. This is three-seven-eight-four-six-two."

"That's right. I want Marion Evans. Who're you?"

"I'm the owner of this house," I said. "The Evanses moved out several weeks ago."

There was a silence, full of disbelief.

"Moved out?" he said finally. "Where to?"

"I've no idea. I never met them and they left no forwarding address."

Another silence, then without so much as a good night, the receiver was banged down.

I set off up the stairs, feeling irritated. The phone rang again.

"Hello!" I shouted.

"You don't sound very happy," said Ann.

"Oh hello, love. Sorry, but I've been working hard."

"So you keep on telling me. What are you doing now?"

"I'm just finishing our bedroom," I said.

"What's it like?"

"Superb. Sensual and soporific at the same time. A symphony of interior decoration."

We talked for a few minutes, then I returned to my work. The pasted length was ruined, of course, and I had to cut a new one. As I snipped at it, I thought nasty thoughts about Frank Evans, whose taste was so abominable, who didn't pay his phone bills and who left no forwarding address.

I finished the room about eleven. Though I say it myself, it really did look superb. This left only one small room to do, a box-room really, which I planned to use as an office. It would take a desk and a filing cabinet, though little else. At the moment it contained my camp bed as I did not care for the paint fumes in the newly decorated rooms.

It also contained the trap-door which led to the attic. I had made a mental note to have a look up there before I started painting the woodwork, and now as I prepared for bed I found my gaze returning again and again to the trap. I felt restless as one often does after bringing a specific task to a successful completion and on an impulse I fetched the step-ladder, ascended to the trap-door and pushed. It opened easily. Handyman Evans kept his hinges oiled.

I stood on the steps, my feet in a world of light and air and my head in a world of musty shadows. To my left loomed the house's central chimneystack and alongside it the water tank. In the dim light filtering from the room below I could see that the floor was boarded between the opening and the tank but elsewhere the bare joists ran out to the shadowy eaves.

I noticed a light switch fitted into the floor next to the trap, but when I clicked it down, nothing happened and I could see no light fitment anywhere among the beams. Perhaps Evans had had to leave before the job was finished, though the switch looked ancient enough.

There was nothing to be seen and the atmosphere was, as it generally is in attics, a trifle uncanny, so why I should have pulled myself wholly on to the patch of boarded floor I do not know. Perhaps because I was aware of an irrational uneasiness and annoyed by it. I told myself I would take a look at the water tank and check that all was well. Every good householder should check his water tank once or twice before he dies!

There were in fact two tanks, both very new. One was the normal cold water tank and the other was for hot water, raised up here to feed the shower unit Evans had installed *en suite* with the main bedroom. Again, I guessed he'd done it all himself. The boards around the tanks and the chimneystack were strewn with old cement sacks. Perhaps he had been such a perfectionist that he'd even been doing some pointing work on the bricks of the chimney, though why he should have felt it necessary, having just installed central heating, I didn't know!

I slid the cover off the cold tank and peered in. All I saw was water and a ball-cock which seemed to be performing its function perfectly adequately. Self-esteem satisfied, I replaced the cover and was about to return to the comfort of my well-lit bedroom when I noticed the trunk.

It was lying across the joists behind the chimneystack and the tank and was thus quite invisible from the trap. I wished it had remained invisible, but having spotted it I had to look more closely. So I stepped off the boarded area and edged my way along the narrow joists, moving with exaggerated care as I had no desire to put a foot through the ceiling of one of my newly decorated bedrooms. I had thought it was dark before, but now the gloom was almost tangible and the square of light from the trap-door seemed very distant and dim.

It was a large trunk, perhaps five feet long and three

deep. I touched it and drew back my hand sharply at its coldness. I had expected wood, not metal. It had been painted a deep green, almost khaki. I wondered if it had some military significance. Perhaps Evans had been an army man and served in far corners of the world with his most precious belongings shut away in this trunk. Perhaps it still contained them. Perhaps . . .

But that was fantasy and a lifetime dealing with figures had given me a practical turn of mind which does not tolerate fantasy for long. The trunk had other implications more important to my present activities. Clearly it belonged to Evans. Had it been left there deliberately or in error? And if in error, suppose he turned up one day and wanted it back?

Simply give it to him, you may answer. There were handles fixed to either end and I bent down and took hold of one of them. Exerting all my strength, I managed to shift the thing a fraction. It would take at least two men to lift it and even then it would require a lot of effort. And how even two strong men would be able to manoeuvre this solid object across the attic and through the trap-door without going through the plaster or damaging the wood and paintwork below, I could not see.

Perhaps emptied, it would provide an easier task.

With a casualness absurd in the absence of witnesses, I tried to raise the lid.

It wouldn't budge.

I stooped and examined it more closely and saw what I had missed at first in the gloom—a hasp with a large and solid-looking padlock.

I felt quite relieved as I made my way back to the comforting square of light. I wouldn't have shied away from opening it if I had been able to, but it was good to have the opportunity denied to me.

As I stood on the step-ladder and pulled the trap-door shut above me, I wondered how on earth Evans had got it up there in the first place.

I was very tired now, but I lay a long time in my narrow and uncomfortable little bed staring up at the ceiling before I finally fell asleep.

The next evening I was a little later than usual and it was dark when I got to the house. The garden was my next job, I thought as I negotiated the rambler rose which lay in ambush between the garage and the front door. Evans had obviously been a keen gardener, too (though the same taste for the garish was apparent in his choice of shrubs and bedding plants), but no one had touched it since he left. The rambler shot out a low branch and caught my ankle and I jerked away angrily and almost stumbled into the arms of a figure who stepped out of the entrance porch.

"Who the hell are you?" I asked in nervous anger.

"I talked to you on the phone last night," he said brusquely. "About Evans."

"Did you? So that's who you are. Well, I told you. He's gone. I don't know where. Excuse me."

I unlocked the front door and stepped inside. I didn't feel inclined to enter into further discussion with this man, and besides I was ill-equipped for hospitality.

"Hold on. I'm not done yet," he said determinedly.

I switched on the hall light and looked at him. He was about my age, mid-thirties; perhaps older. It was hard to say. Experience ages, and his face looked as if it had experienced a lot. It was a good face for winning arguments with and it matched his broad shoulders and aggressive stance.

"I'm sorry. I really can't tell you anything," I repeated in a more conciliatory tone. "I can give you the estate agent's address and that's it."

"I've tried the agent," he said. "I called earlier. You weren't in. One of the neighbours remembered who'd sold the house, though."

I was rather piqued that the fellow had gone to other houses in the street asking questions. There was no way this could reflect on me, but nevertheless I didn't like it.

"And the agent couldn't help? Well, I'm sorry. That's hard luck. You'll just have to advertise for Evans."

"It's not Evans I want. It's his wife."

I raised my eyebrows.

"Marion's my sister."

"Ah!" I said, light dawning. "You must be Ken."

"How the hell do you know that?" he said aggressively and stepped into the hall. Quickly I explained about the letters. He frowned when I described my mistake in opening and reading the first and I felt that perhaps he deserved a little recompense so I took him into the kitchen and offered him some scotch in a tea-cup.

Now he in his turn became conciliatory.

"Yes, I'm Ken Pargeter," he told me. His voice was harsh, his accent northern. "Marion's my kid sister. She were always my favourite. There were six of us in our family, but we were always closest."

"Yes," I said sympathetically. "And she used to visit you, didn't she . . . ?"

My voice tailed off as his eyes fixed me coldly. Hastily I slopped another couple of inches of whisky into his cup.

"I'm sorry," I said. "The letter . . ."

"Oh aye. Well, I'm out now. Parole. It's took a long time but it's come at last. A bloody long time."

He sipped his drink reflectively.

"How long?" I wondered. "I mean, if you don't mind . . ."

"Six years," he said.

"Six, eh?" I said, trying to think how long that meant with remission and parole, and what a man had to do to get himself put away for such a sentence.

"She always came. Regular each month, especially since I've been at Wakefield. It's been handy for her. She'd never miss, no matter what *he* said."

"*He?* Oh, your brother-in-law. You don't care for him?"

He laughed humourlessly and held out his cup for replenishment.

"There's better men inside," he said. "Frank's decent enough on the surface, but I always reckoned there's a nasty streak in him. Our Marion's like me. She'd fly off the handle easy enough, but she'd not bear a grudge. Frank's sneaky. I don't think she'd have wed him if I hadn't been sent down again. She likes to play the field, our Marion. Never short of a man, a good-looking girl like that. So why get stuck with a shit like Evans?"

He was becoming loquacious on my liquor. I'd have placed him as a hard-drinking man, but after six years' lay-off he'd need to get back into training. I had another shot myself.

"Didn't she tell you they were moving?" I asked.

"Not a word," he said. "Not a hint."

"Not to worry," I said confidently. "It's a busy time for a woman. She'll surely get in touch as soon as she's settled."

"It's him," he said. "He's trying to stop her. The bastard."

"You said she's a determined girl," I said. "I mean, she visited you when her husband didn't want her to. So she won't let him stop her from writing to you, will she?"

"Mebbe not," he said, pouring himself another snort. "But you'd think someone'd have her new address."

"Must do," I agreed. I was beginning to take a liking to Pargeter. Through a whisky haze, he was quite a romantic figure. Just out of jail, harsh sentence, debt paid, looking for the sister he loved. I felt I'd like to help him.

"*Someone* knows," I said. "What about his work?"

"He had a shop. Do-it-yourself," said Pargeter scornfully. "I've been there. He'd sold up. No forwarding address."

"Odd," I said. "No assistants?"

"Marion helped. And there was a young fellow, George something. Foxton, aye, that's it. No one knows where he's working now either."

I thought again. He drank. His role was the man of action and I was sure he'd be damned efficient in it. Mine was the thinker. I felt he was relying on me.

"Solicitor!" I said. "He must have used a solicitor. Now, the estate agent will know who it was. Or if not, certainly my solicitor must know! I'll give you his telephone number. Problem solved!"

Triumphantly I poured out what remained in the bottle and we parted on such good terms that we arranged to meet for a pub lunch the following day so that he could tell me what progress he had made.

As he swayed very gently on the doorstep, I was emboldened by the drink and our bond of friendship to ask what he'd been sent down for.

He stopped swaying.

"I was climbing out of a window," he said very clearly. "A policeman stopped me. I broke his jaw. It were an accident."

"Oh, I'm sure, I'm sure," I said.
"Aye. I meant to break his bloody neck. Goo' night!"
Ann rang a couple of hours later.
"How's it going?" she said.
"Fine, fine," I answered. "Have you confirmed everything with the removal men?"
"Yes. Now you're sure you'll be finished?"
"Absolutely," I said.
I felt a little guilty as I lay in bed that night. Not a thing had been done since Pargeter left. I know myself better than to start wielding a paint brush with half a bottle of whisky swilling around inside me. But as I fell asleep I consoled myself with the thought that it was only this one small room that remained to do. One good night would just about finish it.
Hours later I woke up suddenly and lay staring at the trap-door thinking about the green trunk. The only thing that stopped me from getting up and having a glass of whisky was that I knew there was none left.
Next day Pargeter was in the pub waiting when I arrived. To tell the truth, I'd half hoped he wouldn't turn up. Sober, I found him a much less desirable companion.
He was in a morose mood, which didn't help matters. Yes, he had got the address of Evans's solicitors. No, they had not given him Evans's new address because they did not know it. The money from the sales of shop and house had been paid direct into the Evanses' bank account, less solicitors' fees and estate agent's commission, of course.
"What about the bank?" I asked.
He had tried the bank. The people there had not been helpful. People at banks did not believe in giving away information about their clients, not even to their brothers-in-law. He expressed a belief that from time to time bank managers should be severely thumped.
"Well, there's always the police," I said.
He had tried the police. When they'd realized who he was, they had been even less sympathetic than the bank. He wasn't really reporting his sister and her husband as missing persons, was he? Perhaps they didn't want him to know where they were. It was their privilege. Understandable in the circumstances! Unless there was actual suspicion of a crime, there was nothing they could do.

He seemed to think that policemen should be thumped once or twice a day, too, especially by men with experience.

We sat and looked into our drinks for a while. I don't know what he saw but I kept on seeing a green trunk.

"That's it then, I reckon," he said finally.

"Yes. I'm sorry that . . . Look here." I hesitated.

"What?"

"Oh, nothing." I couldn't tell him about the trunk. I'd get the local police to come and look at it, but there was no point in filling this poor devil's mind with a lot of agony, probably for nothing at all.

"Good luck," I said, offering my hand.

He regarded it as if it held a lump of manure.

"What were you going to say?" he demanded.

"Nothing at all."

"I'm not daft," he said. "There's something on your mind. You'd best spit it out, or else . . ."

I felt that I was being lined up with bank managers and policemen with none of the privileges of their positions. People react differently to physical threats. Myself, I almost inevitably give in at once. So I told him about the trunk. I told him as casually as possible, but he took the point at once.

"Let's go," he said.

I protested that I had to go back to work.

"Give us the key then," he said, holding out his hand. I gave in then and went with him. Being late for work was preferable to having Pargeter wandering alone round my beautifully decorated house.

Armed with a torch from my car, I led the way to my bedroom and put up the step-ladder. Visibility in the attic was not so bad even without the torch as quite a lot of daylight crept beneath the eaves, and with two of us standing together up there, everything seemed very ordinary. I think he felt a bit of this, too, as he grinned at me almost sheepishly and said, "Lead on, professor."

As I moved forward the light caught the overhead beams and I saw something which made the situation a little less ordinary. There had once been an electric light fitting here, but it looked as if someone had deliberately severed the wires and removed the socket. The only motive for this that I could think of was to cut down the amount of light up here. In other words to make it more difficult to spot anything concealed. Even a trunk.

"This is it," I said to Pargeter. He nodded, leaned forward and rapped with his knuckles on the lid. I started at the sound and almost put a foot through the ceiling beneath.

"It's not empty," he said.

"No," I agreed. "Try the weight."

He grasped a handle and pulled.

"I see what you mean," he said.

"Old books weigh heavy," I suggested.

"Mebbe," he said.

He examined the padlock for a moment. I stood by respectfully in the presence of an expert. I half expected him to produce some subtle instruments from the lining of his jacket and set about the lock with delicate probings.

Instead he said, "Got a hammer and a cold chisel?"

I had. When I returned with them he struck the lock off with one powerful blow.

"Right," he said. And together we raised the lid.

It was the kind of disappointment I like. Instead of the decomposing body of Pargeter's sister, all that the trunk contained was a load of rubble, mainly bricks. A mixed cloud of soot and cement dust rose and sent me choking backwards so that I almost missed my footing on the joist.

Pargeter reached out and steadied me.

Downstairs the telephone rang.

It was my office. A client was waiting. Had I forgotten? Was I ill?

I rushed to clean myself up, yelling to Pargeter from the bathroom. When he finally appeared, he'd contrived to get himself ten times dirtier than I was and it was going to take him commensurately longer to clean up. I glanced at my watch impatiently and he said, "Never mind me. You go off. I'll let myself out."

I regarded him dubiously. He was after all a criminal and not one whose incarceration had rehabilitated him, so far as I could judge. On the other hand, there was little of value in the unfurnished house. Perhaps I could afford a little trust. Perhaps I even owed him something for putting him through what must have been an agonizing experience.

"All right," I said. "I'm glad we didn't . . . well, things turned out as they did. I hope you find your sister soon."

This time he took my proffered hand and I had to wipe it clean on my handkerchief as I broke the speed-limits for one-handed driving into town. Several times during the afternoon I caught people looking oddly at my blackened handkerchief as I absent-mindedly pulled it from my pocket. And by the end of the afternoon, I was looking at it oddly, too.

When I got home that evening, I went straight upstairs with the car torch which Pargeter had left by the telephone. What I was thinking was absurd, but I'd had the taste of soot in my mouth all afternoon, and there was only one place that it could have come from.

I was moving swiftly in order to keep ahead of my fear. I had a picture very clearly in my mind now of Frank Evans watching with growing jealousy and hatred the developing friendship between his wife and young George Foxton in the shop. Perhaps he followed them. Perhaps he saw things no husband should see. But he sounded as if he were the kind of man who could hold himself in check, maintain the surface of things until the moment should be ripe to strike. I'm not normally a very imaginative man, but once I get going, there's no holding me. I saw it all quite clearly. At last the moment had ripened and Frank had struck. Up here in this very attic, on these very boards over which I now made my way purposefully towards the chimneystack. The chimney would have been prepared in advance, the bricks smashed out and deposited, soot and all, in the trunk, leaving a hole just large enough to push a human body through. Or perhaps two. George Foxton was unaccounted for also. And then roughly plug the hole with cement and shove the trunk up against it to hide the traces. A perfectionist like Frank might have meticulously re-laid the bricks if he'd had time, but even perfectionists will rush things where murder's concerned. Suddenly I was an expert!

Of course I should have rung the police. But I wanted

to be sure before I let those clod-hoppers loose in my lovely house. God knows what else they might want to dig up or knock down if they found nothing first time.

My impetus to action added to my strength also. I managed without too much difficulty to wrestle the trunk away from the stack. My torch showed me that I was well on the way to being right. There at floor level in the chimney was a large semi-circle of rough cement which the weighted trunk had nicely concealed. The hammer and cold chisel lay where Pargeter had left them. I picked them up, applied the chisel and struck home.

I recorded four different sense impressions almost simultaneously.

Touch told me that this cement was still soft and damp as though newly applied.

Scent told me as the hole crumbled open at my gentle pressure that something was decaying close by.

Sight told me what it was.

And sound told me that I was not alone.

"I was hoping you wouldn't be a clever bugger," said Pargeter.

He was standing on the step-ladder with his head and shoulders in the attic.

"Yes," I said. "Well, I'm glad your sister's all right."

I doubt if Frank Evans shared my relief, but then there was little he could say with a mouthful of cement. How did I know it was Evans? My logical mind, I suppose. Who else would wear a red, purple and orange checked tie? Though I preferred it to the other ornament he had round his neck, which was a length of light flex.

Pargeter pulled himself into the attic.

"Me too," he said. "I really thought he'd done her in, while all the time . . . !"

He shook his head admiringly.

"Like me," he said. "Quick, impulsive. Mind you, she must have had help. That lad from the shop, I dare say. Geordie Foxton. She used to tell me he fancied her. Well, it must have gone beyond fancying."

He was moving steadily across the boarded area as he spoke.

"I checked with the estate agent on the phone," he said. "Frank did it all by post, the selling and such.

Well, if my little Marion couldn't scribble his signature, she's no sister of mine! Money in a joint account so she can draw it at will. She's a bright one, our kid! If only she'd thought to warn me, I wouldn't have stirred things up. Or if only you hadn't been so bright. But I reckoned that if I could work it out, it shouldn't be too difficult for a clever bugger like you. So I waited, just to see. I can be a clever bugger, too!"

He laughed. So did I, but a bit hysterically.

"They'll be abroad now, no doubt. Safe and sound."

He sounded quite matter of fact, but I suspected he knew as much about extradition laws as I did. No, the only way his precious sister could be safe and sound was if no one knew about the body in the chimney. Except Pargeter. Strong-willed, quick-tempered, criminally violent Pargeter who was so much like his sister. I glanced again at Frank Evans. That tie really was terrible.

Then I looked back to Pargeter, who had reached the water tank. I had no idea what his precise intentions were but there are some calculations even an accountant doesn't want to waste time working out. Instead my mind was busy with other problems in mathematics. There were eleven joists between the one I stood on and the back of the attic. They were approximately thirty inches apart. Therefore . . .

Pargeter took another step towards me.

I jumped.

My calculations were wrong. I estimated I would come through the ceiling above the landing. Instead of which I crashed to the floor of my beautiful master bedroom in a shower of plaster and ceiling tiles.

Still, it could have been worse, I thought as I bounced to my feet and hurtled through the door, down the stairs and out into the street. One joist to the left and I would have straddled an interior wall with God knows what dreadful consequences!

When the police came, I explained the hole in the ceiling as an accident. There was no proof that Pargeter had intended to silence me. In any case, the angry way in which he was reacting to their questions about Marion suggested he could get himself into a lot of trouble without my help.

The hole came in useful three or four hours later when they decided to remove the trunk to the police station and the body to the morgue. They still had to be manoeuvred down the stairs, and by the time they got them out of the front door there was a long trail of desolation behind them.

I bought another bottle of scotch and settled down to contemplate my next move.

Half a bottle later the phone rang. It was Ann.

"Hello," she said. "What a lousy day I've had! How're things with you?"

"So-so," I replied.

"Everything's fixed at this end. I can't tell you how much I'm looking forward to getting into the new house. Tell me again about our bedroom."

"Words can't describe it," I said.

"You sound a bit funny," she said suspiciously. "What are you doing?"

"Just having a quiet drink."

"Huh!" she snorted indignantly. "How very pleasant! And while you lie around enjoying yourself, your children and I work our fingers to the bone."

"Tell me about it, darling," I said sympathetically.

"Well, for a start, you'll never believe the bother we had getting your trunk down from the attic . . ."

Carefully I poured myself another cup of whisky and settled down to listen.

The Rio de Janeiro Paper

Mr. Chairman, Ladies and Gentlemen,

It has been the custom at the International Criminological Conference to save the best for the last. At least this was the policy pursued by your committee before ill health forced my resignation from it. I think of the men who have occupied this spot in years gone by and I tremble at my effrontery. But perhaps today there is no need. Perhaps during my recent illness the policy has been changed and the last full session of Conference is now reserved for broken-down old professors on the edge of retirement!

Forgive my flippancy. I am deeply moved by the honour you have accorded me. And more than a little scared. Not that I don't like the view from up here. Through that huge window at the back of the hall I can see right across the harbour. The Sugar Loaf seems but a step away and I fancy that if I cared to strain my eyes just a bit, in this clear air, I could see clean across to Africa. It's really quite splendid.

It's only when my gaze drops to take in your own politely expectant faces that I begin to feel afraid.

But I have spoken elsewhere of the psychology of terror and that is not my subject today.

No, today I want to examine a simple proposition that seems to me to derive naturally from any serious criminological study of modern society and one which has implications which must be relevant to all your specializations.

It is that every husband would like to see his wife dead.

Let me start by being non-scientific.

How many married men sitting here in this hall can

look into their own hearts and say they have never felt personally the truth of this proposition?

Come on. Don't be shy. There are no hidden cameras spying on you. Two, three. I can see three. No; four. Thank you, sir. Definitely four. Well, I am disappointed. I had hoped to find greater powers of self-deception among so many eminent men!

So, it seems there might be some popular support for this proposition, *every husband would like to see his wife dead.* Certainly, as I'm sure that Captain Ribeiro of the Rio de Janeiro Police Research Bureau, whose stimulating paper caused so much debate on Tuesday, would confirm, if you show a policeman a female corpse the first thing that comes into his mind is, where's the husband? *Cherchez le mari!* I can't manage it in Portuguese!

I think Dr. Egermann in his excellent paper on *Women's Liberation and the Crime of Violence* put it succinctly when he said that men are killed for many reasons, but women usually because they are women.

In other words because of sex.

Lust, jealousy, disgust, frustration; potency fears, mother fixations, homosexual repression, transvestite envy—you will all recall Dr. Egermann's list of the sources of sexual violence. And is it not self-evident that the marriage relationship as it is understood in Western society, reinforces all these causes where they exist, creates many of them where they do not, and provides, in E. K. Charleshead's well-known phrase, the provocation of opportunity.

To Egermann's list, I myself would add one non-sexual motive to support my present assertions, and that is material gain. In her unpublished Ph.D. thesis on *The Sociology of Wills,* Edna Botibol of Yale shows that while a man is rarely left money by his mistress, wives tend to be much more generous. (A form of compensation, I shouldn't wonder!) But it certainly brings marriage well into our professional view. For it seems to me that in many ways all that Conference has been discussing for the past week, some might say for the past decade, is—which of the two great areas of criminal motivation should be our prime concern: the sexual or the economic? Marriage, I would suggest, unites them uniquely and deserves much more attention from all the criminological specialists gathered here today than it has ever received in the past. It may not be putting it too strongly to say that in marriage there is no such thing as accidental death.

Every husband would like to see his wife dead.

I can see several dubious expressions, and many more that have that air of bright interest with which students are wont to conceal advanced torpor. Perhaps I am being too general. "When in doubt, present a theoretical model" has always been a good maxim for the social scientist and that is what I shall do now.

First, we need a husband. Let's call him Smith. I am, after all, trying to demonstrate, not deceive! But let's bring him within the experimental range of everyone here by making him an academic; Professor Smith, a moderately eminent scholar at a moderately obscure university, the kind of man who at the age of sixty is pretty well known to his contemporaries but will hardly be remembered by their successors. But his voice will be listened to while he speaks.

Now, Professor Smith is a man who values marriage. He must do. He tries it twice. The first marriage follows a conventional course, and the professor reaches his half-century with little cause for complaint and some for congratulation; indeed, he looks an unlikely source of evidence to support my contention that every husband would like to see his wife dead. His children have grown up without too much drama, his first heart attack is still five years away, his home is comfortably and efficiently managed by his comfortable and efficient wife, a still attractive woman, who is a good economist, likes gardening, laughs at his jokes and cooks a fair if underseasoned *canard en croûte* for special occasions.

It is on such a special occasion, the day let us say that his promotion from assistant to full professor is confirmed, that the Smiths first meet Miss X. Christine, let us call her. It sounds less sinister. Christine X.

Christine is eighteen years old, with long blonde hair, a fresh glowing complexion, and the kind of beauty God only gives to eighteen-year-old girls.

She has just joined one of the professor's classes and is enthralled by his material and manner. That day she stays behind to check a reference and, flattered by her interest, Smith takes her home to lend her a book.

She stays to dinner. She is delighted with the *canard en croûte,* which pleases Mrs. Smith. She is also clearly delighted with the professor, which pleases him and amuses his wife, so that after Christine has gone they laugh about it over the washing-up.

The following day Christine X calls on the professor in his office. She is very serious. They talk for an hour. Then they make love on the floor between a filing cabinet and a bookcase with the girl's head pillowed on a pile of examination scripts.

A week later the professor leaves his wife.

In an earlier period there would now have existed a situation in which the professor might very well have wished his wife dead. Such goings-on once could have caused an academic all sorts of problems in his social and professional relationships. But things had changed. I refer you to E. K. Charleshead, who I see has just entered the hall—yes, please, do give him a round of applause; it is rare for one so young to achieve such distinction; let praise be unstinted—I was just referring, Dr. Charleshead, to your monograph on *The Bourgeois Ethic in the Swinging Sixties.* Stimulating. Provocative.

To continue. No, it is not Professor Smith's abandonment of his wife that raises people's eyebrows, it is the ruthlessness with which he expedites the divorce in order to remarry! Who marries these days, except if the accountants advise it?

But once remarried, the professor's happiness seems complete. The only flaw in it is the apparent total alienation of his children. His two daughters shun him completely, while his son suffers some kind of breakdown and is caught in the British Museum Reading Room defacing some of the professor's books with obscene drawings and obscener words.

Smith is filled with guilt and takes all the blame on to himself until five or six years later he has a series of heart attacks which nearly kill him. When he discovers that, as he lay at death's door, not one of his children made enquiry after his state of health, though the doctors had informed them all, his guilt disappears and is replaced by an uncomprehending pain which might have hardened into resentment were there not other more pressing matters to occupy his mind and soul.

His health has been deeply undermined. From being a vigorous, handsome, athletic man in the prime of life, he has become a semi-invalid, fast slipping down the vale of years. He is not confined to bed or anything as extreme as that, but he has to take great care. He must carry a box of pills with him wherever he goes; he must always use the lift, never the stairs; and he knows that love's little death might for him very easily become the real thing.

The passing years change Christine, too.

She wears her hair short and it now strikes the eye with the burnish of ripe barley rather than the soft gold of early corn. Her skin, too, has lost something of its freshness but cunning make-up can highlight the dark eyes and the full lips as well as nature ever did. She, too, has entered the academic life, and when her enemies murmur that she owes her rapid advance to her husband's influence, her friends retort that she is twice as clever as he ever was, and ten times as clever as he has become.

In other words in ten years he has grown old and she has grown up.

You begin to see the shape of our model? Triangulation maps lives as well as landscapes.

Professor Smith, his first wife, and Christine—there's one triangle. Now the time has come for another.

Let's keep things nice and close for the sake of tidiness. Just as in our basic triangle it made sense to locate the second female among the professor's students, now it makes sense to locate the second male among his colleagues. Let us call him C, a young lecturer whose research has won much acclaim and who looks set for a promising career. C has perhaps little grounds for liking or even feeling loyal towards Smith, who (so C alleges) has made a hamfisted effort to appropriate to himself some of C's research results. We have all been research assistants in our younger days and know how narrow the line is between following instructions and finding out new directions for ourselves. Thus there is a cloud between C and the professor which perhaps obscures the moral issue (if moral issues still exist after this morning's seminar on *The Chemistry of Good and Evil!*).

C and Christine are thrown into each other's company, are mutually attracted, at first refuse to admit the attraction, then struggle against it, and finally bring it out into the open to overcome it, which as any student of criminology knows is like stripping a woman naked to combat the temptations of a revealing gown!

The precise circumstances of their fall are not important. It happened, shall we say, two years ago? They are both discreet people, thrown naturally together by their job, and if C has no great concern about the pain he might cause the professor, Christine has enough for both of them. She takes every precaution against discovery and is resolved to stay with her husband until, as seems not unlikely, another heart attack carries him off. He loves her as dearly as ever, so if our starting proposition is to apply here, something must happen which shows him the truth.

It is really very simple. C is a friend of the professor's son, the one who had the trouble at the British Museum. One night they are drinking together and the son, David let's call him, is still complaining after all this time about his father's treatment of his mother. C is happy to join in a general condemnation of Professor Smith at all levels, but when David turns his attention to Christine, he angrily springs to her defense. David is intrigued and either guesses at, or is told of, the relationship. He retails the news to his mother next time they meet and his mother, after a day and a night spent in close discussion of the information with no more than ten or twelve friends, persuades herself that it is her duty to do something. I refer you to the chapter in Arturo Bellario's *Crime in the Third Reich* on "Duty as Pseudo-Motivation."

So the first Mrs. Smith telephones her ex-husband. He is enraged. He slams the phone down. It is a tissue of lies. His former wife is a monster. He will ring the police. He will ring his solicitor and issue a writ for libel. He will summon Christine and invite her to join in his anger. He will not hurt her by telling her anything. He trusts her absolutely. He trusts C. But not absolutely. C dislikes him. He feels uneasy with C. Christine and C spend a lot of time together. C is young. Christine is young. He is old. It is a year since he made love to his wife.

For the time being his thoughts stay there. That night he attempts to make love and fails. Christine assures him it does not matter. He turns away and lies open-eyed in the dark. Suddenly he knows it is true.

Of course as an academic and a scientist he will seek objective evidence. But this is not hard to find.

Captain Ribeiro told us yesterday something of the psychology of interrogation. Two people cannot long deceive a third, especially if they are not yet aware that he suspects them.

So there we have our model complex. I'm sorry if I seem to have laboured over its construction. And I am sorrier still if you feel that all my labour has just brought forth a mouse. For what is he going to tell us now? you ask. That Professor Smith, a sick old man in the throes of jealousy, would like to see his wife dead? Possibly he would! More likely, he would prefer to see C dead. But wishes are not crimes!

No, but they may be translated into crimes. And in this model, it seems to me very likely that the translation would take place.

The situation is more complex than might at first appear. It is not simple jealousy that is at work. Let us examine all the courses that are open to Professor Smith and see that, if he does opt for murder, it is not through a shortage of alternatives.

First, he might carry on as before, concealing his knowledge and hoping that his health might improve or that of the affair deteriorate.

Secondly, he might confront his wife and try to shame her or argue her into giving up her lover.

Thirdly, he might institute divorce proceedings either as a noble gesture aimed at freeing Christine from an intolerable situation, or as a salve to his own hurt pride.

Why does he choose none of these?

Not simply because he is unbalanced by jealousy. On the contrary, he thinks he is behaving perfectly rationally. No, the true reason for his decision to murder his wife might seem odd to a layman but the eminent criminologists here assembled will recall the wise words spoken by E. K. Charleshead in his seminar on *Recidivism as Onanistic Impulse:* "One motive may be more *uncommon* that another, but no motive is more *unlikely* than another."

Professor Smith decides to murder Christine because of the acute pleasure he knows the situation must be giving his first wife and his estranged children.

Better then, you may say, he should murder his first wife. Yes, he thinks of that, of course; but she is distant, access is difficult, he has no desire that his deed should produce consequences unpleasant to himself.

So it has to be Christine.

Thus our model now shows us an extremely complex situation and perhaps I should now extend my opening proposition thus: *a man who has more than one wife would like to see them all dead.*

It has always seemed a shame to me that social scientists discard their models so readily once they have served their purpose. Anything which man has laboured to create deserves more than instant relegation to the scrapheap and I hope you will bear with me if, having brought Professor Smith so far along his road, I follow him a little further.

In any case just as *the wish to see dead* is not the same as the *decision to kill,* so the decision is still not the deed. Professor Smith now needs a method.

Well, if the professor moved in the same circles as we all do, he would not have far to look, for if there's one thing that regular attenders at these conferences get in plenty, it's methods of murder! It's a standing joke, isn't it, how well the homicide seminars are always attended. Of course, what we are considering on these occasions are the sociological and psychological problems, but what one remembers most vividly are things like Herr Doktor Schwarz's diagrams of pressure points, Señor Martinez's dexterity with knife and gun, or (more mundane but no less fascinating) Madame Rive's list of eighteen toxic substances in common domestic use. Whatever the professor's own discipline, such information as this is readily accessible to the academically trained mind. The first thing we all had to learn was how to find things out, was it not? Equally accessible would be all our treatises on police method and police psychology and Professor Smith would know as well as I do that when a wife dies in suspicious circumstances, the first thing the police do is look closely at the husband.

So his first task would, of course, be to create circumstances which did not appear suspicious.

As scholars yourselves, you can easily imagine the meticulous care with which he would approach the task. He would, I'm sure, have read widely enough to know that it is in fact reactions, not circumstances, which usually cause suspicion. I see from your smiles that you recognize I am quoting from my own book, *Crime in Our Time*, the chapter on "Information," though lest I be accused of egotism I should point out that many of my findings were soon afterwards confirmed by no less a talent than E. K. Charleshead. The first thing the provident murderer must do is choose, or arrange, a time when those likely to create an atmosphere of suspicion are as far removed as may be from the sphere of influence. In this case, that would be (in descending order of potential troublesomeness) Christine's lover, C; his son, David; and his first wife. His daughters present little problem, the younger being in California and the elder in a clinic for rehabilitation of alcoholics in, let us say, Yorkshire.

The academic mind always prefers the most elegant solution, so let us create one for our model.

Imagine Professor Smith to have close connections with, say, a Japanese university, whose vice-chancellor, an old friend, is currently visiting England. It is not difficult for him to arrange that C should be invited on very favourable terms to spend a term there—particularly as C is a young man of great promise and growing reputation. The necessary study leave presents no difficulty as it is to all intents and purposes in Professor Smith's gift. But the real elegance of the solution lies in his contriving that the Japanese vice-chancellor, who knew him in his pre-Christine days, should also invite his son and first wife to pay him a visit. C's proposed trip, plus the opportunity en route for visiting the younger daughter, are large inducements respectively, and the ill-assorted trio set off on the same plane.

I do not think we need to exercise our minds much on the method the professor chooses for disposing of Christine. If, as E. K. Charleshead has suggested in his fascinating analyses of death statistics in the decades immediately before and after the Second World War, as much as one per cent of natural causes and up to two point five per cent of domestic accidents are suspect, murder of relatives is second only to Monopoly as a popular family game. Someone as well organized as Professor Smith could have the deed done, the necessary enquiries carried out and the body cremated before word of the tragedy filtered through to Japan.

Now, it was my intention, having constructed this elaborate model, to use it to illustrate the wider criminological implications of my opening contention. But, alas, I fear my recent ill health sapped my strength even more than I was aware. No, no, please, do not agitate yourselves, I am not ill now, just a trifle exhausted and I fear that this, my last lecture, will have to remain more open-ended even than I had intended. Perhaps a happy result of this will be to permit a very free-ranging discussion. The psychologists among you might like, for instance, to consider whether Smith would be able to resist the temptation to make a confession, however obliquely. Academics are notoriously eager to publish their results! But I shall not stay for the discussion. I feel I have earned a good long rest.

And this leads me to conclude on a very personal note. As you all know, I am due to retire from my post at the end of next term. But I have decided for various reasons to bring the date forward and as from the end of this Conference I shall cease to hold my Chair of Criminology. I have spoken to my vice-chancellor on the telephone and he has agreed to accept my resignation, reluctantly he says. I hope, no, I am sure, he will not be so reluctant to accept my nomination of a successor. Indeed, there can only be one man for the job, my former research assistant, my present colleague, and my dear friend, E. K. Charleshead.

Finally, let me say that it is not my intention to return to England. I have few ties there since my recent bereavement, and my resignation has just about cut the last one.

I am contemplating settling down here in Brazil and the authorities have indicated that they would make me most welcome. The attractions are many; a benevolent climate, a beautiful landscape, a lively culture, a sympathetic tax system; perhaps even, as Captain Ribeiro told us in his talk yesterday, the absence of a clearly defined treaty of extradition with the UK! Well, forgive an old man's joke. But I like it here, and here, God willing, I shall rest.

Thank you for the kindness of your invitation, the courtesy of your hearing, and the comfort of your friendship.

I shall not soon forget you. And I hope that I shall be in all of your minds at some times.

And perhaps in some of your minds for ever.

I thank you.

Thank you.

Goodbye.

Threatened Species

I don't care for dogs. They combine creep and crap to a degree only found otherwise in PR men. No, I much prefer cats, the intellectual and hygienic superiors of both breeds.

But I have to admit that when you are woken at two a.m. by stealthy treadings outside your lonely Lake District cottage, it would be some comfort to hear your devoted Doberman slowly rising to his feet at the foot of the bed.

Or even your devoted PR man.

Instead I had to rise slowly myself and my totally undevoted tom cat, Heathcliff, who was only here for the warmth, miaowed in protest. I ignored him, knowing full well that at the first sign of trouble he would be off the bed and under it.

Being dogless, I have always been ready to bark for myself and though I rarely sleep with a pistol under my pillow, I do keep a twelve-bore standing in the corner of my room whenever I'm staying at High Ghyll. There might be less likelihood of trouble on the Cumberland fells than in the middle of London, but if it does come, then there's precious little help available to deal with it. And I had discovered early that it's not female beauty or sensuality that most effectively lights the fire in men's blood; it's being alone.

But you're never alone with a shotgun I thought as my fingers curled round the cold metal. I was thirty-five, widowed once and divorced once (both of which conditions most men consider synonymous with nymphomania), and ready to blast a large hole in any man foolish enough to come uninvited into my Lakeland stronghold.

I fumbled in my dressing-table drawer and found the

two cartridges I kept there. I wasn't yet so neurotic that I kept a loaded gun in my bedroom, particularly as Heathcliff, who used the stock as a scratching-post, usually managed to knock it over at least once a day. It was very dark and without my glasses I find it hard to see at the best of times. I should have collected them first, I decided, as with great difficulty I slid the cartridges into the breech, but as usual I wasn't quite certain where I'd left them.

From the bed Heathcliff, deprived of my warm feet, howled piteously but stopped in mid-note and I saw his dark outline rise, his back arch, his tail fluff out hugely like instant back-combing and his small aristocratic (so *he* claimed) head point accusingly at the window.

I had heard nothing for some moments, indeed had begun to half hope, half believe that the stealthy treader had been nothing more than an insomniac sheep. But Heathcliff if nothing else is a good barometer of foreign presence, and while a sheep might disturb him it wouldn't frighten him. Now with sinking heart I saw my loyal and intelligent pet sum up the situation, step daintily off the bed and disappear beneath it.

Next moment any remaining doubts and hopes were dispersed. I slept with my windows slightly open, partly because of an inherited spartan morality, partly to allow Heathcliff ease of exit, without which he would brutally waken me whenever the urge came on him to clamber over the sill on to the roof of the old single-storeyed farm dairy below and thence to whatever strange trysts he kept on this barren windswept fellside. Tonight the air was comparatively still, hardly enough to flutter the heavy curtains which I had hung to prevent my much-needed sleep from being broken by the morning sun. But now the curtains flapped cumbersomely inward. The window from being ajar a cat's breadth had been pushed wide open, and through the gap between the curtains I saw not the bright star-studded sky, contemplation of which had filled me with adolescent nostalgia three hours earlier, but the shape, monstrous and menacing, of a man, arms raised and spread as he grasped the lintel and dragged himself from the dairy roof on to the sill.

I opened my mouth to say something cool and controlled, instead heard a thin, terrified squeak emerge. He paused, then began to move forward again. His left leg was athwart the sill now. My squeak became a full-blooded scream and I rushed forward, pushed the gun into his face and pulled the trigger.

At that range his head would have been sliced off his shoulders if the cartridge had fired. But all that I heard was a hollow click. Still screaming, I hit him full on the nose with the weapon and either the force of my attack or the noise I was making sent him falling backwards. I thrust my head through the window and saw him lying spreadeagled on the dairy roof. The moon was full and we stared at each other for a long moment. I wished that I had my glasses on so that I could have got a better view of him. Already I was thinking of identity parades and the doubtful pleasure of seeing him put away for a fortnight or whatever the maximum sentence is for the trivial offence of attempted rape. He had a beard, that I could make out, light brown and very curly, perhaps too curly for nature. Also a big nose.

Suddenly he smiled, I saw that clearly. It was a win-a-few, lose-a-few smile which filled me with even greater fury than his attempted break-in. As he pushed himself upright, I remembered I had another barrel still untried. I brought the gun to bear on him; the smile disappeared; he turned and ran to the edge of the roof and as he leapt into space I squeezed the trigger.

This time there was no hollow click but a deafening cordite-stinking explosion and the gun's kick almost knocked me backwards. I'd never fired the weapon at anything more animate than a dead tree before, but I knew that a twelve-bore loaded with no. 5 shot spread so wide that it was hard for even a tyro to miss.

Oh God! I thought, my fury fading faster than the sound of the shot which came bouncing back off the surrounding fells. Oh God! I've killed him!

Then he reappeared, running swiftly through the moonlit field behind the house, his feet kicking up little clouds of silver-edged vapour from the grass. It was an uphill run but he seemed to be making light work of it and I sighed with relief. No seriously wounded man could have moved like that. My aim must have been worse than

I had believed possible. Perhaps a few stray pellets had peppered his backside, but nothing more.

I was beginning to shake now with reaction, and after firmly fastening the window I put on the light and went downstairs to check on my defences and treat myself to a large brandy and five or six cigarettes. I had no telephone at High Ghyll so I would have to wait till morning before I reported what had happened. My car was parked outside but I had no intention of setting off down the long rough track to the main road before full daylight.

Meanwhile it seemed a good idea to reload, so I broke the twelve-bore to remove the cartridges. Instantly I saw why the first barrel had not gone off, and incidentally why the prowler's head was still intact. Out of my dressing-table drawer in the dark I had taken one cartridge and one cylinder of witch-green eye make-up.

Somehow this discovery restored my spirits even more than the brandy and I returned to bed feeling surprisingly ready and able to sleep. My decision had been anticipated and approved by Heathcliff, who was back in his usual position on the foot of the bed, snoring gently. I tickled his tummy and went to bed feeling quite affectionately disposed to him, despite his recent cowardice. Heathcliff himself, of course, was quite indifferent to the vagaries of human feeling, a fact that he proved by butting me awake at six a.m., protesting that the window was closed and he couldn't get out.

Yawning, I rose and threw back the curtains. The morning was misty and the sun's imminence was marked only by a generalized effulgence, but strong enough to bode a good day. I opened the window wide and sucked in a good lungful of cold damp air.

Then I noticed with horror that Heathcliff wasn't going out but was doing his back-arching, tail-fluffing act again.

"Oh no!" I cried, turning for the twelve-bore. But it was too late. His clothes sodden from hours of waiting crouched beneath my window and with dewdrops glinting in his beard, the man was in the room. As my hand reached the gun, he grasped me by the hair and drew me back. I was shrieking hysterically but my mind was cool enough to register Heathcliff stepping daintily through the window without a backward glance.

* * *

Most men don't believe in rape. Without some degree of consent it's not possible, so the apologists claim. Well, bully for them. The stupidity of vast areas of masculine opinion I have, like most women, quietly adjusted to. But though I had read about it and indeed written about it, I had not fully appreciated the degree to which this particular bit of nonsense had biased the law.

I thought it best not to be mealy-mouthed so I told the first police constable I encountered in the station that I'd been raped.

He was very young and he blushed slightly, then asked me if I'd like to sit down. I did and he went away. After that two other young men came out of offices and peered at me from a distance. I had decided to be controlled and detached to ward off motherly offers of tea and sympathy, but I had not expected to be an object of vulgar curiosity.

Finally I was taken to a small windowless room where a seedy detective-sergeant called Ambler started asking questions while a poker-faced WPC sat very upright by the door.

"Name," he said.

"Grant. Mrs. Cora Grant."

"Address."

"At the moment, High Ghyll Farm, Gosforth."

"Permanent address."

Beginning to feel exasperated, I gave him my London address.

"How long have you been staying at High Ghyll, Mrs. Grant?"

"Just since Saturday."

"Alone?"

"Yes."

"Ah," he said, writing at greater length than either the question or my answer seemed to make necessary. Perhaps it was the blotchy ballpoint he was using.

"You own the farmhouse?"

"Yes," I said, then amended, "That is, it belongs to my former husband and myself. We're divorced, but we've kept High Ghyll as a holiday home."

An uneasy compromise, I could have added, after months of each trying to buy the other out. Now we had a strict timetable of visits and left each other sniping notes about the disgusting state in which we found the place.

"*Divorced,*" said Ambler, scribbling again. "Where can we contact Mr. Grant?"

"Mr. Grant? You can't. He's dead."

This stopped the erratic pen for a moment.

"But you said . . ."

"Mr. Grant was my first husband. He died three years ago. I remarried but kept my previous name for professional purposes," I explained.

"Ah. *Widowed,*" he said and the pen was off again.

"So where can we get hold of your ex-husband, Mr. . . . ?"

"Lincoln. James Lincoln."

My nastier friends (the only ones worth having) had opined that I was only attracted to men with the names of American presidents in the hope of ending up with a Kennedy. With my luck I'd get a Nixon.

"Why should you want to get hold of him?" I went on. "I haven't seen Jimmy since the divorce. He works in Manchester, I work in London. We don't want to see each other. The thing is, we don't even like each other. So let's keep Jimmy out of this and concentrate on this maniac who's just raped me!"

He scribbled again, a single word. His writing and the awful pen didn't make it easy to read upside down but it looked very like "hysterical." I couldn't fault him. He was right. That was just how I was beginning to feel.

"Look, don't you want to know what happened?" I demanded.

"Of course we do, Mrs. Grant. But just a few more details. You said you kept your name for professional reasons. What profession would that be?"

"I'm a journalist," I said.

"*Journalist,*" he said. He had a very unpleasant way of making single words vibrate with piled-up overtones of meaning.

"Yes. I'm a freelance mainly. You may even have read some of my pieces in the Sunday papers."

"*Sunday* papers." I have never heard the sabbath touched with such intimations of depravity.

There was a knock at the door. The WPC rose, opened it six inches and slid out. A few seconds later she slid back in.

"The doctor's here," she said.

"Good," said Ambler, rising. "Mrs. Grant, you realize that it's necessary for you to have a medical examination."

I suppose I did in a way. But what I realized even more clearly was that Ambler hadn't been in a hurry to get on with the main business on the agenda until it was firmly established that there was any main business to get on with.

The doctor was a slow, deliberate man who looked old enough to have started his career as a barber.

He showed some signs of distress at what had taken place, but mainly *after* rather than *during* the assault.

"You've had a bath?" he said disapprovingly.

"Yes. And a douche," I answered. "What do you expect? It was the first thing I did after he went."

He continued his examination, shaking his head ponderously as he did so.

Back in the interview room I smoked a cigarette and tried to squeeze some conversation out of the WPC while Ambler had a conference with the doctor.

Finally he returned.

"Tell me what happened," he said.

I told him.

"You didn't think of going for help the first time he came?" he asked.

"I wasn't going to leave the house!" I assured him. "I was locked up, safe and sound."

"But you opened your window in the morning," he said.

"That was to let the cat out," I protested. "I never thought he'd come back. To tell you the truth, I'd half forgotten about him."

"Forgotten," he said.

"Yes," I said.

"That was shortly after six. Yet it was nearly nine when you came to the station."

"Yes. After he left, I locked the window again. Then I just sat around for a while, smoking, drinking. I couldn't believe it had happened, I suppose. Then when it finally got through to me, I ran a bath and just lay there soaking for God knows how long."

"Yes. The doctor said you'd had a bath," he said neutrally.

"I felt filthy," I protested. "I just wanted to lie there for ever. Finally I got dressed, let Heathcliff, my cat, in and gave him his breakfast . . ."

"You gave your cat his *breakfast,*" he said.

"Yes," I said defensively. "It's very difficult not to give a cat his breakfast. They're very insistent. After that I got in the car and drove here."

"I see. Why didn't you go to the local constable?"

"I did," I said triumphantly. "But he wasn't in. So I drove on into town. I thought that anyway I'd need to come here for the full treatment."

"For the full treatment," he said. This time I sympathized with him. It had been a poor choice of phrase.

"This man," he said. "Did you know him?"

"I told you, I'd never seen him before."

"Can you describe him?"

I did the best I could. Brown curly hair and beard, big nose, medium height, well built.

"Clothes?" he asked.

"Some kind of cord trousers," I said. "Brown. And a brown leather jerkin."

"I see. No more detail than that?" he asked. "Did the jerkin have a zip or buttons? Was there any design on it, any of these hell's angels things, for instance? Skull and crossbones? Born to die?"

"No," I said. "Though it's probably peppered with a bit of shot."

"I thought you said you missed," he said.

"I don't think I hurt him, but I don't think I could have missed altogether."

"He gave no impression of being wounded when he was . . . er . . ."

"No, he bloody didn't!"

"I see," said Ambler. "I'll want to see that gun when I come up to the farm, of course."

"You don't have to go that far," I answered. "I've got it in the car."

"What?" For the first time he showed an emotion other than sceptical diffidence.

"Yes," I said. "You didn't think I was going to go out of the house without it, did you?"

"Can we have your keys, Mrs. Grant?"

"No need. It's not locked, Sergeant."

The WPC rose. As she went out I called after her, "It's on the passenger seat."

Ambler drummed his fingers on the desk.

"We hope it's on the passenger seat, Mrs. Grant," he said ominously. "You do have a licence?"

"A licence," I said, playing him at his own cunning game. "Perhaps we should wait till we see if I still have a gun. Tell me, Sergeant, is there any chance that you might eventually start investigating this crime?"

"I don't follow you, Mrs. Grant. I'm getting your statement down. It's important we establish the facts."

"Yes indeed," I said indignantly. "Though it's becoming clear that my facts and your facts aren't altogether coinciding!"

The WPC returned with my shotgun. Ambler took it from her and cautiously sniffed at the barrels.

"It's been fired," he said.

"Yes," I said. "Fortunately I didn't take that into the bath with me."

"No," he said. "Well, it's as well you made a mistake with the loading first time, Mrs. Grant. This is a powerful weapon. The consequences could have been serious."

Something in my expression must finally have got through to him for he hastily changed the subject, saying in an almost conciliatory tone, "I don't know your work, I'm afraid, Mrs. Grant."

"No," I said. "I tend to write features for the more intellectual papers."

"Really?" he said, un-put-down. "What have you done recently?"

"Mainly a series of three articles in one of the colour supplements. I'm sorry you missed them."

"What were they about?" he asked.

"Rape," I said.

At last I had got to him.

"Rape," he echoed. "Oh. From what point of view? I mean . . ."

"Generally speaking," I said, "I was against it."

That night I went to the theatre. In the circumstances it might seem a curious thing to do. Sergeant Ambler certainly looked at me disapprovingly and said *"Theatre"* when I mentioned it to him. This obviously confirmed his growing suspicion that I was not so much a hysterically hallucinating woman as a cold and calculating journalist paving the way to a profitable personal-angle follow-up to my "rape" articles. Still, give the police their due, they went through the motions and I went back to High Ghyll accompanied by Ambler (for my protection) and the WPC (for Ambler's, I supposed). To tell the truth, I was glad of their company though Heathcliff made it clear that he did not welcome the intrusion.

Ambler looked sagely around my bedroom and even climbed through the window on to the dairy roof. Out of the police station, much of his seediness seemed to disappear and he responded to the chilly air of the fells as though to a tonic. In his case I felt it was a pity that generally speaking crime is a sea-level activity.

"He went across the field?" he said.

"That's right," I said.

The field ran away from the house at an increasingly steep angle so that by the time it reached the drystone wall at its far end, grazing animals needed to be equipped with great tenacity of purpose. But it was recognizably a field, fairly even of surface and carpeted with long lush-green grass. Beyond the wall, the terrain was unequivocably fellside.

"Did you see him climb the wall?"

"No. It's too far. It was dark and I didn't have my specs."

"I see. Is all this land yours?"

"Oh no. Just the house and that patch of grass as far as the end of the dairy. It was tumbling down when we bought it, no one had lived here for years."

"Ah," he said.

"What will you do now?" I asked.

"Check round to see if we can find where he came

from. If he had a car, he must have left it somewhere within walking distance. You'd have heard anything coming up the lonning, I suppose?"

"Oh, certainly," I said. "Noise carries up here, especially strange noises."

"He could be living out, of course," continued Ambler. "Camping, perhaps. We'll check that, too. If he is, well it's a pity you didn't get on to us quicker. As it is, he'd got a couple of hours' start before we began looking."

"Sorry," I said meekly.

"Well, Mrs. Grant, what about you now?" He looked at me dubiously.

"What about me?"

"You won't want to stay up here by yourself," he said. "Do you have any friends locally that might join you? Or perhaps you could stay with them?"

"I don't think that will be necessary, Sergeant," I said boldly.

"Perhaps not now, Mrs. Grant. But tonight . . ." He paused and glanced at the WPC. "Constable Slater here could hang on for a couple of hours, I'm sure, till we see how you feel . . ."

"That's very kind, but no," I said. I guessed it was his distrust of me that was making him so conscientiously solicitous, but I was touched all the same.

"I *am* seeing some friends tonight," I went on. "They're taking me to the theatre."

"The *theatre,*" he said as though I'd confirmed all his suspicions.

"At Rosehill. I'm sure I can make some arrangements with them."

"As you wish," he said, suddenly losing interest. "We'll keep in touch."

I watched their car bump out of sight down the lonning, then went inside and made myself a cup of tea.

The play was a revival of the famous dramatization of John Aubrey's *Brief Lives.* I'd seen it before in London, but it was well worth a second visit and the audience loved it.

Afterwards we went back to the large modern bungalow near St. Bees where my hosts for the evening, Sheila and Mike Underdown, lived. Sheila, a skinny hectic blonde with buck-teeth that men found very sexy (so she claimed), had shared a flat with me during my early years in London. I had seen Mike develop from a rather gauche young man with a huge appetite for our food to the present smooth property dealer with a huge appetite for his own scotch. He was a partner in a local estate agent's but his own speciality was finding, buying, renovating and either selling or letting properties as second or holiday homes. High Ghyll had come to me via Mike, so while politically I vaguely disapproved of his activities, personally I had benefited greatly. Until last night, of course.

We talked about the play as Mike poured drinks.

"The one I liked best," said Sheila, "was the man, Sir William something who got caught short in Cheapside and told his servant, hide my face, for they shall never see my arse again."

"No, no," said Mike. "That's an old story. I bet it existed in Latin and Greek, too, and ancient Egyptian before that. My favourite is that fellow, Captain Carlo Fantom. He sounds a complete original. A Croatian, very quarrelsome and a great ravisher."

"Yes, that would appeal to you," said Sheila.

I took my drink from Mike and drank deeply. I had not spoken yet of what had happened at High Ghyll earlier that day. It had proved strangely difficult, don't ask me why. I'm not usually bothered by considerations of delicacy, particularly among friends. But I hadn't been able to say anything when we met in the theatre bar and it wasn't something I felt we could chat about during the interval. I took a deep breath.

"Talking of ravishing," I said.

I thought I was being self-possessed and objective about the business but half-way through my account I found that I was crying. I did not break down or sob and my narrative was quite uninterrupted, but tears ran steadily down my cheeks and occasionally splashed audibly into my scotch.

I found myself watching their reactions closely. What, I wondered, would I say if it were Sheila doing the telling?

"Good God!" said Mike. "Why didn't you tell us before?"

He sounded faintly put out as though his place in the pecking order of confidences had been usurped. But he topped up my tear-diluted drink, which showed some sense of priorities.

Sheila had gone pale and quiet.

"That's monstrous," she said finally. "Monstrous. The bastard should be castrated."

I realized I had voiced some deep and secret terror of Sheila's. Men seem to believe that women fantasize (usually with an element of fearful pleasure) about rape all the time, but the research I had done for my articles didn't throw up much evidence of this. I suppose the fact that I kept a shotgun in my bedroom at High Ghyll might seem to indicate that some thoughts on the subject had crossed my mind. Perhaps so, but never consciously and never as imaginative titillation. Even tonight, only twelve hours or so after it had happened, there had been moments during the play when the nasty memory had gone quite out of my mind. I couldn't say that I'd found the piece about Carlo Fantom, the Croatian Ravisher, particularly amusing, but yes, Mrs. Lincoln could say that, apart from that, she'd enjoyed the play.

Sheila was angrier than I've ever seen her and I found my own equilibrium was quickly regained in my efforts to placate her. My tears dried up as suddenly as they'd started and Sheila led me from the room to repair my face and give me a chance to say anything I might not have said in front of Mike. There wasn't in fact anything I wanted to say, but I gave her a few grisly details to keep her unhappy, though in reality the whole affair was already strangely distant and I had to draw heavily on my imagination.

They wanted me to stay the night and I might have succumbed if later while Sheila was out of the room Mike had not said to me in his serious voice, "Listen, Cora, someone's got to say this, I hope you won't let this experience put you off, I mean, it's rotten I know but . . ."

"Like falling off a horse?" I said. "The thing to do is get right back on?"

"Yes. In a way." He looked at me sideways over his

glass. I was, I realized, going to have a lot of men looking at me like that if I wasn't careful. Suddenly I regretted having told the Underdowns anything and I became adamant in my intention of going back to High Ghyll. In any case, Heathcliff would be worried. About his meals, of course.

They drove back with me. Mike searched the house while Sheila made another big thing about spending the night with me, but I wasn't having that either. Mike reappeared with that look men wear when they've done something practical for a helpless woman.

"All clear," he pronounced.

I promised to have coffee with Sheila in the morning, thanked them for their kindness and finally got them over the doorstep. My relief at their departure was already becoming tinged with a little regret as I watched their headlights sway and shake down the lonning. I went inside and locked the front door. The long-case clock in the hall made two of the chokey sounds which had been chimes before my desire for uninterrupted sleep had introduced a gag. It was just twenty-four hours since the prowler's first visit had awoken me.

I yawned widely and went into the living-room.

Some shocks are too great even to shock. You just don't believe them and your panic responses are dulled by your mind signalling error! error!

Sitting in my favourite well-worn leather armchair, smiling as though to welcome his dearest friend, was the man with the curly beard.

Two things prevented me from screaming and running. One was that he had my shotgun across his knees. The other was that he had Heathcliff draped round his shoulder, purring contentedly.

"Forgive me if I don't get up," he said.

"I should prefer it," I answered tremulously.

"The thing is, I feel I owe you an explanation."

His voice was educated, his tone conversational.

"You couldn't make it an apology, I suppose?" I said. Irony was always my first resort in times of stress.

He considered, then shook his head.

"No. It would be hypocritical to apologize for something I enjoyed, wouldn't it?"

I was glad he'd said it. It's odd, isn't it? Two seconds of chat in a nice educated voice and already I needed reminding I was talking to a nut.

"Do you fancy coffee?" I said in my best Home Features manner. Put your guest at ease. And once you're in the kitchen either pick up a carving knife or open the back door and run like mad.

"No, thanks," he said. "A scotch would be nice though. How did you find the police?"

"Just picked up one of those big pointed hats and there was one underneath," I said as I poured two very stiff drinks.

"Ha ha. Bad as you anticipated?"

"Anticipated?"

"In your articles," he said. "You didn't have many good words to say for them, did you?"

"You've read my articles?"

"Oh yes," he answered, smiling. "In a manner of speaking, you could say that's why I'm here."

"A fan, no less," I said, handing him his drink. I'd half thought of chucking it in his face but the kind of start that that was likely to give me would hardly get me to the front door.

"In a way," he said. "This must all be marvellous copy for you!"

"Gee, thanks. I'm glad I'm not a war correspondent."

"Don't be nervous," he said sympathetically. "Enjoy your drink and I'll tell you all about it."

Sympathy from a psychopath is like being cuddled by a tarantula. But I didn't say that. I sipped my stiff drink and hoped it would make me brave while his made him drunk.

"Those articles of yours caused great interest down at the club," he said.

"Club?"

"The golf club. They were quite a talking point in the bar after our Sunday morning round. Well, they would be, with Jimmy being a member."

"Jimmy . . . ?" I was getting as bad as Ambler with my one-word echoes.

"Jimmy Lincoln, your ex."

"*Jimmy!* You mean Jimmy put you up to this!"

"Oh no," he said, shocked. "It was just that with Jimmy being a member, it added an extra something to our discussions. A sort of expert witness, you know."

I felt surprisingly distressed, though it should have come as no surprise that Jimmy with a few drinks in his belly would be capable of giving the details of our sex life a public airing in a golf-club bar.

"The general feeling was that you were being a bit hard on the men," he went on. "I know you're a journalist and journalists can't afford little artistic luxuries like accuracy and objectivity, but in that last piece, what did you call it?—"Looking Down—the Masculine View"—well, there you really *did* become rather hysterical, we thought. I put the point to Jimmy."

"Oh, good old Jimmy," I said, pouring more drink. "What did good old Jimmy have to say?"

"Methinks the lady doth protest too much," said the man. "That's all he said. This sort of confirmed the general feeling that what women like you really needed—you know, anti-men and women's libbers, that sort of thing—what you needed was a sample of the goods you were complaining about. Not to put too fine a point on it, it was our unanimous conclusion that anyone raping you would be doing mankind at large a not inconsiderable favour."

"Jesus!" I cried in horror. "You mean you were deputed to come up here and . . ."

"Oh no!" he said, smiling. "At the golf club we just talk. Interesting ideas—shoot Arthur Scargill, drop H-bombs on Moscow, set fire to Ireland—but they're just words. Only this time, somehow the idea really got into my mind. I was coming up to Carlisle on business and I knew you'd be in the cottage . . ."

"How the hell did you know that? How did you know where High Ghyll was, anyway?" I demanded.

"Why, I've been here a couple of times with Jimmy," he answered. "Weekends walking. Great! I love it here. I mentioned to Jimmy I was going to be in this part of the world this week and suggested we rendezvoused here at the weekend but he said he was sorry but you would be in occupation and he didn't feel he could ask you to change your plans. He's a bit scared of you, is Jimmy."

I poured myself yet another whisky. He smiled and shook his head and refused.

"So, let's get it straight," I said. "You decide, all on your own, to slip out of your comfy hotel, drive forty miles, park the car, walk across the fells at night, and do a bit of raping! Christalmighty! Is this a regular hobby of yours?"

"Oh no!" he said. "This was the first time. Unless you count a couple of parties, and that was sort of half and half, if you know what I mean. But the thing is, and this is why I'm here, what do you feel about it now? I planned to wait and see what you wrote in your article—I felt pretty sure you'd make an article out of it—but I couldn't wait. It's been on my mind all day, my colleagues thought I must be ill! I had to hear it straight from you, as soon as possible, while it's fresh in your mind and before you sensationalize it for the press. What do you *really* think about it now?"

He looked at me with the apprehensive eagerness of an L-driver waiting the result of his test. I was by now drunk enough to want to giggle at the lunacy of the situation. Then my eyes saw that his right hand was coiled so tightly round the trigger guard of my shotgun that his knuckles were white, and the impulse to giggle faded and died. A couple of years earlier I had worked on a series about the treatment of the criminally insane. In fact, because of the paper who'd commissioned it, the series had really been an anthology of instances of patients whose first action on being released, ostensibly cured, had been to commit another act of violence. Like most journalists I accept, within bounds, that whoever pays the piper calls the tune. At the same time (again, like most journalists) whatever the market I make sure that the topic is as meticulously researched as I can manage. And I'd come out of that series with the firm conviction that it wasn't the convicted loonies we'd locked up that should worry us but the undetected loonies going happily about their everyday business waiting for the call.

This fellow's call had come. Perhaps it was inevitable. Or perhaps if he'd joined another golf club he'd have stayed happy with his fantasies and a bit of half-and-half at parties. My task in the next few minutes was simply to convince him that it was as safe to leave me alive and well and able to talk as it was to leave me with a big hole in my head.

"Are you sure you won't have another drink?" I said.

He shook his head impatiently.

"By the way, what's your name?" I burbled. "I can't sit here just calling you 'you,' can I?"

I merely wanted to establish a climate of confidence, but I wished I'd kept my mouth shut.

He regarded me narrowly. I'd often wondered what that meant, but now I saw. It means the kind of close scrutiny you get from a man who thinks you're trying to tell him he got you pregnant at the office party last Christmas.

"Forget it," I said. "I'll stick with 'you.' "

"Oh no," he said. "You're right. I mean, you could always find out by having a chat with someone at the golf club, couldn't you? Patrick's the name. Patrick Craik."

"Patrick Craik," I echoed. "Well, who worries about euphony these days?"

"Now we know all about each other and are both sitting comfortably, why don't you begin," he said. He made a slight movement with the shotgun. He might just have been adjusting his position in the chair, but I wasn't going to put the rent on it. I began.

"Look, it was a shock, I was terrified, there's no way of getting away from that," I said. Disarm him with honesty, then flatter him with lies, that was my chosen line.

"How terrified were you?" he asked with great interest.

"Out of my wits!" I said. "Who wouldn't be! *You* would be if you woke up in the middle of the night and heard someone trying to get in at your window."

"That's right," he said. "And if I'd had a shotgun in my hands when they appeared, I'd have used it! But you didn't."

"Yes I did!" I protested indignantly.

"Oh no," he said, smiling in a very superior kind of way. "Not when you had me full in your sights. And even when you did blast off after me, you made sure you missed!"

So my aim *had* been that bad, I thought ruefully. And, of course, this loony didn't know that his head remained on his neck only by courtesy of a tube of witch-green eye make-up!

It didn't seem the moment to disillusion him.

"Well, you don't just kill people dead," I said feebly. "Not when you haven't been introduced."

"Precisely!" he said triumphantly. "But I would have fired. Any man would. You didn't *want* to harm me. And what did you do next?"

I considered.

"I shut the window, had a drink, and went back to bed," I replied.

"You see!" he said. "You see! Why didn't you go for help?"

Because there was a bloody lunatic roving around outside! I shouted internally.

"I don't know," I said. "I thought I'd wait till the morning, that was all."

"Because it'd be safer in daylight?" he said.

"Yes. That's right," I said, beginning to let my irritation show. "Because it'd be a bloody sight safer in daylight. Wouldn't you agree about that?"

"Oh yes. I'd agree," he said, smiling. "But tell me, why then before it was fully light did you get up out of bed and open your window again? Go on, explain that, eh? Explain that!"

He was bouncing up and down on his seat in excitement. Heathcliff opened an eye and gave a silent miaow of admonition. I imitated him and let out a silent shriek of anger and indignation and incredulous disgust. But the expression on my face was (I hoped) one of interested reflection.

"You mean that perhaps it was because I hoped you might still be out there and wanted to let you in?" I said.

"It could be," he said, nodding at me encouragingly like a dedicated teacher leading on a slow-thinking pupil. "All right. At first you're terrified. It's dark and you wake up suddenly and there's someone at your window. For all you know it's a gang of burglars!"

He said this as if fear of being robbed was the most intense feeling known to man! Perhaps it is. They make the laws, and crimes against property have always carried the top penalties.

"But even then, you don't try to hurt me," he went on. "You don't go for help either. You just lock yourself in! And a couple of hours later after you've got over the initial terror, what do you do? You get up and open the window!"

"I see, I see!" I said. "Yes, now you put it like that, I can see you're probably right!"

The journalist's motto is, he who writes and runs away lives to write another day. Occasionally my colleagues have gone to jail for a few days rather than reveal their sources, but if there'd been a bit of pain involved, there'd have been more spilt beans than at a spastics' tea-party. Me, I was as far away from Joan of Arc as you can get. Oh yes, me lud, it's them bloody bell-ringers, and I'll certainly have my ears syringed!

So I poured myself another drink and showered Craik with praise for his masterly analysis of my behaviour in the face of his most kind and courteous assault on me the night before.

For a few moments he modestly accepted my plaudits, then his face went all solemn and that narrow look appeared again.

"But you *did* go the police, didn't you? I heard you talking to those people who came back with you tonight. You'd told *them*, too. You were trying to get me caught. That doesn't fit."

"Good Lord!" I said, with a light laugh. "You don't want to take any notice of that."

"Why not?" he demanded.

I shook my head at him sorrowfully. I was getting quite good at this.

"Of course I went to the police. It wasn't that I was really bothered by what had happened. And I understand why I wasn't bothered now you've explained it to me. But I'm a journalist, aren't I? Like you said, there's good copy in this for me, especially coming right after my series. But I can hardly claim to have been raped if I didn't go the police about it, can I? I mean, it'd sound a bit thin!"

His look became less narrow, but only marginally. My creative powers were bubbling merrily, however.

"And another thing," I went on. "You know what?

Now I see you again, Patrick, I realize I gave the police an entirely misleading description of you. Not deliberately, you understand. But deep down, I can't have wanted you to be caught. I told them you were ginger. Would you credit it? With sort of greeny eyes and a hooked nose!"

"Like Jimmy?" he said.

"You're right!" I cried. "Just like dear old Jimmy."

He began to laugh. I began to laugh, too. Soon we were both howling hysterically. Heathcliff opened both his eyes and regarded me scornfully from Patrick's shoulders. I roared even louder. It was the laughter of relief. There was still a long way to go, but I felt that the danger of this loony killing me had now been reduced to a minimum.

"You know," said Craik, wiping away his mirthful tears, "I think I'll have another drink now."

I reached the whisky bottle over to him, but he shook his head.

"Could I have a brandy, please? Just to round off the evening?"

I'd have uncorked a thousand-pound claret if I'd had one and he'd asked for it! I got up, went over to the sideboard, produced a huge balloon glass, sloshed a couple of inches of the *fine champagne* into it, and turned, still chortling.

I found myself looking down the barrels of my shotgun. And Craik had stopped laughing.

"What's the matter?" I said.

He shook his head sadly.

"As with all women and most journalists," he said, "you have only a very coarse appreciation of the way that human beings work. I think that of all the reasons you give me for disliking you, and they are many, the most offensive is the insultingly obvious way you have tried to humour me. Now you imagine I'm going to sip my brandy and then go out into the night which you will fill with sleepy policemen at the first opportunity. But you're wrong."

"Am I?" I said. "That's twice in a year!"

"Indeed you are. I got to thinking last night after I'd

left here that I'd put myself in your hands. The hands of a vicious opinionated female!"

"That's one way of looking at it," I said.

"I wasn't lying when I said I'd thought of you all day, but the picture I had was of your finger pointing at me and your hysterical voice screeching, "That was the man!" I have a reputation, a wife, a family to think of. You have all the power of an immoral and irresponsible press behind you. I came back tonight to finish what I really ought to have finished last night. I wasn't very hopeful, I must confess. It didn't seem likely I'd find you still here, and certainly not alone!"

"Perhaps I was hoping you'd return," I said. "Perhaps I was expecting it."

"Still humouring me?" he said. "It's absurd, isn't it, that something so trivial and unimportant as a man behaving as nature intended should be able to destroy his whole life? Don't you agree?"

"You're right, you're right. Or a woman's either. Let's call it quits," I said eagerly.

"Really? Perhaps before I finish it, I'll test the sincerity of your conversion," he said. "Come here."

He beckoned me with the gun. I approached slowly.

"Stop there," he said when I was right in front of him. "Now, take your clothes off."

I was ready to do it. Anything which would delay matters long enough to let a chance of escape present itself. But I couldn't start undoing buttons while I still had the brandy in my hand. I offered it to him but his eyes were hot for the strip-show now and he impatiently motioned it away with the gun barrel.

So instead I threw it in his face.

I was as bad a shot with the brandy as I'd been with the gun. I just about missed him altogether as he jerked his head aside. But Heathcliff I didn't miss. The fiery liquid caught him full in his startled and dignified face. And his howl of protest turned to a scream of pain as the spirit burned in his eyes. His feet shot out and his claws ripped bloody channels down Patrick's cheek. The man shrieked and half rose, trying to dislodge the cat. But Heathcliff was not about to let himself be hurled to dangers he could not see and he anchored himself firmly into

Patrick's neck and face and sank his teeth into the man's nose for extra purchase.

There was no way for Craik to resist that onslaught and keep hold of the shotgun, too. He couldn't use it against the cat without blowing his own head off, so he dropped it and tried to drag Heathcliff loose with his bare hands. I let it lie on the floor for a few moments while man and cat spun together around the room in a snarling, swearing, bloodstained dance. Furniture went flying, ornaments were shattered, the drinks tray overturned. I had read of the cat of Barnburgh which killed the armoured knight and now I could well believe it. Finally Craik tripped and fell heavily and Heathcliff, sensing the nearness of the floor, released his grip and scuttled under the sideboard.

Now I flung myself toward and grabbed at the shotgun. Not that Craik was offering much competition. He staggered to his feet with his bloody hands clutched to his face. I was glad I couldn't see what lay beneath them. I levelled the gun, but he ignored it. I don't know whether he believed what he'd said earlier about my reluctance to use it, or whether he was having as much difficulty as Heathcliff in seeing. Whatever the case, he moved drunkenly towards the door and though I shrieked at him to stop, this time I wasn't able to pull the trigger. I followed him to the doorway. It was a wild gusty night, and what looked like a tremendous storm was bubbling up out of Ennerdale. Already the low clouds were trailing wild tresses across the brow of the humble fell behind the cottage. This was the direction the shambling figure of the wounded rapist took. I guessed he had his car parked on the track which ran up the next little valley, a distance of less than two miles and a pleasant stroll at most times, but not a journey I would have cared to undertake now. He disappeared from view very quickly, not because of the speed at which he was moving but because of the speed at which the cloud was rolling down the fell. Well, he would have to look after himself. I had someone more important to worry about.

Anxiously I re-entered the cottage, fearful that the brandy and the fight might have seriously injured Heathcliff. It was with great relief that I saw he had emerged from under the sideboard and was busy foraging among the debris for the peanuts and crisps which had fallen to the floor with the drinks tray. He turned a pair of very bloodshot but obviously functioning eyes on me and miaowed reproachfully. I could find no sign of injury on his body, though I shuddered when I looked closely at his claws. Half an hour later with his eyes bathed, his fur brushed and his claws cleaned, he was willing to accept a tin of pilchards from me as a sufficient mark of atonement and I was able to start clearing up the room.

As I busied myself straightening rugs, moving furniture and sweeping up broken glass, I debated my next move. I knew that what I ought to do was get in the car and go and roust Ambler out of his bed so that Patrick Craik could be caught, red-faced if not red-handed, before the night was out. But the howl of the wind and the lash of rain against the windows, combined with the thought of all that explaining, those looks of disbelief, the ghastly hours spent hanging around that musty police station, all this was strong argument in favour of a postponement till the morning. The day had started with me being raped and it had finished with me being almost murdered. Surely that was enough for any single day!

My mind was churning like a washing-machine. I had to put a stop to it. I took a couple of the sleeping pills the doctor had prescribed when the divorce was at its most unpleasant. They must have reacted in a most peculiar way with all the scotch I had swilled. For a few moments I thought the house had taken off in the storm and was flying out towards the Irish Sea. Then everything stopped and began to go dark and I scarcely had time to reach my bed, and certainly no time to get in it, before I fell asleep.

I was awoken the next day by a furious knocking at the door and voices anxiously calling my name.

When I got downstairs I found it was Mike and Sheila, who greeted me with the mingled relief, indignation, and covert disappointment of those who have been made to worry unnecessarily.

"You said you'd come and have coffee with me," said

Sheila. "When it got to lunch-time I began to get worried."

"Lunch-time!" I said. My watch had stopped, but through the window, in the well-washed denim-blue sky which the storm had left behind, I could see the sun was in a most peculiar place for nine a.m., my usual rising time.

"Yes, it's half past two," said Mike accusingly. "I should have been showing a client round a house!"

"Oh, shut up, Mike," said Sheila. "Cora, are you all right? You look a bit distraught."

"Hang-over," I said. "I had a nightcap and took a couple of pills. They didn't mix!"

I wasn't lying, merely postponing the moment when I told them what had taken place the previous night. Perhaps I should talk to Ambler first in any case. But I could see him looking at his watch in vast disbelief and saying, "He tried to murder you last night and you've waited till tea-time before reporting it!"

But the interview with Ambler was to take place before that. As Sheila busied herself in the kitchen making coffee and Mike sat next to me on the sofa with his hand on my knee preparatory (I presumed) to a second get-back-in-the-saddle-straightaway pep-talk, another car came bumping up the lonning and the sergeant got out.

"Come to see I survived the night, Sergeant?" I asked as I opened the door. I thought I might provoke some little ironic rejoinder which he'd be thoroughly ashamed of when he heard about my experiences. Instead he addressed me in a manner which was almost apologetic and asked if he might have a word.

"The thing is, Mrs. Lincoln—er, Grant—first thing this morning Tom Graham, you'll know him, the farmer you bought your cottage from, well, he was out on the backside of the fell there, checking how his sheep had weathered the storm, when he found a man's body."

"Good God," said Mike. "Anyone we know?"

Ambler ignored him.

"He was quite close to the foot of the fell and in the lonning that runs down to the main road there was a car parked. It looks as if this fellow had got out of his car and gone for a walk up the hill for some reason or other."

"Wanted a pee. Or just liked fell-walking. A lot of people do," said Mike.

"Oh, shut up, Mike," said Sheila, who'd come in from the kitchen with a tray full of coffee things. "What did he die of, Sergeant? A fall?"

"No," said Ambler. "He was drowned."

"Drowned?"

"Yes. He must have fallen and banged his head. He was in a shallow channel, you know, the kind of thing which usually carries just a trickle of water. But last night's rain turned everything into a torrent for a while. And unfortunately for him his head was facing uphill with his mouth open."

"Ugh," said Sheila.

"Yes. Nasty. A funny thing was his face was very badly scratched, too, as though he'd been attacked by some wild animal. Perhaps after he'd died, something had had a go at him."

"Ugh, again," said Sheila. "Do you know who he is? Was."

"Yes. That was easy. Stuff he had on him and in the car. A Mr. Patrick Craik. He was from Manchester. Had been staying in Carlisle on business, it seems. He went out yesterday evening and just didn't come back."

"Well, he wouldn't, would he?" observed Mike.

"Does the name mean anything to you, Mrs. Grant?" asked Ambler.

This was the first time I'd been invited to contribute. My mind was doing its washing-machine churn again. I had to tell him, I supposed, but before I could speak Mike decided to do his protective friend act and said in his most pukka voice, "Just what has this got to do with Cora, Sergeant? After what she's been through, I think she needs a bit of peace and rest."

"I agree, sir," said Ambler. "It's just that this man Craik, well, he bears some resemblance to the description Mrs. Grant gave me of the man who assaulted her. And as he was found not too far from the cottage as the crow flies, I thought that . . ."

"You'd like me to take a look at the body, Sergeant," I said.

He nodded.

"I'll get myself ready," I said, and left the room.

I suppose you could say that the journalist and the private person were fighting inside me. The journalist knew she had a super story, the private person would be happy to get quietly out of this without any fanfares of publicity. I postponed a verdict till I'd seen the remains. For all I knew there was some other completely different bearded man with a face covered with scratches roaming around the fells last night!

But it was him all right. I looked down at that face and tried to hate it and could only manage a very small twinge.

"Well?" said Ambler impatiently.

A uniformed sergeant came in at that moment and whispered in his ear. Ambler frowned and nodded.

"Will you come outside now, Mrs. Grant?" he said to me.

As we went along the corridor, a door opened and a pale-faced woman with a frightened-looking boy of about sixteen holding her arm stepped out. The uniformed sergeant addressed her.

"This way please, Mrs. Craik."

I looked at Ambler.

"His wife. And son. There's two younger daughters, too, I believe."

"Tough on them," I said. "Still, it happens all the time, doesn't it?"

"It doesn't make it any less painful," he said. "Well, Mrs. Grant. Was that the man?"

He regarded me steadily. Not narrowly, just steadily. I thought of my story and I thought of that pale-faced woman and the frightened boy and the two girls probably still in school, not yet knowing what might have happened to them.

"Oh no," I said. "You'll have to keep on looking, Sergeant. That certainly wasn't my boy."

"You're sure?"

"You seem to find it very hard to take my word for anything, Sergeant," I said.

"I'm sorry if I give that impression, Mrs. Grant," he said. "Coincidence then?"

"What? Oh, you mean the beard? They're more common than bare faces these days, surely!"

"The beard, yes. Coincidence enough," he said, frowning at a sheet of paper he had produced from his pocket. "But there can't be all that many men walking the fells wearing leather jerkins with half a dozen pellets of lead shot embedded in them."

So my aim hadn't been totally inaccurate after all! For a second I wished Craik had been alive to hear that I really had tried to kill him.

"Coincidences happen, Sergeant," I said. "Police and newspapermen should know that better than most."

"True," he said. "Tell me, Mrs. Grant. Normally in matters like this, we're very discreet. But in your case, being a journalist and all, I wondered if we're likely to be getting a lot of questions asked."

He studied the ground at his feet as he spoke. He really did look as if he needed a tonic!

"Not through me you're not," I assured him. "As far as I'm concerned, you can close the file and get back to parking offences."

Now he looked straight at me and smiled. It altered his face as the fresh air and open vistas of High Ghyll had done.

"I'm sorry we had to meet in such circumstances, Mrs. Grant," he said. "But I'm pleased to have made your acquaintance. I'll look out for your articles in future. Are you working on anything special at the moment?"

"I'm thinking of doing something on conservation. You know, threatened species, that sort of thing. Like peregrines and golden eagles in the fells."

He looked at me in alarm.

"You won't be mentioning locations of nests, will you?" he said anxiously. "Once they know where it is, there's some people will stop at nothing to rob a nest. Especially up here where everything's so exposed."

"Don't I know it," I said.

Snowball

Alice had been baking jam tarts. If there was one thing Alice could do really well, it was bake. If you wanted another thing she could do really well, you were in trouble. But she was certainly a great baker.

I smelt the tarts even before I entered the kitchen after my morning walk. I always took a morning walk when I stayed at Rose Cottage, not because I liked the exercise but because it gave me a chance to get rid of Alice's breakfast out of my *Times*. Normally I'm a *Mirror* man, but a tabloid's no good for concealing a breakfast. Alice's jam tarts were superb, but her fried eggs defied description. Or dissolution, as I had discovered after an unhappy half-hour trying to flush one down the loo on my first visit the previous summer. So I had had to seek other methods of disposal and now the countryside round the village of Millthwaite was littered with caches of Alice's fried eggs.

I could, of course, merely have rejected the breakfasts, but Alice was a very touchy person. She distrusted me on principle, as she distrusted all men who showed an interest in her poor widowed niece, Sally. But if distrust ripened into dislike, I was finished. So I praised the breakfasts and ordered *The Times* whenever I came to Millthwaite.

I stood and looked at the tarts, cooling on the kitchen table. There were two dozen of them, intended, I surmised, for the Women's Institute Fête that afternoon. I breathed in the rich seductive smell of warm pastry and hot jam. And I was tempted.

Why a man as eager to be liked as I was should have let himself be tempted is hard to explain. All I can say is four-and-twenty looks pretty like an infinity of tarts and also I was very hungry. After all, I'd had no breakfast.

I picked one up. It made a single delicious mouthful. I had a second in my hand when I realized I was being observed.

Standing outside the window was the monster, Lennie. His wavy jet black hair curled down over his brow, almost hiding the cold grey eyes which I felt rather than saw staring at me accusingly. At five years old Lennie gave every promise of becoming as morally unscrupulous as his father.

I smiled reassuringly at him and offered him a tart. He was, after all, Sally's son and the apple of Alice's eye and I would do well to keep in his good books. But the little monster shook his head and said "Fête," or it might have been "fate." Either way it sounded like a threat.

With a sigh I reached into my pocket and found it was empty, an all too common discovery of late. I had never realized how much our little contracting business depended on my partner, Leonard, until he fell off the scaffolding. I had tried to keep Sally's share up at the old level as I didn't want Alice to get a sniff of my inefficiency, but it left me perpetually short. Young Lennie did not have the mien of a child ready to be fobbed off with promissory notes. Debating what was best, I glanced idly round the kitchen and my eyes fell on a fifty-pence piece in a saucer on the shelf behind the cellar door. I picked it up. Lennie brushed his black locks aside to get a better view and when I lobbed it through the window he plucked it out of the air like an on-form slip fielder. Then he was gone.

Just like his father, I thought as I went upstairs. You didn't have to spell things out for him.

I met Sally coming out of the bathroom. She liked rising late when she could, which was useful to me as it meant I could breakfast alone. Sally was almost as sensitive on Alice's behalf as the ancient beldame herself, and I wouldn't have cared for her to catch me at my sleight of hand with *The Times*. I'd never thought of Sally as a particularly "loyal" person; in fact, as far as Leonard went, my experience had pointed quite the other way. But it turned out that she was a scion of one of those old blood-is-thicker-than-water bucolic families and after Leonard's death she hadn't hesitated to accept Aunt Alice's invitation to come and stay till she "got herself sorted." I had done all I could to help Sally bear her tragic loss and would have done a great deal more, but her sojourn at Millthwaite had somehow reawoken a whole ocean of sleeping Krakens, notably a sense of family and (worse still) a sense of propriety. No, she hadn't gone off me, she explained, as I tried to arrange a tryst in her bedroom on my first visit, but it wasn't right, not here, in Aunt Alice's house. And when I suggested what Aunt Alice might care to do, our relationship almost came to a close there and then. Left to herself, I had no doubt that in the end she would marry me. But Leonard's death hadn't left her to herself. It had left her to Lennie and to Alice and I wasn't about to get my share without their express approval.

There was, besides, a more comfortably mercenary motive. Alice's small fortune ("in the funds," would you believe?) was going to come Lennie's way, via his mother—but not if she rushed into a foolish second marriage. And even after three visits to Millthwaite my suitability was still very much under scrutiny—and (though it hurt to admit it) not only by Alice!

Sally looked very fetching in her nightie and I couldn't resist giving her a passionate embrace, which she permitted only because we could hear Alice in the hall below trying to make contact with the idiot girl who looked after the village's tiny telephone exchange. My own recognition of the need for caution couldn't survive such close contact with that soft flesh and I was trying to manoeuvre Sally back into the bathroom when Alice's voice rose sufficiently to penetrate even the drumbeat of hot blood in my ears.

"Constable Jarvis!" she bellowed. "That's who I want . . . No reply? What if I was being assaulted? . . . No, I'm not! I'll try later."

She slammed the phone down as I descended the stairs, having abruptly abandoned my assault on Sally much to her surprise and, I hope, disappointment.

"Anything wrong, Alice?" I asked casually.

She regarded me with distaste. She was a big-boned,

grey-haired countrywoman in her late fifties and anger turned her face a greyish-purple and drew the sides of her mouth down till they almost touched her chin.

"You didn't eat any of my tarts, did you?" she demanded.

No one in his right mind would have admitted it at that moment.

"No!" I said emphatically. "Are some missing?"

"Four," she said.

Four! I'd only taken two! The monster, Lennie, must have returned and taken the others. How like his father, to add theft to blackmail!

Without compunction I suggested, "Perhaps Lennie helped himself?"

"No," she said, shaking her head. "The milkman's money's gone from the shelf, too. He'd not do that."

But you still asked me! I thought indignantly. What a world it was where children received more trust than their elders. Especially a child whose criminal inheritance stood out like a love-bite on a nun.

"No, I know who it'd be," she continued grimly. My blood chilled. "I saw that tramp, the one they call Old Tommy, hanging around earlier. He kept going when he saw me, he knows there's nothing for the likes of him at my house. He must have come back through the kitchen garden later. I'll get Jarvis after him as soon as he bothers to answer his phone."

So saying, she picked up the telephone once more. I went through the kitchen, avoided the temptation of the depleted but still heavily loaded tray of tarts, and strolled out into the morning sunshine. It seemed like a good time for a walk. If I could have spotted young Lennie, I'd have invited him along not because of his sparkling conversation but merely to have him out of the way when PC Jarvis arrived. But he was nowhere in sight, so I had to be content with making myself scarce. Not that there was much to bother about. I'd seen this tramp, Old Tommy, pretty frequently on my egg-disposal expeditions along the country by-ways and he looked a natural suspect for all petty crime in the district. So I strolled along enjoying the warm sunshine, the lush green fields gilded with buttercups, and the warbling of innumerable birds. Even the distant pop of a shotgun as some unsentimental farmer tried to cut down on the warbling seemed to blend in with the overall rich sensuous pattern of Nature.

The pattern became a little threadbare round the next corner. There, sitting in the hedgerow like a pile of house-hold rubbish dumped by a passing vandal, was Old Tommy. Some tramps are picturesque at a distance. Close or far, Tommy was revolting. Such skin as could be seen through the layers of rags and the tangles of lank gingery hair was a mottled grey, like mouldy bread. He was stuffing some sort of food he held wrapped in an old newspaper into the mouth which doubtless lay beneath the beard and he didn't even look up as I passed. I would have ignored him also if it hadn't been for a sudden shock of recognition.

That was no ordinary food he was eating! That was one of Alice's solid fried eggs!

Surely a man could get no lower than this? I stopped and shared the horror of his degradation.

Now he looked up and acknowledged my presence.

"I would appreciate a little more salt," he said. "If you could manage that one morning."

Now my shock was doubled, or even trebled. He knew who I was! No wonder I'd seen him so frequently on my post-breakfast trips. Whenever I was at Millthwaite, it must have been like room service to him!

But worse still was his voice. This was no mumbling, half-witted derelict, but an educated man. *The Times* was not just a container. He was holding it the right way up and reading the grease-stained news.

"Watch it, mate!" I blistered. "I'll have the law on you."

I dare say he looked surprised beneath the hair.

"What for!" he said. "Stealing your breakfast? You shouldn't leave it lying around in ditches, should you? Now push off, will you. I want to get on with my paper."

So saying, he opened it wide and I observed the words "Rose Cottage" scribbled plainly on the front page. If Jarvis questioned him about the money and the tarts, not only did he have the articulacy to defend himself, he had the evidence to support a counter-attack. If this got back to Alice, her fury would be formidable.

I could see that there was little profit to be gained from arguing with Old Tommy. Threats weren't going to work and I lacked the wherewithal to bribe him. In any case, as I'd found with young Lennie, bribery only got you in deeper. So with an affectation of indifference, I began to retrace my steps.

The countryside round Millthwaite is thickly wooded and it was easy to step off the road round the first bend and find a vantage point among the trees from which I could observe what Old Tommy did next. The ground sloped sharply here. Far above me I could still hear the farmer stuffing pigeons full of buckshot. Behind me in a small field carved out among the beechwoods, a couple of dozen sheep grazed, baa-ing contentedly as they chewed the lush grass. Bees buzzed, birds chirruped, leaves rustled. And over all the sun shone hotter and hotter.

God, how I hate the bloody countryside!

My fear was that Old Tommy might succumb to the general somnolence, but after only a minute or two, I saw him rise. If I read him aright, he was very willing to argue the toss with impotent civilians, but empty though he believed my threat of the law to be, he preferred not to run the risk of an encounter with PC Jarvis. Or perhaps it was my connection with Rose Cottage and the ultimate deterrent of Aunt Alice which inspired him. Whatever the case, he began to walk with unwonted briskness along the lane in a direction which would ultimately bring him to the arterial road about two miles distant, and once over that he was off Jarvis's patch.

I watched him out of sight with a lightening heart and whistled merrily as I strolled through the sheep in the little field and out of the gate back on to the road.

But it seemed to be the fate of my bubbles of joy that summer morning to be rapidly burst.

As I came in sight of Rose Cottage again, I saw the lean and hungry figure of Constable Jarvis leaning on the gate in deep conversation with Alice. But it wasn't just the sight of the constable that bothered me, it was what accompanied him.

On all my previous visits, Jarvis had moved majestically around the countryside on a very old, very upright and very slow bicycle. The young and the hale could leave him far behind, and many of the old and the halt could give him a good run for his money.

But now a profligate state had seen fit to provide him with a shiny new motor-scooter! Since Leonard's death I had frequently come into close and unpleasant contact with the Inland Revenue, and this blatant waste of tax-payers' money filled me with rage.

It also filled me with apprehension. If Jarvis set off in the right direction, he could easily overtake Old Tommy before the tramp was safely over the arterial. I hadn't been seen by the pair at the gate, so I quickly retreated. It was my simple intention if Jarvis came this way to flag him down and engage him in conversation as long as I possibly could. But when I came in view once more of the little field nestling among the wooded hills, I saw that not all the sheep were safely grazing inside any more. Some fool had left the gate ajar. It was probably me. I was never very hot on the country code, I'm afraid. Anyway, two or three sheep were already out on the road and the others were queuing up to follow. Guiltily I set about trying to shoo the escapers back in. Then it struck me that here was the perfect excuse for delaying Jarvis if he came. Not that a couple of sheep would cause a country policeman much trouble. Was that the distant putt-putt of a motor-scooter I could hear?

Acting with sudden resolution, I opened the gate wide, went into the field and began waving my arms and shouting. For a few seconds, the stupid animals merely regarded me indifferently. Then as if someone had pressed a panic button, suddenly they turned as one and stampeded out of the gate and down the road.

At exactly that moment PC Jarvis came sailing round the corner. They must have used more of the tax-payers' money to give him a first-class training, for he displayed a high degree of skill, gently colliding with no more than four or five of the leading animals before his machine came to rest in the hedgerow as, shortly afterwards, he did himself.

It was no time to come forward and pretend I had been

trying to restore the sheep to their field, I decided. A quiet withdrawal was best. Jarvis was on his feet. He was bleeding slightly and looked rather dazed, but in the best traditions of the great force to which he belonged, he was applying himself instantly to the immediate task which seemed to involve viciously kicking every sheep that was foolish enough to remain within range.

It would be a long time before he was ready to resume the chase after Old Tommy. Well satisfied, I climbed out of the field into the surrounding wood and began to make my way back towards the cottage across country. I smiled as I walked at the thought of all those sheep running wildly in all directions. They would take hours to round up. Foolish animals! Unlike the rational part of creation, their only reaction to danger was flight. Had I been a sheep and not a man, I would doubtless have been running madly towards the railway station by now (I smiled at the thought), instead of which I was going to stay on at Rose Cottage, conquer Alice's suspicions, win Sally's hand, and live happily ever after.

Another bubble! Townie though I am, I have a sharp enough ear for danger to catch a discordant note in the great symphony of Nature. And now I paused and listened.

I was right. Something was approaching fast, some large heavy beast galloping down the slope towards me, paying scant attention to the undergrowth or any other obstacle. A wild boar? I wondered, ready to believe anything of a landscape which could house Aunt Alice.

Then I saw a figure and heard a distant voice. It was almost incomprehensible with anger and the thick local accent but I heard enough to catch his general drift.

". . . -ing bugger . . . ! my -ing sheep . . . ! -ing shoot . . . ! -ing police . . . !"

This might have been the not totally unattractive programme of some new anarchist party, but I guessed not. No, it seemed more likely this was the same pigeon-shooter I had heard earlier, probably one of the local farmers, a fearsome tribe of primitives, fit consort for the likes of Alice. And I guessed from his broken speech that the sheep were his, and from some vantage point on the hill he'd observed my apparent attempt to rustle them!

I could only hope he'd been too distant for identification. From the time he'd taken to appear on the scene, it seemed likely. Without further ado, I took to my heels, scrambling madly through the undergrowth which, innocuous a moment earlier, now seemed to coil thorny tentacles around my calves and thighs at every step.

Behind me the voice ceased its abusive babble and a single more terrible sound filled its place, the soft explosion of a shotgun cartridge. The leaves above my head hissed as though drilled by jets of boiling rain, frightened birds rose noisily into the air, and I fell to the ground with all the speed I could muster.

"Come on out, you varmint!" roared that awful voice. (He may or may not have said "you varmint," but this was in fact the kind of thing these local farmers were able to say with no self-consciousness whatsoever.)

I had no intention of coming out. I knew enough about country matters to recognize that he had let loose only one barrel of his shotgun and I felt sure that the other was anxiously seeking the slightest sign of movement on my part. My best bet was to lie low. The undergrowth around me was so thick and rustly that I should be able to keep close track of his movements if he began to approach.

Why this should have seemed a comfort I don't know! When next he moved, I certainly heard him, but he was so near that he must just as certainly hear me if I attempted to retreat. Now he'd stopped again. I pictured him standing close by, beady eyes gleaming, ears and gun cocked for my slightest movement.

I could bear it no longer. I had to get out of there!

Slowly I rose, using a Walt Disney beech tree for cover. I had a strange sense that he was directly on the other side of it, but it didn't matter. Nothing could be worse than this terror of waiting!

Then from under my feet a rabbit started! The poor beast must have been crouching only a couple of feet away from me, petrified by an equal terror. Now it was off in a noisy panic-stricken dash through the dark brush. I leaned against the tree startled half out of my mind, and suddenly the farmer, attracted by the noise of the rabbit's flight, jumped out from behind the beech.

He looked exactly as I'd imagined him. I held my breath. He peered after the rabbit, gun levelled. I thought I was going to die. He hadn't seen me yet, but he was only a yard away. I felt myself choking. Any moment he must turn!

I did the only thing possible.

Raising both my arms I leapt forward and brought my clenched fists crashing down on the base of his thick red neck.

For the next few seconds I staggered around in complete agony, certain I must have broken my wrists. When the pain eased slightly and the tears cleared from my eyes, I discovered the unfortunate farmer was lying flat on his face in a tangle of whin and briar. I must have unknowingly struck some particularly susceptible point of the body. It was the kind of thing I had frequently viewed with blasé disbelief in the cinema. I still do. They never show you the hero nursing his sprained wrists.

To my relief, he began to make groaning noises and even essayed a movement of the arms to push himself upright. It was unsuccessful but the next one might not be. His shotgun lay at my feet. I did not feel he was going to be a safe person, either physically or mentally, to bear arms for a few hours, so I picked it up and set off at a brisk trot.

The trees thinned out after a while and I could make almost as rapid progress as I would have done in the open. Eventually the wood became a mere meadow and this ran all the way to the hedge which marked the furthest boundary of Alice's kitchen garden.

Flitting from tree to tree, I crossed the meadow with a mixture of speed and circumspection, my mind very much concerned with the twin necessities of getting under cover as quickly as possible and of getting into the house without being spotted. It was the monster, Lennie, I feared the most of all. Discovery by Alice would be more completely devastating, I knew, but in terms of sheer probability Lennie was the real danger. Alice was a large woman, slow moving, easily spottable, while Lennie wandered hither and thither like an infant poltergeist, perceptible only by the trail of damage he left. He could be sitting behind the hedge at this very moment watching my progress with that cold curiosity of his, wondering what profit was in it for him.

I stopped and regarded the hedge uneasily, victim of my own imaginings. But my luck was holding. As I watched, I heard the noise of a car and out of the old lean-to garage at the far side of the house pulled Sally's Mini. I caught a clear glimpse of two heads, one topped by Sally's dear long blonde hair, the other by Lennie's raven-black tangle, before the car turned into the road and set off for Millthwaite village, which fortunately lay in the opposite direction to the angry policeman, the assaulted farmer, the educated tramp and the rustled sheep.

This left only Alice, and a glance at my watch told me that it was more than likely she, too, would be out. About this time most mornings she took a short walk over the fields to practise good works on Widow Tyler, who was too old to resist or too imbecile to resent the dreadful condescension with which Alice's gifts of caramel custards, nourishing broths or home-made wine (all on a par with her fried eggs) were given.

Saying a little prayer of anticipatory thanks, I dashed across the few remaining yards of the meadow, clambered over the hedge, trod with fearful care between the rows of Alice's vegetables (how hard do our old terrors die!) and entered the kitchen.

It was empty. The twenty tarts still lay on the table. The empty saucer still stood on the shelf by the cellar door.

I realized I was still holding my borrowed shotgun and I put it down on the table. It took only a couple of moments to assure myself that there was no one in the living-room or upstairs. Now all I had to do was clean off the traces of my passage through the woods and change my clothing to make identification more difficult. But first I returned to the kitchen to retrieve the tell-tale shotgun. It looked quite domestic lying there on that rustic table amid a squad of jam tarts. I picked it up, turned to go, then for the second time that day temptation assailed me.

The snowball had started rolling here. Alice's tarts, Lennie's blackmail, the milkman's money; the accused tramp, the escaped sheep, the crashed constable; the assaulted farmer and the stolen gun. And all for the sake of a couple of jam tarts.

Surely I deserved another?

Of course I did.

I took it and raised it to my mouth. Behind me I heard a noise. My nerves had gone beyond rapid reaction. Slowly I turned.

Standing in the cellar doorway with a bottle of elderberry wine in her hand and an expression of self-righteous triumph on her face was Alice.

"I knew it were you!" she cried. "I knew it!"

This was nonsense, of course, and mere wish fulfillment. I opened my mouth to say as much, when I observed the triumph fading to be replaced by another less positive expression. For a second I was puzzled till I realized that as I had turned the shotgun had turned with me and the barrel was pointed straight at Alice's ample bosom. Flushed with effort, gashed by briars, and grim with guilt, I must have looked quite a frightening sight.

I savoured the moment, knowing that I could scarcely hope twice in a lifetime to have the ascendancy over Alice.

Popping the tart in my mouth, I brought both hands to bear on the gun and curled my finger around the forward trigger. Her eyes bulged. I smiled and squeezed.

"Boom!" I said through a mouthful of pastry.

She shrieked and stepped backwards, then disappeared from view as though she'd dropped into a hole. I heard Widow Tyler's bottle of elderberry smash to pieces on the cellar floor. And I heard no more.

After a moment, I moved slowly forward and peered down the steep flight of worn stairs.

It was a very lucky escape for Alice, I realized. If I'd squeezed the other trigger, she'd have got the loaded barrel right through her whalebone corset. As it was, I thought as I carefully closed the cellar door, her parting from this world was tragic rather than scandalous. That would have been the way she wanted it, Alice would have hated being relegated to the status of mere victim.

When Sally and Lennie returned, I was clean, immaculate and relaxed, standing by the kitchen window eating jam tarts. Lennie looked at the tray with uncharacteristic bewilderment. There were only ten left.

Sally made no comment but put the kettle on. Her face wore that characteristic half smile which few of the world's upsets could remove for long. She was a dear girl, able to take everything in her stride, neither asking for, nor attending to, explanations.

"I'll make a pot of tea," she said. "We'll have it in the garden. Or would you prefer a bottle of Aunt Alice's potato wine?"

I considered the option.

"No," I said. "Tea will be fine."

I had another jam tart. Lennie's eyes never left me. I thought of cause and effect; small causes, large effects; single steps and journeys of a thousand miles. I had not known what I was doing when I took the tarts that morning any more than I could have foreseen the consequences that other morning (so long ago it now seemed) when I helped myself to a couple of quid from the petty-cash box. Such a fuss Leonard had made! Poor, soft, amiable, hard-working Leonard, to make such a fuss about a few pounds when for years I had been milking every penny I could out of the business! He'd been very upset. I'd told the coroner so, though I naturally did not particularize the cause. Pressure of work was mentioned. Pressure of heel as he clung to the outer scaffolding was not. The heart has its laws which the law might misunderstand.

Lennie was breathing heavily over the remaining tarts.

"Help yourself," I said magnanimously. He considered this for a moment, the deep grey eyes under the shock of black hair inward-looking as he weighed up the situation. Then he arrived at his decision, smiled broadly, and grabbed two.

I, too, smiled, feeling almost fond of the little monster. Perhaps, I thought, preening myself slightly as I regarded my reflection in the kitchen window, perhaps he had inherited some of his father's good qualities, too.

My reflection nodded agreement and a lock of my jet black hair flopped down over my deep-set grey eyes. I pushed it back and thought that perhaps it was as well

Leonard had not lived to see the way young Lennie developed.

"We are all children of fate," I mused as we went out into the garden.

"Fête?" said Sally. "This afternoon's, you mean?"

Lennie, bringing up the rear with the last of the jam tarts on a plate, said nothing.

But I felt that he understood.

Exit Line

There is a chair.

There is a table.

There is an iron bedstead.

There is a bucket.

There is no window.

The walls, ceiling and floor are of the same untreated concrete. Only gravity distinguishes them. Even the door does not help much. It is flush with the wall like the door of a squash court and it is set in the centre of the wall about four feet from the ground and equidistant from the ceiling.

The only light in the room comes from a single bulb set above the door. It is protected by a metal muzzle. There is no switch. It goes out when I get into bed and comes on when I get up.

The door is made of some very hard wood. There is no handle or keyhole and it fits so snugly into the wall that no crack remains wide enough to admit even a sheet of paper.

I sleep wrapped in a square grey blanket on the metal mesh of the bedstead. The temperature of the room never varies. I would put it around 65 Fahrenheit.

Hunger, fatigue and the movement of my bowels are my only clock.

There are a few inches of chemical solution in the bucket, but despite this the room must smell abominably. Fortunately I cannot tell.

My bucket is emptied and my rations supplied while I sleep. My rations consist of a soft plastic jug of water, a cob loaf, a lump of cheese, two apples and a bone with a few scraps of meat on it.

I try to stay awake as long as possible after going to bed, but always sleep comes and I have neither seen nor heard any sign of those who clean out my bucket and bring my food.

I exercise each day, following a routine of press-ups, stretches, running on the spot and deep breathing. I think I am still fairly fit despite everything they have done to me, but I have no mirror to check my appearance.

I cannot work out why the door is in the middle of the wall. Perhaps there was once a flight of steps leading up to it. I can find no trace of them, however.

There is always paper on the table and newly sharpened pencils. I have to write every day. If I do not write, I get no food, only water.

The door is made of very hard wood and has no handle or keyhole. If I am to get out of here I must find some means of opening it.

I have to write the story of my life. Each morning I look to see if what I wrote the previous day has gone. If it is still there, then I know I must re-write it. Sometimes I have done the same episode a dozen times before it is accepted. Sometimes the alteration of a single word is enough.

These notes are the framework of my sanity.

My clothes consist of a pair of blue denim trousers with zipped flies and no belt, a loose shirt, or rather smock, of grey cotton, a pair of open sandals without buckles or laces. I also have a wristwatch on a canvas strap. The face is cracked and it does not work. Hunger, fatigue and the movement of my bowels are my only clock.

Sometimes I think that the walls of the room are getting closer together. I have measured the breadth and width of the room with my feet, placing one in front of the other from corner to corner. It is fifteen foot-lengths square. I do this measurement at least once every day. I know it will not change, but I cannot sit writing for any length of time without doing the measurement.

I have tried banging on the door with my chair but no one comes and the door shows no sign of damage. It sounds so solid that perhaps no noise is audible outside. Not that that matters. I do not doubt I am watched all the time.

I have developed a habit of doodling and scribbling on sheets of paper. Then sometimes I tear and fold these sheets to make aeroplanes, dancing men, flowers or cockleshell boats. But always I contrive to secrete that one of the torn scraps which has my note on it. I dare not write more but I need what I write. These notes are the framework of my sanity.

Any hope I have lies in that door. I laid a trap, putting my toilet bucket directly beneath it. It wasn't much of a trap and absolutely worthless if I am being watched. I tried to lie awake but eventually fell asleep. The bucket was emptied and back in its usual place when I woke.

I suspect I am being injected with drugs as I sleep. I have noticed tiny punctures appearing in my skin and I can think of no other explanation. Perhaps they are trying to make me dependent on some drug so that withdrawal will force me to talk. About what?

I must make contact. Only through contact can there be a future for me.

I need these notes to keep some check on the present. Without them I would not know if things change. I keep them concealed beneath my smock. My broken watch has a luminescent dial. By this tiny light I read my notes under the blanket before I fall to sleep. Without them I think I should be mad. Even with them, I have no certainty of survival. Above all I fear those punctures in my skin. I must force them to show themselves.

Yesterday I stood on my chair and poured cold water through the protective muzzle on to the light bulb. It cracked and went out. I then stood by the door holding the chair ready to attack anyone who entered. But no one came. The room was in pitch darkness. I waited for what seemed several hours, then I grew so fatigued that I sat on the floor. Eventually I fell asleep. When I awoke the light was on again.

I need these notes to keep some check on the present. I have scarcely any memory of the recent past. My broken watch is stopped at a quarter to four. I cannot recall how it got broken. Perhaps I do not want to. But the more autobiography I write, the more my childhood comes back to me. I write in such detail that I shall be old before I reach my youth. Yet whenever I omit anything the writing is not accepted.

My fears that the room is contracting are with me always. I must make contact. I shall refuse to write until they contact me or I starve.

I have written nothing for three days. On the third day I woke up very weak from lack of food and found I was lying on the ceiling of the room. Up above, or down below, I could see the chair, the table, the bucket and the bed. I tried to crawl down the walls to them but I stuck to the ceiling like a fly. Finally I either fainted or fell asleep. When I awoke I was in my bed again and there was food on the table. I ate and started writing immediately.

The door is set in the centre of the wall. There is no crack big enough to admit even a razor blade. It is so solid that it cannot be broken down. Perhaps it will burn. I have an idea for starting a fire. But I have had ideas for so many things.

I have been trying to write of the death of my mother for the past three? four days? Each time what I write is rejected. Why? What do they want of me? I shall write no more.

I have to write again. More and more I think of death but it must be quick. I have no will to die of starvation. My attempt to start a fire was a fiasco. I cleared everything from my table, picked a few small splinters of wood from the surface with my fingernails, then held a pencil between both my palms and rubbed violently, trying to generate heat where the pencil point touched the woodwork. It got warm but nothing more.

I have written that I was not wholly sorry at my mother's death. This is a lie but they have accepted it. They have accepted a lie. How many other lies have they made me tell? I must make an end to this while I still can.

I have decided to hang myself. There is no other way. I thought of slashing my wrists as I lay under my blanket one night, but I have nothing to use. I tried to break my water jug but it just bounces. If I had the courage I could bite through the veins but even in my despair that thought revolts me. But I shall use my teeth to cut through the bound edge of my blanket so that I can tear off a strip to make a noose.

The only light in the room comes from a single bulb set above the door. It is protected by a metal muzzle fitted into the wall. This must be my gallows. The thought frightens me more than I can say, but I see no alternative. I write lies all the time now, descriptions of childhood hatreds and deceptions and odious lusts and imaginings, all lies, all lies. Yet they are accepted, every one of them.

I have my noose. I wish it had not to be this way. How much better to slash my wrists as I lie on my bed and feel the life pour softly from me.

I keep my noose around my waist. All is ready. I climbed on my chair today and examined the light. Let them think what they will. I had to make sure I had the right length of "rope." No point in ending up on tiptoe slowly strangling. Oh God! but I will strangle. The drop cannot be deep enough to break my neck.

Perhaps they will come if they see me strangling. Perhaps my piece of blanket will break or stretch and leave me flat-footed on the ground. If only I could be certain. Sometimes in the past I have had in my rations a flat brittle shoulder-bone. If I had one of these now I could break a splinter off and stab myself with it or slash my wrists. I must have certainty. I cannot face being hauled back from the brink.

More lies today. And another knuckle-bone. I cannot go on much longer.

Oh God! Today a shoulder! They will wonder at my appetite to see me gnawing and cracking at it. I have a long thin splinter, surprisingly strong but with a point like a needle. I feel as joyous as if someone had given me freedom.

Was it yesterday I was so joyful? Yet I am still here. A noose round my waist, a dagger of bone at my side, yet I am still here. Is it illusion that I think I remember a time when I had will and courage and conviction? If there was a button on the table before me which I merely had to press to obliterate all this place and me with it, could I reach out my finger and press it? Perhaps I have arrived where they want me to arrive. Perhaps now all I have to do is wait.

* * *

My dear friends, for what else should I call those who have watched over me with such unstinting care all these weeks? months? years?—my dear friends, these are the last words I shall write in this stinking cell. Yesterday you saw me sitting like a zombie staring blindly into space. Today you will be interested to observe this sudden last outburst of creative energy. And when it is finished you shall at last see me make my suicide attempt. All will be as you have doubtless forecast. Why should it not be, for you must be clever men? But you must not retain to yourself sole claim on the power of prognostication. We on our side have been trained also. And whose school is the better?

I laid my plans within a couple of days—so far as I can gauge—of arriving here. I knew I had to. It's all a question of taking the initiative. Sit and wait, and very soon you are totally under control. This business of autobiography is very seductive. By the time I came to the politically significant period in my life I've no doubt I would have been providing you with dense detail just to convince you of my accuracy! So against your routine I had to set a counter-routine. But *I* am not so stupid as to imagine *you* are so stupid as not to look for this. So I worked out a double routine, the top layer of which you could penetrate easily enough. All those little notes of mine with their hints of breakdown, their wild hopes, their repetitions, did you imagine I would not guess that you would read them? More! I have lain there and felt your hands remove them from under my smock, then replace them after they'd been copied. That surprises you? There is much to surprise you!

I let all my hopes for escaping from here seem to centre on the door. But within a very short while I'd worked out that the door was a dummy. A little piece of hair stuck across the wood and the wall confirmed that it never opened or shut. I then set about discovering the real door. My exercises enabled me to examine most of the floor area without being too obvious and my "shrinking cell" fears allowed me to pace slowly right into the corners and stand there, as if making sure that the walls weren't moving. Really, of course, what I wanted to discover was that the walls did move! But your interior decorator is pretty good and it took another hair in the corner to convince me that the section of wall behind my bed must slide or swing open.

The next thing was to confirm this. I'd worked out that I was certainly being drugged to put me to sleep so soundly that your visits did not disturb me. This meant the food or the water had been tampered with, probably both. Not to eat would draw too much attention, I thought, but you co-operated to the extent of withdrawing my food if I did not write. So I deliberately did not write one day and this just left me with the problem of the water. I had noticed the calibrations on the inside of the jug and I knew it was not enough merely to pretend to drink—this was not just a one-off thing. I would need to repeat it at least once, probably twice, till all my theories were checked. So I decided to kill two birds with one stone and see if I could put the light out of action.

It worked beautifully. When the cold water cracked the hot bulb I crouched in the darkness as though waiting to attack the first man through that dummy door. Gradually, as you would expect having seen me apparently drink quite a lot of water before my experiment, I pretended to grow drowsy. Finally I flopped over as if asleep. I could have embraced the man who came through the wall and picked me up, even when he stuck a pin in me to check the depth of my sleep! Fortunately I had already worked out what this rash of punctures meant and I was ready for it. I hope my fears of being turned into a junkie entertained you. Fear and the human imagination are all the drugs the expert interrogator needs.

Now I needed to do this once more to establish the routine. I hope I kept you amused with my attempts to break down the door and set fire to it! How natural that at last full of despair I should turn to thoughts of suicide. And how equally natural, I hope, that in my search for a weapon I should attempt to shatter my jug and thus spill all the water again—on a day, of course, when I was foodless for being naughty.

Again I had to go through the motions of drowsiness and finally sleep. I hope I got the timing right, but as this must be uncertain in any case as it's related to the amount of water I drink, perhaps it didn't matter. But it mattered thereafter.

Counting seconds, I reached eighty minutes before the wall slid open. I have had to take what happened then as the routine sequence for I do not dare risk another trial run.

The light went on as the wall slid open (I'm writing this for my benefit, dear friends, not yours!), a single figure entered, stuck a pin into me as before. Ready though I was I twitched slightly and he tried again. This time I showed no reaction and this satisfied him. That must be some drug you're using!

His job seemed to be pretty menial so far as I could make it out. He simply removed the jug and the toilet bucket. As he left, another two men arrived. They removed my notes from their hiding-place and photographed the latest one before returning them. Then they photographed what I had written during the day. (The original I found on the table still when I got up, so clearly rejection has nothing to do with content. It is merely aimed at setting up doubts and anxieties in the writer so that the search for detail is pursued with greater vigour each time. *What* clever men you must be!)

I knew that these two were not you, my dear friends, for they talked like underlings. Not indiscreetly, of course, for they, too, would be on your video screen, but of ordinary things like the foulness of the weather and the approach of Christmas.

As they finished, the first man (I assume) returned with my bucket and my next day's rations. I had written that day, so my food was restored.

Now I had all the information I needed or at least was likely to get to enable me to escape. So now the plan could really get under way.

I wrote more and more of suicide. I made a noose. I was interested to observe that although you knew I had a noose, you didn't take it off me. So I wondered if you could be provoked into giving me a weapon, that is the bone dagger.

I bet this caused some debate between the two of you. Yes, I've come to the conclusion that there are probably two of you sitting up there like gods watching my behaviour on a flickering grey screen. One of you will be a military man, concerned with security, duty, following orders, protecting the state. He wouldn't be very happy at the thought of my having anything which could be called a weapon.

The other must be a scientist, fascinated by the opportunity to acquire new knowledge and to test old. This is no weapon, but a token, he would say. The prisoner has no real intention of committing suicide. To give the possibility of death is to give the hope of life and it is from this that true confessions will spring. Besides what if I did die? Even failed experiments are useful. The unexpected becomes expected once it has happened.

So I got my weapon. A bonus of bone! See, I can still make jokes, scientist. What does that prove of the human spirit? But it really was a bonus. The main function of my suicide pretensions has been to permit me to play around with the light again. You've seen me examine it, ostensibly as a hook to hang myself on. Shortly you shall see me get back up there once again, and I doubt if you'll be surprised. I must look as if I'm building up to some climax of action, which indeed I am. Yesterday I sat as if in a coma, staring into space. Today I have been scribbling in an agitated fashion. I bet you can hardly wait to see what I've been writing, scientist!

Very shortly I shall jump up and begin to pace around the room looking as if I'm breaking up. Then suddenly I will push the chair under the light. Next I shall unwind my noose of blanket from my waist and examine it as though both fascinated and horrified. I shall put my hand to my throat, have a bout of coughing as though the very *thought* of hanging restricts my breathing. (I bet you make a note of that!) Picking up my jug, I shall take a draught of water to stop the coughing. And finally I shall climb on the chair and loop the noose over the light fitment.

This is the big moment. The soldier may want to interfere (they can be very humane, soldiers. They like to kill to timetables). The scientist will say *wait*. The struggle will show itself in every angle of my body.

And life will win. I will relax, sob convulsively, almost be sick. The scientist will preen himself.

And I shall be squirting the water held in my mouth

into the little cockleshell of paper I have tied into the noose. The keel of this paper boat, of a kind you've grown very used to seeing over the past few weeks, has a tiny hole in it. As I clamber off the chair, the water will already begin to seep through. I shall look exhausted. Who wouldn't be in my circumstances, drained of emotion and topped up with drugged water?

I shall stagger across the room and fall on the bed. The light will go out. (Is it economy or convention that makes you switch off when I go to bed?) And a moment or so later, if all goes well and the fates who have so maligned me these past months decide to wink, while the bulb is still red hot the water will drip through and crack the glass and you up aloft in your God-like observation post will not be aware of it.

So in one hour and twenty minutes (if he is as punctilious as my military friend must surely require) the man with the pin will open the door. Only this time no light will go on and I shall be waiting with my pin also.

After that, who knows? If once I get outside, I'm sure that I shall find myself in remote enough terrain to make escape possible. The way my photographer friends talked about the rough winds and snow on the hills gives me a picture of a countryside with plenty of undulations to hide in, lots of flowing water to shake off dogs, lots of trees (pine forests, perhaps?) to ward off helicopters.

We shall see. You, my friends, I should have liked to meet. But I shall not be able to arrange it, I fear. If I escape, distance—and if I don't, death—will separate us beyond hope of encounter. Either way, you my soldier with all your schemes of security, and you my scientist with all your charts of the human mind, you both will have been defeated. You deserve death also, but perhaps defeat will serve as well for your puffed-up egos. Let the curtain rise.

"The thing about the human mind," said the scientist with great satisfaction, "is that even its deceits are forecastable. A lie is as good as the truth to the discerning eye."

"If you were so sure 128 was going, I wouldn't have

a man in hospital with a punctured lung,'' growled the soldier.

''I'm sorry about that,'' said the scientist. ''But I had to let things run their course. All those notes! What ingenuity. I look forward to observing the reaction to recapture.''

''If there is a recapture,'' said the soldier.

''What on earth do you mean? You assured me security was complete!'' said the scientist.

''It is,'' said the soldier. ''Look at the map on the screen. That bleep and flashing light comes from the bugs. Every item of 128's clothing has got one attached. Lose a sandal, it makes no difference. My men can track every movement. Only . . .''

''Only what?''

''Only there's nothing but your fancy theories to say that it won't be a corpse they bring back!''

''I've told you,'' said the scientist. ''128's not suicidal. All this talk of death or escape is self-deceit. That light seems to be following the line of the stream, doesn't it?''

''Yes. The usual pattern. We could have worked it out even without the bugs. The letter told us, though we hardly needed that either. A valley for concealment, running water to throw the dogs off the scent. Dogs! They must think we live in the dark ages.''

''The light's moving pretty fast.''

''It's a fast-moving stream.''

''You don't mean 128's actually in the water?'' said the scientist, suddenly alarmed.

''Why not? Swimming, floating, it's the fastest way down to the sea.''

''Let's have a look at the file,'' said the scientist. ''Nothing here about being a strong swimmer.''

''You don't have to be,'' said the soldier with grim satisfaction. ''Dead or alive, that water'll move you fast. Don't look so worried! There's a net across the mouth of the stream and my men are waiting there.''

''I hope so. I hope so,'' said the scientist. ''But nets are more holes than string.''

''There's no way through. And even if there were, no one's going to stay alive for long in the Irish Sea on a winter's day. Poor sod. The things I do for England. Look, there you are! Like I said, in the net."

The light had halted where the line of the stream intersected the line of the shore.

A telephone rang.

"Back in the fold," said the soldier, picking it up.

He listened for a few moments and then said, "Good God!"

"What's up?" demanded the scientist. "Not dead?"

"No," said the soldier. "All they found was a bundle of clothes tied to a log."

"Maximum security screen!" he barked into the mouthpiece. "Then start searching. I'm coming down."

He replaced the receiver.

"Maximum security?" sneered the scientist.

The soldier paused at the door.

"Has it struck you yet that the letter was probably just as big a smoke-screen as the notes?" he asked coldly. "So much for psychology."

"Rubbish," said the scientist, peering into the thick file before him. "No one's that controlled. Show 'em freedom or vengeance, every time they'll run."

The soldier said nothing but gave a little gasp and stepped back a pace from the open doorway.

The scientist looked up from the file.

"You OK?" he asked.

The soldier turned. His hands clutched his belly. About his tight-laced fingers was coiled a thread of blood. "Psychology!" he whispered scornfully.

Then he fell.

Behind him in the doorway stood a naked woman. She stepped into the room.

In her hand was a dagger of bone.

Dalziel's Ghost

"Well, this is very cosy," said Detective-Superintendent Dalziel, scratching his buttocks sensuously before the huge log fire.

"It is for some," said Pascoe, shivering still from the frosty November night.

But Dalziel was right, he thought as he looked round the room. It *was* cosy, probably as cosy as it had been in the three hundred years since it was built. It was doubtful if any previous owner, even the most recent, would have recognized the old living-room of Stanstone Rigg farmhouse. Eliot had done a good job, stripping the beams, opening up the mean little fireplace and replacing the splintered uneven floorboards with smooth dark oak; and Giselle had broken the plain white walls with richly coloured, voluminous curtaining and substituted everywhere the ornaments of art for the detritus of utility.

Outside, though, when night fell, and darkness dissolved the telephone poles, and the mist lay too thick to be pierced by the rare headlight on the distant road, then the former owners peering from their little cube of warmth and light would not have felt much difference.

Not the kind of thoughts a ghost-hunter should have! he told himself reprovingly. Cool calm scepticism was the right state of mind.

And his heart jumped violently as behind him the telephone rang.

Dalziel, now pouring himself a large scotch from the goodly array of bottles on the huge sideboard, made no move toward the phone though he was the nearer. Detective-superintendents save their strength for important things and leave their underlings to deal with trivia.

"Hello," said Pascoe.

"Peter, you're there!

"Ellie love," he answered. "Sometimes the sharpness of your mind makes me feel unworthy to be married to you."

"What are you doing?"

"We've just arrived. I'm talking to you. The super's having a drink."

"Oh God! You did warn the Eliots, didn't you?"

"Not really, dear. I felt the detailed case-history you doubtless gave to Giselle needed no embellishment."

"I'm not sure this is such a good idea."

"Me neither. On the contrary. In fact, you may recall that on several occasions in the past three days I've said as much to you, whose not such a good idea it was in the first place."

"All you're worried about is your dignity!" said Ellie. "I'm worried about that lovely house. What's he doing now?"

Pascoe looked across the room to where Dalziel had bent his massive bulk so that his balding close-cropped head was on a level with a small figurine of a shepherd chastely dallying with a milkmaid. His broad right hand was on the point of picking it up.

"He's not touching anything," said Pascoe hastily. "Was there any other reason you phoned?"

"Other than what?"

"Concern for the Eliots' booze and knick-knacks."

"Oh, Peter, don't be so half-witted. It seemed a laugh at The Old Mill, but now I don't like you being there with him, and I don't like me being here by myself. Come home and we'll screw till someone cries *Hold! Enough!*"

"You interest me strangely," said Pascoe. "What about *him* and the Eliots' house?"

"Oh, sod him and sod the Eliots! Decent people don't have ghosts!" exclaimed Ellie.

"Or if they do, they call in priests, not policemen," said Pascoe. "I quite agree. I said as much, remember . . . ?"

"All right, all right. You please yourself, buster. I'm off to bed now with a hot-water bottle and a glass of milk. Clearly I must be in my dotage. Shall I ring you later?"

"Best not," said Pascoe. "I don't want to step out of my pentacle after midnight. See you in the morning."

"Must have taken an electric drill to get through a skirt like that," said Dalziel, replacing the figurine with a bang. "No wonder the buggers got stuck into the sheep. Your missus checking up, was she?"

"She just wanted to see how we were getting on," said Pascoe.

"Probably thinks we've got a couple of milkmaids with us," said Dalziel, peering out into the night. "Some hope! I can't even see any sheep. It's like the grave out there."

He was right, thought Pascoe. When Stanstone Rigg had been a working farm, there must have always been the comforting sense of animal presence, even at night. Horses in the stable, cows in the byre, chickens in the hutch, dogs before the fire. But the Eliots hadn't bought the place because of any deep-rooted love of nature. In fact Giselle Eliot disliked animals so much she wouldn't even have a guard dog, preferring to rely on expensive electronics. Pascoe couldn't understand how George had got her even to consider living out here. It was nearly an hour's run from town in good conditions and Giselle was in no way cut out for country life, either physically or mentally. Slim, vivacious, sexy, she was a star-rocket in Yorkshire's sluggish jet-set. How she and Ellie had become friends, Pascoe couldn't work out either.

But she must have a gift for leaping unbridgeable gaps for George was a pretty unlikely partner, too.

It was George who was responsible for Stanstone Rigg. By profession an accountant, and very much looking the part with his thin face, unblinking gaze, and a mouth that seemed constructed for the passage of bad news, his unlikely hobby was the renovation of old houses. In the past six years he had done two, first a Victorian terrace house in town, then an Edwardian villa in the suburbs. Both had quadrupled (at least) in value, but George claimed this was not the point and Pascoe believed him. Stanstone Rigg Farm was his most ambitious project to date, and it had been a marvellous success, except for its isolation, which was unchangeable.

And its ghost. Which perhaps wasn't.

It was just three days since Pascoe had first heard of it. Dalziel, who repaid hospitality in the proportion of three of Ellie's home-cooked dinners to one meal out had been entertaining the Pascoes at The Old Mill, a newly opened restaurant in town.

"Jesus!" said the fat man when they examined the menu. "I wish they'd put them prices in French, too. They must give you Brigitte Bardot for afters!"

"Would you like to take us somewhere else?" enquired Ellie sweetly. "A fish and chip shop, perhaps. Or a Chinese takeaway?"

"No, no," said Dalziel. "This is grand. Any road, I'll chalk what I can up to expenses. Keeping an eye on Fletcher."

"Who?"

"The owner," said Pascoe. "I didn't know he was on our list, sir."

"Well, he is and he isn't," said Dalziel. "I got a funny telephone call a couple of weeks back. Suggested I might take a look at him, that's all. He's got his finger in plenty of pies."

"If I have the salmon to start with," said Ellie, "it won't be removed as material evidence before I'm finished, will it?"

Pascoe aimed a kick at her under the table but she had been expecting it and drawn her legs aside.

Four courses later they had all eaten and drunk enough for a kind of mellow truce to have been established between Ellie and the fat man.

"Look who's over there," said Ellie suddenly.

Pascoe looked. It was the Eliots, George dark-suited and still, Giselle ablaze in clinging orange silk. Another man, middle-aged but still athletically elegant in a military sort of way, was standing by their table. Giselle returned Ellie's wave and spoke to the man, who came across the room and addressed Pascoe.

"Mr. and Mrs. Eliot wonder if you would care to join them for liqueurs," he said.

Pascoe looked at Dalziel enquiringly.

"I'm in favour of owt that means some other bugger putting his hand in his pocket," he said cheerfully.

Giselle greeted them with delight and even George raised a welcoming smile.

"Who was that dishy thing you sent after us?" asked Ellie after Dalziel had been introduced.

"Dishy? Oh, you mean Giles. He *will* be pleased. Giles Fletcher. He owns this place."

"Oh my! We send the owner on errands, do we?" said Ellie. "It's great to see you, Giselle. It's been ages. When am I getting the estate agent's tour of the new house? You've promised us first refusal when George finds a new ruin, remember?"

"I couldn't afford the ruin," objected Pascoe. "Not even with George doing our income tax."

"Does a bit of the old tax fiddling, your firm?" enquired Dalziel genially.

"I do a bit of work privately for friends," said Eliot coldly. "But in my own time and at home."

"You'll need to work bloody hard to make a copper rich," said Dalziel.

"Just keep taking the bribes, dear," said Ellie sweetly. "Now when can we move into Stanstone Farm, Giselle?"

Giselle glanced at her husband, whose expression remained a blank.

"Any time you like, darling," she said. "To tell you the truth, it can't be soon enough. In fact, we're back in town."

"Good God!" said Ellie. "You haven't found another place already, George? That's pretty rapid even for you."

A waiter appeared with a tray on which were glasses and a selection of liqueur bottles.

"Compliments of Mr. Fletcher," he said.

Dalziel examined the tray with distaste and beckoned the waiter close. For an incredulous moment Pascoe thought he was going to refuse the drinks on the grounds that police officers must be seen to be above all favour.

"From Mr. Fletcher, eh?" said Dalziel. "Well, listen, lad, he wouldn't be best pleased if he knew you'd forgotten the single malt whisky, would he? Run along and fetch it. I'll look after pouring this lot."

Giselle looked at Dalziel with the round-eyed delight of a child seeing a walrus for the first time.

"Cointreau for me please, Mr. Dalziel," she said.
He filled a glass to the brim and passed it to her with a hand steady as a rock.
"Sup up, love," he said, looking with open admiration down her cleavage. "Lots more where that comes from."
Pascoe, sensing that Ellie might be about to ram a pepper-mill up her host's nostrils, said hastily, "Nothing wrong with the building, I hope, George? Not the beetle or anything like that?"
"I sorted all that out before we moved," said Eliot. "No, nothing wrong at all."
His tone was neutral but Giselle responded as though to an attack.
"It's all right, darling," she said. "Everyone's guessed it's me. But it's not really. It's just that I think we've got a ghost."
According to Giselle, there were strange scratchings, shadows moving where there should be none, and sometimes as she walked from one room to another "a sense of emptiness as though for a moment you'd stepped into the space between two stars."
This poetic turn of phrase silenced everyone except Dalziel, who interrupted his attempts to scratch the sole of his foot with a bent coffee spoon and let out a raucous laugh.
"What's that mean?" demanded Ellie.
"Nowt," said Dalziel. "I shouldn't worry, Mrs. Eliot. It's likely some randy yokel roaming about trying to get a peep at you. And who's to blame him?"
He underlined his compliment with a leer straight out of the old melodrama. Giselle patted his knee in acknowledgement.
"What do *you* think, George?" asked Ellie.
George admitted the scratchings but denied personal experience of the rest.
"See how long he stays there by himself," challenged Giselle.
"I didn't buy it to stay there by myself," said Eliot. "But I've spent the last couple of nights alone without damage."
"And you saw or heard nothing?" said Ellie.
"There may have been some scratching. A rat per-

haps. It's an old house. But it's only a house. I have to go down to London for a few days tomorrow. When I get back we'll start looking for somewhere else. Sooner or later I'd get the urge anyway."

"But it's such a shame! After all your work, you deserve to relax for a while," said Ellie. "Isn't there anything you can do?"

"Exorcism," said Pascoe. "Bell, book and candle."

"In my experience," said Dalziel, who had been consuming the malt whisky at a rate which had caused the waiter to summon his workmates to view the spectacle, "there's three main causes of ghosts."

He paused for effect and more alcohol.

"Can't you arrest him, or something?" Ellie hissed at Pascoe.

"One: bad cooking," the fat man continued. "Two: bad ventilation. Three: bad conscience."

"George installed air-conditioning himself," said Pascoe.

"And Giselle's a super cook," said Ellie.

"Well then," said Dalziel. "I'm sure your conscience is as quiet as mine, love. So that leaves your randy yokel. Tell you what. Bugger your priests. What you need is a professional eye checking on things."

"You mean a psychic investigator?" said Giselle.

"Like hell!" laughed Ellie. "He means get the village bobby to stroll around the place with his truncheon at the ready."

"A policeman? But I don't really see what he could do," said Giselle, leaning towards Dalziel and looking earnestly into his lowered eyes.

"No, hold on a minute," cried Ellie with bright malice. "The Superintendent could be right. A formal investigation. But the village flatfoot's no use. You've got the best police brains in the county rubbing your thighs, Giselle. Why not send for them?"

Which was how it started. Dalziel, to Pascoe's amazement, had greeted the suggestion with ponderous enthusiasm. Giselle had reacted with a mixture of high spirits and high seriousness, apparently regarding the project as both an opportunity for vindication and a lark. George had sat like Switzerland, neutral and dull. Ellie had been smilingly baffled to see her bluff so swiftly called. And Pascoe had kicked her ankle savagely when he heard plans being made for himself and Dalziel to spend the following Friday night waiting for ghosts at Stanstone Farm.

As he told her the next day, had he realized that Dalziel's enthusiasm was going to survive the sober light of morning, he'd have followed up his kick with a karate chop.

Ellie had tried to appear unrepentant.

"You know why it's called Stanstone, do you?" she asked. "Standing stone. Get it? There must have been a stone circle there at some time. Primitive worship, human sacrifice, that sort of thing. Probably the original stones were used in the building of the house. That'd explain a lot, wouldn't it?"

"No," said Pascoe coldly. "That would explain very little. It would certainly not explain why I am about to lose a night's sleep, nor why you who usually threaten me with divorce or assault whenever my rest is disturbed to fight *real* crime should have arranged it."

But arranged it had been and it was small comfort for Pascoe now to know that Ellie was missing him.

Dalziel seemed determined to enjoy himself, however.

"Let's get our bearings, shall we?" he said. Replenishing his glass, he set out on a tour of the house.

"Well wired up," he said as his expert eye spotted the discreet evidence of the sophisticated alarm system. "Must have cost a fortune."

"It did. I put him in touch with our crime prevention squad and evidently he wanted nothing but the best," said Pascoe.

"What's he got that's so precious?" wondered Dalziel.

"All this stuff's pretty valuable, I guess," said Pascoe, making a gesture which took in the pictures and ornaments of the master bedroom in which they were standing. "But it's really for Giselle's sake. This was her first time out in the sticks and it's a pretty lonely place. Not that it's done much good."

"Aye," said Dalziel, opening a drawer and pulling out a fine silk underslip. "A good-looking woman could get nervous in a place like this."

"You reckon that's what this is all about sir?" said Pascoe. "A slight case of hysteria?"

"Mebbe," said Dalziel.

They went into the next room, which Eliot had turned into a study. Only the calculating machine on the desk reminded them of the man's profession. The glass-fronted bookcase contained rows of books relating to his hobby in all its aspects from architectural histories to do-it-yourself tracts on concrete mixing. An old grandmother clock stood in a corner, and hanging on the wall opposite the bookcase was a nearly lifesize painting of a pre-Raphaelite maiden being pensive in a grove. She was naked but her long hair and the dappled shadowings of the trees preserved her modesty.

For a fraction of a second it seemed to Pascoe as if the shadows on her flesh shifted as though a breeze had touched the branches above.

"Asking for it," declared Dalziel.

"What?"

"Rheumatics or rape," said Dalziel. "Let's check the kitchen. My belly's empty as a football."

Giselle, who had driven out during the day to light the fire and make ready for their arrival, had anticipated Dalziel's gut. On the kitchen table lay a pile of sandwiches covered by a sheet of kitchen paper on which she had scribbled an invitation for them to help themselves to whatever they fancied.

Underneath she had written in capitals BE CAREFUL and underlined it twice.

"Nice thought," said Dalziel, grabbing a couple of the sandwiches. "Bring the plate through to the living-room and we'll eat in comfort."

Back in front of the fire with his glass filled once again, Dalziel relaxed in a deep armchair. Pascoe poured himself a drink and looked out of the window again.

"For God's sake, lad, sit down!" commanded Dalziel. "You're worse than a bloody spook, creeping around like that."

"Sorry," said Pascoe.

"Sup your drink and eat a sandwich. It'll soon be midnight. That's zero hour, isn't it? Right, get your strength up. Keep your nerves down."

"I'm not nervous!" protested Pascoe.

"No? Don't believe in ghosts, then?"

"Hardly at all," said Pascoe.

"Quite right. Detective-inspectors with university degrees shouldn't believe in ghosts. But tired old superintendents with less schooling than a pit pony, there's a different matter."

"Come off it!" said Pascoe. "You're the biggest unbeliever I know!"

"That may be, that may be," said Dalziel, sinking lower into his chair. "But sometimes, lad, sometimes . . ."

His voice sank away. The room was lit only by a dark-shaded table lamp and the glow from the fire threw deep shadows across the large contours of Dalziel's face. It might have been some eighteenth-century Yorkshire farmer sitting there, thought Pascoe. Shrewd; brutish; in his day a solid ram of a man, but now rotting to ruin though his own excesses and too much rough weather.

In the fireplace a log fell. Pascoe started. The red glow ran up Dalziel's face like a flush of passion up an Easter Island statue.

"I knew a ghost saved a marriage once," he said ruminatively. "In a manner of speaking."

Oh Jesus! thought Pascoe. It's ghost stories round the fire now, is it?

He remained obstinately silent.

"My first case, I suppose you'd call it. Start of a meteoric career."

"Meteors fall. And burn out," said Pascoe. "Sir."

"You're a sharp bugger, Peter," said Dalziel admiringly. "Always the quick answer. I bet you were just the same when you were eighteen. Still at school, eh? Not like me. I was a right Constable Plod I tell you. Untried. Untutored. Hardly knew one end of my truncheon from t'other. When I heard the shriek I just froze."

"Which shriek?" asked Pascoe resignedly.

On cue there came a piercing wail from the dark outside, quickly cut off. He half rose, caught Dalziel's amused eye, and subsided, reaching for the whisky decanter.

"Easy on that stuff," admonished Dalziel with all the

righteousness of a temperance preacher. "Enjoy your supper, like yon owl. Where was I? Oh aye. I was on night patrol. None of your Panda-cars in those days. You did it all on foot. And I was standing just inside this little alleyway. It was a dark narrow passage running between Shufflebotham's woolmill on the one side and a little terrace of back-to-backs on the other. It's all gone now, all gone. There's a car park there now. A bloody car park!

"Any road, the thing about this alley was, it were a dead end. There was a kind of buttress sticking out of the mill wall, might have been the chimneystack, I'm not sure, but the back-to-backs had been built flush up against it so there was no way through. No way at all."

He took another long pull at his scotch to help his memory and began to scratch his armpit noisily.

"Listen!" said Pascoe suddenly.

"What?"

"I thought I heard a noise."

"What kind of noise?"

"Like fingers scrabbling on rough stone," said Pascoe.

Dalziel removed his hand slowly from his shirt front and regarded Pascoe malevolently.

"It's stopped now," said Pascoe. "What were you saying, sir?"

"I was saying about this shriek," said Dalziel. "I just froze to the spot. It came floating out of this dark passage. It was as black as the devil's arsehole up there. The mill wall was completely blank and there was just one small window in the gable end of the house. That, if anywhere, was where the shriek came from. Well, I don't know what I'd have done. I might have been standing there yet wondering what to do, only this big hand slapped hard on my shoulder. I nearly shit myself! Then this voice said, "What's to do, Constable Dalziel?" and when I looked round there was my sergeant, doing his rounds.

"I could hardly speak for a moment, he'd given me such a fright. But I didn't need to explain. For just then came another shriek and voices, a man's and a woman's, shouting at each other. "You hang on here," said the sergeant. "I'll see what this is all about." Off he went, leaving me still shaking. And as I looked down that gloomy passageway, I began to remember some local stories about this mill. I hadn't paid much heed to them before. Everywhere that's more than fifty years old had a ghost in them parts. They say Yorkshiremen are hard-headed, but I reckon they've got more superstition to the square inch than a tribe of pygmies. Well, this particular tale was about a mill-girl back in the 1870s. The owner's son had put her in the family way which I dare say was common enough. The owner acted decently enough by his lights. He packed his son off to the other end of the country, gave the girl and her family a bit of cash and said she could have her job back when the confinement was over."

"Almost a social reformer," said Pascoe, growing interested despite himself.

"Better than a lot of buggers still in business round here," said Dalziel sourly. "To cut a long story short, this lass had her kid premature and it soon died. As soon as she was fit enough to get out of bed, she came back to the mill, climbed through a skylight on to the roof and jumped off. Now all that I could believe. Probably happened all the time."

"Yes," said Pascoe. "I've no doubt that a hundred years ago the air round here was full of falling girls. While in America they were fighting a war to stop the plantation owners screwing their slaves!"

"You'll have to watch that indignation, Peter," said Dalziel. "It can give you wind. And no one pays much heed to a preacher when you can't hear his sermons for farts. Where was I, now? Oh yes. This lass. Since that day there'd been a lot of stories about people seeing a girl falling from the roof of this old mill. Tumbling over and over in the air right slowly, most of 'em said. Her clothes filling with air, her hair streaming behind her like a comet's tail. Oh aye, lovely descriptions some of them were. Like the ones we get whenever there's an accident. One for every pair of eyes, and all of 'em perfectly detailed and perfectly different."

"So you didn't reckon much to these tales?" said Pascoe.

"Not by daylight," said Dalziel. "But standing there

in the mouth of that dark passageway at midnight, that was different."

Pascoe glanced at his watch.

"It's nearly midnight now," he said in a sepulchral tone.

Dalziel ignored him.

"I was glad when the sergeant stuck his head through that little window and bellowed my name. Though even that gave me a hell of a scare. "Dalziel!" he said. "Take a look up this alleyway. If you can't see anything, come in here." So I had a look. There wasn't anything, just sheer brick walls on three sides with only this one little window. I didn't hang about but got myself round to the front of the house pretty sharply and went in. There were two people there besides the sergeant. Albert Pocklington, whose house it was, and his missus, Jenny. In those days a good bobby knew everyone on his beat. I said hello, but they didn't do much more than grunt. Mrs. Pocklington was about forty. She must have been a bonny lass in her time and she still didn't look too bad. She'd got her blouse off, just draped around her shoulders, and I had a good squint at her big round tits. Well, I was only a lad! I didn't really look at her face till I'd had an eyeful lower down and then I noticed that one side was all splotchy red as though someone had given her a clout. There were no prizes for guessing who. Bert Pocklington was a big solid fellow. He looked like a chimpanzee, only he had a lot less gumption."

"Hold on," said Pascoe.

"What is it now?" said Dalziel, annoyed that his story had been interrupted.

"I thought I heard something. No, I mean really heard something this time."

They listened together. The only sound Pascoe could hear was the noise of his own breathing mixed with the pulsing of his own blood, like the distant sough of a receding tide.

"I'm sorry," he said. "I really did think . . ."

"That's all right, lad," said Dalziel with surprising sympathy, "I know the feeling. Where'd I got to? Albert Pocklington. My sergeant took me aside and put me in the picture. It seems that Pocklington had got a notion in his mind that someone was banging his missus while he was on the night shift. So he'd slipped away from his work at midnight and come home, ready to do a bit of banging on his own account. He wasn't a man to move quietly, so he'd tried for speed instead, flinging open the front door and rushing up the stairs. When he opened the bedroom door, his wife had been standing by the open window naked to the waist, shrieking. Naturally he thought the worst. Who wouldn't? Her story was that she was getting ready for bed when she had this feeling of the room suddenly becoming very hot and airless and pressing in on her. She'd gone to the window and opened it, and it was like taking a cork out of a bottle, she said. She felt as if she was being sucked out of the window, she said. (With tits like yours and a window that small, there wasn't much likelihood of that! I thought.) And at the same time she had seen a shape like a human figure tumbling slowly by the window. Naturally she shrieked. Pocklington came in. She threw herself into his arms. All the welcome she got was a thump on the ear, and that brought on the second bout of shrieking. She was hysterical, trying to tell him what she'd seen, while he just raged around, yelling about what he was going to do to her fancy man."

He paused for a drink. Pascoe stirred the fire with his foot. Then froze. There it was again! A distant scratching. He had no sense of direction.

The hairs on the back of his neck prickled in the traditional fashion. Clearly Dalziel heard nothing and Pascoe was not yet certain enough to interrupt the fat man again.

"The sergeant was a good copper. He didn't want a man beating up his wife for no reason and he didn't want a hysterical woman starting a ghost scare. They can cause a lot of bother, ghost scares," added Dalziel, filling his glass once more with the long-suffering expression of a man who is being caused a lot of bother.

"He sorted out Pocklington's suspicions about his wife having a lover first of all. He pushed his shoulders through the window till they got stuck to show how small it was. Then he asked me if anyone could have come out of that passageway without me spotting them. Out of the question, I told him.

"Next he chatted to the wife and got her to admit she'd been feeling a bit under the weather that day, like the 'flu was coming on, and she'd taken a cup of tea heavily spiked with gin as a nightcap. Ten minutes later we left them more or less happy. But as we stood on the pavement outside, the sergeant asked me the question I'd hoped he wouldn't. Why had I stepped into that alley in the first place? I suppose I could have told him I wanted a pee or a smoke, something like that. But he was a hard man to lie to, that sergeant. Not like the wet-nurses we get nowadays. So after a bit of humming and hawing, I told him I'd seen something, just out of the corner of my eye, as I was walking past. "What sort of thing?" he asked. Like something falling, I said. Something fluttering and falling through the air between the mill wall and the house end.

"He gave me a queer look, that sergeant did. 'I tell you what, Dalziel,' he said. 'When you make out your report, I shouldn't say anything of that. No, I should keep quiet about that. Leave ghosts to them that understands them. You stick to crime." And that's advice I've followed ever since, till this very night, that is!"

He yawned and stretched. There was a distant rather cracked chime. It was, Pascoe realized, the clock in Eliot's study striking midnight.

But it wasn't the only sound.

"*There!* Listen," urged Pascoe, rising slowly to his feet. "I *can* hear it. A scratching. Do *you* hear it, sir?"

Dalziel cupped one cauliflower ear in his hand.

"By Christ, I think you're right, lad!" he said as if this were the most remote possibility in the world. "Come on! Let's take a look."

Pascoe led the way. Once out of the living-room they could hear the noise quite clearly and it took only a moment to locate it in the kitchen.

"Rats?" wondered Pascoe.

Dalziel shook his head.

"Rats gnaw," he whispered. "That sounds like something bigger. It's at the back door. It sounds a bit keen to get in."

Indeed it did, thought Pascoe. There was a desperate insistency about the sound. Sometimes it rose to a crescendo, then tailed away as though from exhaustion, only to renew itself with greater fury.

It was as though someone or something was caught in a trap too fast for hope, too horrible for resignation. Pascoe had renewed his acquaintance with Poe after the strange business at Wear End and now he recalled the story in which the coffin was opened to reveal a contorted skeleton and the lid scarred on the inside by the desperate scraping of fingernails.

"Shall I open it?" he whispered to Dalziel.

"No," said the fat man. "Best one of us goes out the front door and come round behind. I'll open when you shout. OK?"

"OK," said Pascoe with less enthusiasm than he had ever OK'd even Dalziel before.

Picking up one of the heavy rubber-encased torches they had brought with them, he retreated to the front door and slipped out into the dark night.

The frost had come down fiercely since their arrival and the cold caught at his throat like an invisible predator. He thought of returning for his coat, but decided this would be just an excuse for postponing whatever confrontation awaited him. Instead, making a mental note that when he was a superintendent he, too, would make sure he got the inside jobs, he set off round the house.

When he reached the second corner, he could hear the scratching quite clearly. It cut through the still and freezing air like the sound of a steel blade against a grinding-stone.

Pascoe paused, took a deep breath, let out a yell of warning and leapt out from the angle of the house with his torch flashing.

The scratching ceased instantly, there was nothing to be seen by the rear door of the house, but a terrible shriek died away across the lawn as though an exorcized spirit was wailing its way to Hades.

At the same time the kitchen door was flung open and Dalziel strode majestically forward; then his foot skidded on the frosty ground and, swearing horribly, he crashed down on his huge behind.

"Are you all right, sir?" asked Pascoe breathlessly.

"There's only one part of my body that feels any sensitivity still," said Dalziel. "Give me a hand up."

He dusted himself down, saying, "Well, that's ghost number one laid."

"Sir?"

"Look."

His stubby finger pointed to a line of paw prints across the powder frost of the lawn.

"Cat," he said. "This was a farmhouse, remember? Every farm has its cats. They live in the barn, keep the rats down. Where's the barn?"

"Gone," said Pascoe. "George had it pulled down and used some of the stones for an extension to the house."

"There you are then," said Dalziel. "Poor bloody animal wakes up one morning with no roof, no rats. It's all right living rough in the summer, but comes the cold weather and it starts fancying getting inside again. Perhaps the farmer's wife used to give it scraps at the kitchen door."

"It'll get precious little encouragement from Giselle," said Pascoe.

"It's better than Count Dracula anyway," said Dalziel.

Pascoe, who was now very cold indeed, began to move towards the kitchen, but to his surprise Dalziel stopped him.

"It's a hell of a night even for a cat," he said. "Just have a look, Peter, see if you can spot the poor beast. In case it's hurt.

Rather surprised by his boss's manifestation of kindness to animals (though not in the least at his display of cruelty to junior officers), Pascoe shivered along the line of paw prints across the grass. They disappeared into a small orchard, whose trees seemed to crowd together to repel intruders, or perhaps just for warmth. Pascoe peered between the italic trunks and made cat-attracting noises but nothing stirred.

"All right," he said. "I know you're in there. We've got the place surrounded. Better come quietly. I'll leave the door open, so just come in and give a yell when you want to give yourself up."

Back in the kitchen, he left the door ajar and put a bowl of milk on the floor. His teeth were chattering and he headed to the living-room, keen to do full justice to both the log fire and the whisky decanter. The telephone rang as he entered. For once Dalziel picked it up and Pascoe poured himself a stiff drink.

From the half conversation he could hear, he gathered it was the duty sergeant at the station who was ringing. Suddenly, irrationally, he felt very worried in case Dalziel was going to announce he had to go out on a case, leaving Pascoe alone.

The reality turned out almost as bad.

"Go easy on that stuff," said Dalziel. "You don't want to be done for driving under the influence."

"What?"

Dalziel passed him the phone.

The sergeant told him someone had just rung the station asking urgently for Pascoe and refusing to speak to anyone else. He'd claimed what he had to say was important. "It's big and it's tonight" were his words. And he'd rung off saying he'd ring back in an hour's time. After that it'd be too late.

"Oh shit," said Pascoe. "It sounds like Benny."

Benny was one of his snouts, erratic and melodramatic, but often bringing really hot information.

"I suppose I'll have to go in," said Pascoe reluctantly. "Or I could get the Sarge to pass this number on."

"If it's urgent, you'll need to be on the spot," said Dalziel. "Let me know what's happening, won't you? Best get your skates on."

"Skates is right," muttered Pascoe. "It's like the Arctic out there."

He downed his whisky defiantly, then went to put his overcoat on.

"You'll be all right by yourself, will you, sir?" he said maliciously. "Able to cope with ghosts, ghouls, werewolves and falling mill-girls?"

"Never you mind about me, lad," said Dalziel jovially. "Any road, if it's visitors from an old stone circle we've got to worry about, dawn's the time, isn't it? When the first rays of the sun touch the victim's breast. And with luck you'll be back by then. Keep me posted."

Pascoe opened the front door and groaned as the icy air attacked his face once more.

"I am just going outside," he said. "And I may be some time."

To which Dalziel replied, as perhaps Captain Scott and his companions had, "Shut that bloody door!"

It took several attempts before he could persuade the frozen engine to start and he knew from experience that it would be a good twenty minutes before the heater began to pump even lukewarm air into the car. Swearing softly to himself, he set the vehicle bumping gently over the frozen contours of the long driveway up to the road.

The drive curved round the orchard and the comforting silhouette of the house soon disappeared from his mirror. The frost-laced trees seemed to lean menacingly across his path and he told himself that if any apparition suddenly rose before the car, he'd test its substance by driving straight through it.

But when the headlights reflected a pair of bright eyes directly ahead, he slammed on the brake instantly.

The cat looked as if it had been waiting for him. It was a skinny black creature with a mangled ear and a wary expression. Its response to Pascoe's soothing noises was to turn and plunge into the orchard once more.

"Oh, no!" groaned Pascoe. And he yelled after it, "You stupid bloody animal! I'm not going to chase you through the trees all bloody night. Not if you were a naked naiad, I'm not!"

As though recognizing the authentic tone of a Yorkshire farmer, the cat howled in reply and Pascoe glimpsed its shadowy shape only a few yards ahead. He followed, hurling abuse to which the beast responded with indignant miaows. Finally it disappeared under a bramble bush.

"That does it," said Pascoe. "Not a step further."

Leaning down he flashed his torch beneath the bush to take his farewell of the stupid animal.

Not one pair of eyes but three stared unblinkingly back at him, and a chorus of howls split the frosty air.

The newcomers were young kittens who met him with delight that made up for their mother's wariness. They were distressingly thin and nearby Pascoe's torch picked out the stiff bodies of another two, rather smaller, who hadn't survived.

"Oh shit," said Pascoe, more touched than his anti-sentimental attitudes would have permitted him to admit.

When he scooped up the kittens, their mother snarled in protest and tried to sink her teeth into his gloved hand. But he was in no mood for argument and after he'd bellowed, "Shut up!" she allowed herself to be lifted and settled down comfortably in the crook of his arm with her offspring.

It was quicker to continue through the orchard than to return to the car. As he walked across the lawn towards the kitchen door he smiled to himself at the prospect of leaving Dalziel in charge of this little family. That would really test the fat man's love of animals.

The thought of ghosts and hauntings was completely removed from his mind.

And that made the sight of the face at the upstairs window even more terrifying.

For a moment his throat constricted so much that he could hardly breathe. It was a pale face, a woman's he thought, shadowy, insubstantial behind the leaded panes of the old casement. And as he looked the room behind seemed to be touched by a dim unearthly glow through which shadows moved like weed on a slow stream's bed. In his arms the kittens squeaked in protest and he realized that he had involuntarily tightened his grip.

"Sorry," he said, and the momentary distraction unlocked the paralysing fear and replaced it by an equally instinctive resolve to confront its source. There's nothing makes a man angrier than the awareness of having been made afraid.

He went through the open kitchen door and dropped the cats by the bowl of milk which they assaulted with silent delight. The wise thing would have been to summon Dalziel from his warmth and whisky, but Pascoe had no mind to be wise. He went up the stairs as swiftly and as quietly as he could.

He had calculated that the window from which the "phantom" peered belonged to the study and when he saw the door was open he didn't know whether he was pleased or not. Ghosts didn't need doors. On the other hand it meant that *something* was in there. But the glow had gone.

Holding his torch like a truncheon, he stepped inside. As his free hand groped for the light switch he was aware of something silhouetted against the paler darkness of the window and at the same time of movement elsewhere in the room. His left hand couldn't find the switch, his right thumb couldn't find the button on the torch, it was as if the darkness of the room was liquid, slowing down all movement and washing over his mouth and nose and eyes in wave after stifling wave.

Then a single cone of light grew above Eliot's desk and Dalziel's voice said, "Why're you waving your arms like that, lad? Semaphore, is it?"

At which moment his fingers found the main light switch.

Dalziel was standing by the desk. Against the window leaned the long painting of the pre-Raphaelite girl, face to the glass. Where it had hung on the wall was a safe, wide open and empty. On the desk under the sharply focused rays of the desk lamp lay what Pascoe took to be it contents.

"What the hell's going on?" demanded Pascoe, half relieved, half bewildered.

"Tell you in a minute," said Dalziel, resuming his examination of the papers.

"No, sir," said Pascoe with growing anger. "You'll tell me now. You'll tell me exactly what you're doing going through private papers without a warrant! And how the hell did you get into that safe?"

"I've got you to thank for that Peter," said Dalziel without looking up.

"What?"

"It was you who put Eliot in touch with our crime prevention officer, wasn't it? I did an efficiency check the other morning, went through all the files. There it was. Eliot, George. He really wanted the works, didn't he? What's he got out there? I thought. The family jewels? I checked with the firm who did the fitting. I know the manager, as it happens. He's a good lad; bit of a ladies' man, but clever with it."

"Oh God!" groaned Pascoe. "You mean you got details of the alarm system and a spare set of keys!"

"No, I didn't!" said Dalziel indignantly. "I had to work it out for myself mainly."

He had put on his wire-rimmed National Health spectacles to read the documents from the safe and now he glared owlishly at Pascoe over them.

"Do you understand figures?" he asked. "It's all bloody Welsh to me."

Pascoe consciously resisted the conspiratorial invitation.

"I've heard nothing so far to explain why you're breaking the law, sir," he said coldly. "What's George Eliot supposed to have done?"

"What? Oh, I see. It's the laws of hospitality and friendship you're worried about! Nothing, nothing. Set your mind at rest, lad. It's nowt to do with your mate. Only indirectly. Look, this wasn't planned, you know. I mean, how could I plan all that daft ghost business? No, it was just that the Fletcher business was getting nowhere . . ."

"Fletcher?"

"Hey, here's your income tax file. Christ! Is that what your missus gets just for chatting to students? It's more than you!"

Pascoe angrily snatched the file from Dalziel's hands. The fat man put on his sympathetic, sincere look.

"Never fret, lad. I won't spread it around. Where was I? Oh yes, Fletcher. I've got a feeling about that fellow. The tip-off sounded good. Not really my line, though. I got Inspector Marwood on the Fraud Squad interested, though. All he could come up with was that a lot of Fletcher's business interests had a faint smell about them, but that was all. Oh yes, and Fletcher's accountants were the firm your mate Eliot's a partner in."

"That's hardly a startling revelation," sneered Pascoe.

"Did you know?"

"No. Why should I?"

"Fair point," said Dalziel. "Hello, hello."

He had found an envelope among the files. It contained a single sheet of paper which he examined with growing interest. Then he carefully refolded it, replaced it in the envelope and began to put all the documents read or unread back into the safe.

"Marwood told me as well, though, that Fletcher and Eliot seemed to be pretty thick at a personal level. And he also said the Fraud Squad would love to go over Fletcher's accounts with a fine-tooth comb."

"Why doesn't he get himself a warrant then?"

"Useless, unless he knows what he's looking for. My tipster was too vague. Often happens with first-timers. They want it to be quick and they overestimate our abilities."

"Is that possible?" marvelled Pascoe.

"Oh aye. Just. Are you going to take that file home?"

Reluctantly, Pascoe handed his tax file back to Dalziel, who thrust it in with the others, slammed the safe, then did some complicated fiddling with a bunch of keys.

"There," he said triumphantly, "all locked up and the alarm set once more. No harm to anyone. Peter, do me a favour. Put that tart's picture back up on the wall. I nearly did my back getting it down. I'll go and mend the fire and pour us a drink."

"I am not involved in this!" proclaimed Pascoe. But the fat man had gone.

When Pascoe came downstairs after replacing the picture, Dalziel was not to be found in the living-room. Pascoe tracked him to the kitchen, where he found him on his hands and knees, feeding pressed calves-tongue to the kittens.

"So you found 'em," said Dalziel. "That's what brought you back. Soft bugger."

"Yes. And I take it I needn't go out again. There's no snout'll be ringing at one o'clock. That was you while I was freezing outside, wasn't it?"

"I'm afraid so. I thought it best to get you out of the way. Sorry, lad, but I mean, this fellow Eliot is a mate of yours and I didn't want you getting upset."

"I *am* upset," said Pascoe. "Bloody upset."

"There!" said Dalziel triumphantly. "I was right, wasn't I? Let's get that drink. These buggers can look after themselves."

He dumped the rest of the tongue on to the kitchen floor and rose to his feet with much wheezing.

"There it is then, Peter," said Dalziel as they returned to the living-room. "It was all on the spur of the moment. When Mrs. Eliot suggested we spend a night here to look for her ghosts, I just went along to be sociable. I mean, you can't be rude to a woman like that, can you? A sudden shock, and that dress might have fallen off her nipples. I'd no more intention of really coming out here than of going teetotal! But next morning I got to thinking. If we could just get a bit of a pointer where to look at Fletcher . . . And I remembered you saying about Eliot doing your accounts at home."

"Income tax!" snorted Pascoe. "Does that make me a crook? Or him either?"

"No. It was just a thought, that's all. And after I'd talked to Crime Prevention, well, it seemed worth a peek. So come down off your high horse. No harm done. Your mate's not in trouble, OK? And I saw nowt in his safe to take action on. So relax, enjoy your drink. I poured you brandy, the scotch is getting a bit low. That all right?"

Pascoe didn't answer but sat down in the deep old armchair and sipped his drink reflectively. Spur of the moment, Dalziel had said. Bloody long moment, he thought. And what spur? There was still something here that hadn't been said.

"It won't do," he said suddenly.

"What's that?"

"There's got to be something else," insisted Pascoe. "I mean, I know you, sir. You're not going to do all this *just* on the off-chance of finding something to incriminate Fletcher in George's safe. There *has* to be something else. What did you expect to find, anyway? A signed confession? Come to that, what *did* you find?"

Dalziel looked at him, his eyes moist with sincerity.

"Nowt, lad. Nowt. I've told you. There'll be no action taken as a result of anything I saw tonight. None. There's my reassurance. It was an error of judgement on my part. I admit it. Now does that satisfy you?"

"No, sir, to be quite frank it doesn't. Look, I've got to know. These people are my friends. You say that they're not mixed up in anything criminal, but I still need to know exactly what is going on. Or else I'll start asking for myself."

He banged his glass down on the arm of his chair so vehemently that the liquor slopped out.

"It'll burn a hole, yon stuff," said Dalziel, slandering the five-star cognac which Pascoe was drinking.

"I mean it, sir," said Pascoe quietly. "You'd better understand that."

"All right, lad," said Dalziel. "I believe you. You might not like it though. *You'd* better understand *that.*"

"I'll chance it," replied Pascoe.

Dalziel regarded him closely, then relaxed with a sigh.

"Here it is then. The woman Giselle is having a bit on the side with Fletcher."

Pascoe managed an indifferent shrug.

"It happens," he said, trying to appear unsurprised. In fact, why was he surprised? Lively, sociable, physical Giselle and staid, self-contained, inward-looking George. It was always on the cards.

"So what?" he added in his best man-of-the-world voice.

"So if by any chance, Eliot did have anything which might point us in the right direction about Fletcher . . ."

Pascoe sat very still for a moment.

"Well, you old bastard!" he said. "You mean you'd give him good reason to do the pointing! You'd let him know about Giselle . . . Jesus wept! How low can you get?"

"I could have just let him know in any case without checking first to see if it was worthwhile," suggested Dalziel, unabashed.

"So you could!" said Pascoe in mock astonishment. "But you held back, waiting for a chance to check it out! Big of you! You get invited to spend the night alone in complete strangers' houses all the time! And now you've looked and found nothing, what are you going to do? Tell him just on the off-chance?"

"I didn't say I'd found *nothing,*" said Dalziel.

Pascoe stared at him.

"But you said there'd be no action!" he said.

"Right," said Dalziel. "I mean it. I think we've just got to sit back and wait for Fletcher to fall into our laps. Or be pushed. What I did find was a little anonymous letter telling Eliot what his wife was up to. Your mate *knows*, Peter. From the postmark he's known for a few weeks. He's a careful man, accountants usually are. And I'm sure he'd do a bit of checking first before taking action. It was just a week later that my telephone rang and that awful disguised voice told me to check on Fletcher. Asked for me personally. I dare say you've mentioned my name to Eliot, haven't you, Peter?"

He looked at the carpet modestly.

"Everyone's heard of you, sir," said Pascoe. "So what happens now?"

"Like I say. Nothing. We sit and wait for the next call. It should be a bit more detailed this time, I reckon. I mean, Eliot must have realized that his first tip-off isn't getting results and now his wife's moved back into town to be on Fletcher's doorstep again, he's got every incentive."

Pascoe looked at him in surprise.

"You mean the ghosts . . ."

"Nice imaginative girl, that Giselle! Not only does she invent a haunting to save herself a two hours' drive for her kicks, but she cons a pair of thick bobbies into losing their sleep over it. I bet Fletcher fell about laughing! Well I'm losing no more! It'll take all the hounds of hell to keep me awake."

He yawned and stretched. In mid-stretch there came a terrible scratching noise and the fat man froze like a woodcut of Lethargy on an allegorical frieze.

Then he laughed and opened the door.

The black cat looked up at him warily but her kittens had no such inhibitions and tumbled in, heading towards the fire with cries of delight.

"I think your mates have got more trouble than they know," said Dalziel.

Next morning Pascoe rose early and stiffly after a night spent on a sofa before the fire. Dalziel had disappeared upstairs to find himself a bed and Pascoe assumed he would still be stretched out on it. But when he looked out of the living-room he saw he was wrong.

The sun was just beginning to rise behind the orchard and the fat man was standing in front of the house watching the dawn.

A romantic at heart, thought Pascoe sourly.

A glint of light flickered between the trunks of the orchard trees, flamed into a ray and began to move across the frosty lawn towards the waiting man. He watched its progress, striking sparks off the ice-hard grass. And when it reached his feet he stepped aside.

Pascoe joined him a few minutes later.

"Morning, sir," he said. "I've made some coffee. You're up bright and early."

"Yes," said Dalziel, scratching his gut vigorously. "I think I've picked up a flea from those bloody cats."

"Oh," said Pascoe. "I thought you'd come to check on the human sacrifice at dawn. I saw you getting out of the way of the sun's first ray."

"Bollocks!" said Dalziel, looking towards the house, which the sun was now staining the gentle pink of blood in a basin of water.

"Why bollocks?" wondered Pascoe. "You've seen one ghost. Why not another?"

"One ghost?"

"Yes. The mill-girl. That story you told me last night. Your first case."

Dalziel looked at him closely.

"I told you that, did I? I must have been supping well."

Pascoe, who knew that drink had never made Dalziel forget a thing in his life, nodded vigorously.

"Yes, sir. You told me that. You and your ghost."

Dalziel shook his head as though at a memory of ancient foolishness and began to laugh.

"Aye, lad. My ghost! It really is my ghost in a way. The ghost of what I am now, any road! That Jenny Pocklington, she were a right grand lass! She had an imagination like your Giselle!"

"I don't follow," said Pascoe. But he was beginning to.

"Believe it or not, lad," said Dalziel. "In them days I was pretty slim. Slim and supple. Even then I had to be like a ghost to get through that bloody window! But if Bert Pocklington had caught me, I really would have been one! Aye, that's right. When I heard that scream, I was coming out of the alley, not going into it!"

And shaking with laughter the fat man headed across the lacy grass towards the old stone farmhouse where the hungry kittens were crying imperiously for their breakfast.

About the Author

Reginald Hill has been widely published both in England and in the United States. Among his novels are *Another Death in Venice* and *A Very Good Hater,* and in the famous Pascoe-Dalziel series, *Deadheads, A Clubbable Woman, Exit Lines* (all available in Signet) and *An April Shroud.* He lives with his wife in Yorkshire, England.